The

Philip William Stover lives on the Upper Eastside in New York City. He has previously ghosted for a best-selling women's fiction author and published middle-grade novels for Simon & Schuster but this is his first male/male romantic commercial fiction novel. He grew up tearing the covers off the romance novels he devoured so he wouldn't get teased at school. Now he enjoys traveling the world with his husband of over twenty years and would never consider defacing any of the books he loves.

THE PROBLEM WITH PERFECT

PHILIP WILLIAM STOVER

hera

First published in the United Kingdom in 2023 by

Hera Books
Unit 9 (Canelo), 5th Floor
Cargo Works, 1–2 Hatfields
London SE1 9PG
United Kingdom

A CIP catalogue record for this book is available from the British Library.

Print ISBN 978 1 80436 329 4
Ebook ISBN 978 1 80436 328 7

Look for more great books at www.herabooks.com

Printed and bound in Great Britain by Clays Ltd, Elcograf S.p.A.

1

For my husband, WBC, who in my eyes is perfect.

Chapter 1

I always assumed that if I were in *The Wizard of Oz*, I'd be the lovable scarecrow or the glamorous Glinda, or even Dorothy if I didn't have to wear gingham — the devil's plaid. But lately I've realized I'm none of those characters. Instead, I'm the guy frantically pulling levers and pushing buttons, hiding behind a curtain to create the myth of the great and inspiring leader of Oz. In my case, the Emerald City is the hit queer lifestyle show, *Myles of Style*, and at this moment, I would like to take the show's star, Chase Myles, and drop a house on him.

'Ethan, nooo,' Chase whines, tugging at the collar of the silk, Gatsby-inspired purple and midnight paisley smoking jacket that's tailored to fit his muscular frame. He puts his hands on his hips and pouts. It would be hard for most people to tell if he's pouting since his lips have a natural plumpness that's part of his overwhelming physical appeal.

'Chase, what's wrong now? Can we just get through this segment today so that the staff and crew can go home before their grandchildren graduate college?' It's one thing to torture me. As the executive producer, that's part of the job description, but many talented people work very hard to make the show a success. I don't see any reason they have to suffer due to one of Chase's tantrums. The crew is like a family to me, and they've dedicated countless hours to making this show a success. I won't let them down and especially not right before a holiday weekend.

'Ethan, I want you to come over here and put this in your mouth.' He picks up a delicate piece of prosciutto that has been folded into the shape of a rook, ruining the chess-inspired charcuterie board that the food stylists spent hours on. Everyone on the crew from Tina, my small and tightly wound assistant, to Mike, the lead cameraman and former UFC fighter and war veteran, looks petrified.

'What's wrong with it, Chase?' I ask plainly, trying not to get sucked into any type of blow-up.

'Ethan, you must see for yourself. It's too salty. It's an experience of the mouth.' He speaks to me like I'm a small child who doesn't understand why I can't put my hand on the hot stove when in fact I taught him how to keep his fingers safe from the burner, not to mention the importance of using a good cuticle remover.

Every shoot involves the same strange ritual of ridicule. Chase throws a tantrum about some inconsequential detail. Then he tries to humiliate me in front of the entire team. With multiple days of taping to get through, I can't let him do this. At least not so soon. It took days to build the speakeasy set complete with plush burgundy velvet couches and dark wood-paneled walls to evoke the mood for a Roaring Twenties-themed Pride Eve cocktail soiree. Not to mention tailoring all of the prohibition era-inspired wardrobe and researching the perfect hors d'oeuvres and signature drinks for Chase's special countdown to Pride. I did consider a 1960s theme to coincide with Stonewall but I couldn't really see myself developing a fun twist on granola and bell bottoms should never be seen again, so we landed on lush deco-decadence for this segment, but it's taken longer than I anticipated. Not to mention there's still social media shoots and B-roll segments for the live telecast to get in the can. I assumed in the days before the Pride Parade Chase would be a complete nightmare, but I hoped we could end day one with him as a tamable beast. We just finished cleaning up the cantaloupe he spit out on the couch after proclaiming it was 'too ripe' and now he's an expert in cured meats despite not knowing the difference between bologna and pastrami.

In fact, I have tasted this brand of prosciutto and it's fine. It lacks some of the nuance of imported artisanal brands, but Oh Mama That's Italian Inc. is a significant sponsor and the network overlords have made it clear that we are to feature their products. I would never promote a product that's beneath my standards. Unfortunately, I don't always get to decide where the bar is set and that part of the job is almost as stressful as dealing with the petulant prima donna in front of me.

Chase repeats, 'Ethan, I want you to put this. In. Your. Mouth.'

'It's television. No one will be able to taste it. What does it matter?'

'What does it matter?' he asks as if we're discussing a Supreme Court nomination. Then Chase slowly and deliberately takes off the black apron we had altered to make his lithe yet muscular body even more alluring to viewers, and dramatically lifts it in the air before throwing it down. He pushes his jet-black bangs with purple high-lights away from his eyes and behind his ears. 'I'll have you know, Chase Myles stands for something. People look up to me. Young people. I'm a queer role model like Ellen DeGeneres or Harley Milk. I will not compromise.'

3

I wonder if he tells people he rides a Harvey. I don't have time to give Chase yet another lesson in gay history. 'Yes, you are the *Harley* Milk of fashion, food and culture. A gay Marie Curie who can plan a swinging party. Can we just *please* get this next shot?'

The set is silent. The often boisterous crew is frozen like some evil queen has cast a spell on them and perhaps one has. I stare at Chase and he stares back at me. Neither of us moves an inch when his tinted purple bangs fall from behind his ear. The tension couldn't boil faster if it were set on an induction cooktop. I look at the clock. In about twenty minutes, we will have to pay overtime and we still have three shots left. Even an hour of overtime can throw the production budget into a tailspin. To be honest I would much rather sit here and have a conversation about the relationship between salt and fat in Italian meat products, but when you're on a successful show the higher you go in the production the further you get from the content. Sometimes I overhear a group of production assistants discussing a segment in great detail going over the nuances of a recipe or the color palette of an outfit and I wonder how I got so far removed from those conversations. Now I keep things moving, meet deadlines and make sure everything looks perfect. 'Should we just take it from the last mark?' I ask, my voice pleading. I'm not above begging in this moment.

'No,' he says, shaking his head. 'I can't work if I'm not taken seriously.' He sits down on the stool behind the counter and crosses his arms in front of him. I look at my watch and see the seconds flying away and the dollar signs adding up. I've got to nip this in the bud. We have too much to do.

'Taken seriously?' I finally respond. 'Are *you* serious right now?' We're behind on shooting and over budget. If I don't get through the production schedule, there's no chance of being ready for the Pride Parade live stream. And if the live stream isn't a success, I can forget about becoming a network executive.

The pressure is too much and I explode.

'You hit the genetic jackpot. Being hot is not a talent. If you were a queer style icon, you would know the difference between gin and vodka, you would know that coq au vin is not made with cocoa and you would know that in 1980 the first openly gay person to be elected to public office in San Fransisco was named *Harvey* Milk, not Harley. I've had it.'

For a long moment Chase keeps his steely eyes, framed by his bi-weekly waxed brows, on me. What have I done? I just poked the bear when I should have been telling him how nice his fur looks. I know how to handle Chase. What was I thinking? The next month has too much riding on it for me to push back with Chase like this.

I'm about to dial it back and take my usual approach of appeasement when Chase calls out, 'Tina!' My assistant who has been hiding behind the craft services table appears. 'Please tell Mr Wells that I will be in my dressing room.' He walks off set, the heels of his custom Italian leather oxfords clicking against the floor the only sound in the studio.

Tina shuffles over to me. 'Excuse me, Ethan. Chase said to tell you that...'

'Tina,' I snap. 'I am already aware of the location of Mr Myles.' Her lips quiver. I can tell she's about to cry. 'I'm sorry. It's not you. You know that. I'm not mad at you.'

'I know,' she says, blinking away the tears. 'It's just that I hate any type of confrontation.'

'Tina, you majored in conflict resolution at NYU.'

'I only did that because I didn't want to confront my parents.' She looks down at her brown loafers.

'Focus, Tina. I need your help. I can't go into his dressing room alone.'

'Why not?' she asks.

'I need a buffer,' I say. 'With you there we are both more likely to be on our best behavior.' I walk down the hall, Tina on my heels, and knock on the door gently. 'Chase, can we talk?'

I hear him tearing around his dressing room. Usually he just does crunches or whatever calisthenics make his body so perfectly beyond human. But I don't hear the usual whoosh of air from his exhale. I knock again. 'Chase, are you all right?'

'What do you care?' he shouts through the door.

'Of course I care.' I care about getting him back to set.

'Mr Myles. It's Tina. Tina Wong. We all care about you, Mr Myles.'

'Tina, he knows who you are,' I say. I know she's trying to be helpful. I suddenly hear closet doors and drawers slamming. What *is* he doing?

'Chase, I'm coming in,' I warn him. I open the door, unprepared for what I see.

'No!' I shout. 'No. No. No. What do you think you're doing?'

He's packing. He has the gorgeous ocean blue Hermès leather duffel bag I got him for Christmas last year open and perched on his makeup chair.

'Ethan, you told me you've had it. Well, you know what? So have I.' He grabs a vintage Hugo Boss seaweed green linen shirt that cost more than my first car and crumples it into a ball before stuffing it into the bag.

'Chase! Don't!' My immediate panic is over the shirt. Some people think it's fine to wear slightly wrinkled linen. These people are going to hell. Then I realize a larger disaster is unfolding, so I ignore the lack of attention to garment care that's making a vein in my forehead twitch. 'Chase, we have so much to do.' I should focus on persuading him to calm down but I can't help myself and reach for the linen shirt, take it out of the bag and honor it with a proper fold.

'It's a holiday weekend and I want a holiday,' he says.

'Chase, you know we need to do all the social media shoots this weekend.'

'I can't,' he says.

'Yes, you can,' I say. I can feel the panic rising in my chest. I dig in my pocket for the small package of colorful antacids I keep on hand. Chase has put off this shoot for the past month. One week he wanted to go to a spa, another time there was a sale at Saks he couldn't miss and last weekend his astrologer told him he should not engage in anything requiring him to stand. The contract is clear that we need these posted by the end of Memorial Day weekend. 'Chase, we can pick up today's shots next week. Tina, could you rework the schedule?' I ask.

'Yes, of course,' she says. I can always count on Tina.

'But we need the socials done this weekend. You can't go anywhere.'

'Ethan, it's a holiday. I'm not going to spend Veteran's Day taking orders from you.'

'This is Memorial Day. The last weekend in May. Veteran's Day is a different holiday. In November,' I say.

Chase lets out an exasperated roar. 'See, it always has to be your way. Your holiday. Your dates. Your timeline.'

'Are you out of your mind?' I ask even though I already know the answer to that question. 'I don't control the dates of federal holidays.'

'You'd like to,' he says, grabbing his jacket.

He's not wrong. I would never put Labor Day on a Monday. Give people a Friday off for a change. And who can keep track of President's Day? It needs to be more consistent. I'd be very good at revising the federal holiday calendar.

Chase zips the duffel closed with a dramatic swing of his arm. At least the linen is safe. 'It's been three years and I'm sick of you always thinking you know everything.'

Three years ago, I met Chase Myles at Cafe Loop when I was researching an article titled 'Ten Things You Don't Know About the New Lettuce'. The restaurant where Chase worked had developed a reputation for exciting salads. Chase showed up at my table with a plate of bitter greens and jicama covered in artisanal honey and goat cheese. I've lived in and around New York most of my life and I had met a lot of exceptional-looking men at the gym, on the train, on the street, but when Chase came over to take my order he was simply breathtaking. He wasn't my type at all. At that time I was dating a film professor with a thick dark moustache who thought narrative film was an abomination and he was on the fence about the use of dialogue. It ended quickly.

I ordered three salads from Chase because I had to study each combination. That was my favorite part of the job, comparing the subtle nuances of each variation. 'Are these all for you?' he asked.

'I'm researching a piece on the new lettuce.'

'There's a *new* lettuce? I thought there was just lettuce. How can you grow a new lettuce?'

'You can't,' I told him. 'You can't grow one but you can create one. That's what I do.' I explained my job was to take things and make them trends. I had been working as a freelance food stylist and was producing some lifestyle pieces on a few television shows. My plan was to soak up as much as I could so I could open an elegant home furnishing shop or a designer clothing boutique, or maybe even a chic little cafe where I could have complete control over the experience from the font on the menu to the design on the foam of an after-dinner cappuccino. Learning about what people liked and how to shape trends was supposed to be the first step toward that. It was never my goal to become a television producer but sometimes the yellow brick road leads you in a direction you weren't always headed.

'It was my article on ramen noodle burgers that helped create that big trend,' I told Chase, trying to impress him.

'What big trend?'

'The ramen noodle burger trend?'

'That's a trend?' he asked.

'Yes, a big trend,' I told him.

'Wow,' he said, his voice full of awe. 'That's awesome.'

I knew that a popular and expanding streaming channel was looking to create a new lifestyle program for gay audiences. Their first foray into the rainbow waters. Someone had suggested I audition to be the host but that was laughable. I certainly knew the material but I could never be on camera. I can barely get through singing 'Happy Birthday' in a crowd, and during a middle school production of *Oliver* I got so nervous before going onstage that I pulled the fire alarm and walked out through the audience.

Now Chase on the other hand, Chase could do it with me behind him. He was eager and you could still smell Wisconsin on him. He wasn't the sharpest knife in the kitchen but I didn't want some fancy steel-forged Santoku blade. I needed the dullest edge possible so I could sharpen it myself. Most importantly, he had that X-factor that made him the natural center of attention. I pitched the idea to Chase and worked to transform some of his cluelessness into an aloof veneer with my witty writing and detailed lifestyle insights. Chase brought the eye candy and I developed the secret sauce. At first Chase was a loveable airhead, easy to work with and willing to do whatever he was told. That first season we worked well together. The critical and commercial response was overwhelmingly positive. We were a hit.

But like all monster stories, the beginning seems so innocent. Surely Godzilla won't eat the fine citizens of Tokyo. Overnight Chase went from being one of the many handsome faces on the streets of New York to the person everyone recognized. Random strangers asked for selfies or stopped to tell him how much they loved him on the show. The ratings and Chase's ego seemed to ride the same wave and I was sucked out to sea by the undertow.

'Ethan, do you have any idea how exhausting it is being your puppet?' Chase asks, snapping my thoughts back to the fact that I have to stop him from leaving or the entire production will come to a grinding halt. I can't wax nostalgic about a time when the most pressure I felt was where to eat that night.

'Chase, we have multiple segments to finish before the parade. The entire LGBTQ world will be watching your live stream in fifteen different countries. Not to mention you're the one cutting the ribbon. You can take a vacation the minute the parade ends and we're on hiatus,' I say and this time my eyes stay parallel with the horizon.

'Do you know what I found on my face yesterday?'

I want to say, 'A sailor's ass,' but I refrain.

'This,' he says, pointing to the area to the side of his eye. I don't see anything. Maybe a light freckle under the makeup. 'It's a stress line and if I don't have a break there will be another and another and another. When does it stop?' I almost feel sorry for Chase. He's always been beautiful but never used to give a thought to what he was wearing or how his bangs fell across his forehead. Now he's obsessed with every inch of his appearance. Chase looks down at his phone and then says, 'There's a car arriving in four to nine minutes. I'm done. I won't stay here and have you control me. I'm not just an amazing body and a chiseled jawline.'

'Of course you aren't,' I plead. 'You also have great hair.' It's true. His hair is like vines of thick, dark weeds that just grow and grow. Rapunzel would scratch his eyes out.

'Ethan! I want to do the show my way. I have ideas too. It's been years of taking orders from you. You shut down every idea I have.'

'I do not,' I say sincerely, although of course I do. His ideas are terrible.

'You do. Like the segment about getting rid of wrinkles.'

'You wanted to use a real iron on your face,' I remind him.

'So what? I wasn't going to plug it in.'

'We can't have millions of people ironing their crow's feet,' I say. Was I supposed to budge on that one? The thought of the lawsuits and scars makes me shudder.

'What about my idea for the raw foods segment?'

'Raw food I am down with. Salads, dips, cold soups. You wanted to do a raw chicken and egg sandwich.'

'I still stand behind that. The amount of protein in it was incredible. But you just proved my point. You never use any of my ideas and I'm sick of it. I want to be appreciated for who I am, not who you think I am when you are telling me who I am and that is not who I am. I am who I think I am.' If Dr Seuss were a narcissus he might have written those words himself. Chase is such a child despite being a year older than I am.

'Chase…' I try to think of something to say to him to get him back to set and stop his tantrum but I'm so sick of him that a part of my brain refuses to go into overdrive the way it usually does to turn things around.

'Goodbye, Ethan,' he says. He grabs his bag and walks out the door. Tina bursts into tears.

'Tina, don't cry,' I say, turning to her and putting my hand on her shoulder for comfort. Chase is just having one of his famous tantrums. He's had them dozens of times before. It's standard operating procedure around here. 'He'll come back. He always comes back,' I say. 'Tomorrow we will all be back at it and this will have been forgotten. I promise.' I give Tina a reassuring look, but inside I feel like the tornado has just begun and someone's about to drop a house on my head.

Chapter 2

The next morning I text Chase to soften things a bit and make sure he's on his way to set. I don't hear anything back but I don't panic. He likes to make me sweat it out. Fine, I'll let him soak up all the attention he needs. I send a few more texts but I don't beg. Chances are he's still asleep at home.

I get out of bed and grab a few antacids from the bottle I keep in arm's reach. Granted, in my tiny studio everything is within arm's reach – the sink, the fridge, the window. I never intended to stay here more than a few months but that was more than a few years ago. I'm never here anyway so what's the point of upgrading to a place I'd rarely enjoy. Most of my time is spent on set shooting the show or in meetings discussing the show. I've been told it's important to have a steady work–life balance but that isn't an issue. I don't have a life so there's nothing to balance. I have a steady diet of *Myles of Style* and antacids. No one ever tells you that getting to the top and staying on top are two very different games. One is an exhilarating climb, the other is a tightrope walk carrying a basket of live chickens.

Instead of racing into the studio I'm up early enough to have a physical and emotional workout. I could call my best friend Kiara but I know she's opening her salon early so she can close early for the holiday weekend. I grab my phone and jump on the cycle I keep squashed in the corner. It's an actual Exercycle from the 1970s with a fan for the front wheel, not a fancy Peloton with a screen and some Adonis telling me to be my best and reach my goals. I don't need that. I have Uncle Clams.

'What's wrong?' he asks as soon as he picks up the phone.

'Nothing is wrong,' I say despite the fact that I could be minutes away from a complete breakdown. But there's no need to trouble him with Chase's latest tantrum. 'And I haven't even said anything so why do you think something is wrong?'

'I can hear it in your breathing. This is exactly how you sounded when your cousin Sheila gave her Barbie Styling Head that mullet haircut.'

'Oh please, you were more upset than I was,' I say, huffing and puffing into the phone as the fan on the bike makes everything not nailed down in my apartment flutter.

'True,' he says. 'I mean, who does that to a natural blonde like Barbie...' He starts coughing.

I wait a second for him to catch his breath, but it takes him longer than I would like. I get off the cycle. 'Uncle Clams? Are you all right? Has the nurse arrived?' I'm already swiping through screens to text the nurse on duty. It's Friday morning so that means it's Paula, but she doesn't usually arrive until a bit later. Uncle Clams lives in a rent-controlled apartment on 7th Street in the East Village. He has diabetes and he broke his ankle four months ago so his daughter Sheila and I decided Clams needed someone to help out from time to time until he is fully recovered.

'Stop. Do not text Paula. She's already here and in the kitchen. I'm totally fine. You would not believe what that jerk of an ex-husband did to her this weekend.'

I listen carefully to make sure he's telling the truth about being all right. I know his entire nursing schedule and have the private phone numbers of every staff member who is part of the rotating group of home health aides we've hired. If he suffers even a moment of discomfort they have me to answer to. The fact is they're all sweethearts. I'm not sure if that's due to their natural dispositions or the fact that Uncle Clams makes everyone feel like they're his best friend.

As he tells me about the latest episode with Paula and the fight over custody of a guinea pig named Mr Pope she's having with her ex, I resume my workout. His voice is clear and steady so my concern about any immediate issue abates. All my life Uncle Clams has been a rock in my life, so seeing him struggle with his health has made me very concerned.

When things were hard growing up Uncle Clams was always the one telling me things would get better. The summer after my dad walked out, never to be heard from again, my mom let me stay with him for a week in New York City and I was hooked. The East Village was only sixty miles from our house in suburban New Jersey but it could have been on another planet. That summer Uncle Clams taught me how to haggle over a piece of fish on Fulton Street, why you should always use the side entrance to The Metropolitan Museum of Art and the importance of having a few basic black well-tailored staples in your closet. He showed me a world of beauty and style that existed beyond the strip malls and chain restaurants that dominated my hometown where I felt like such an outsider. Uncle Clams showed me how to create my own perfect world and that made me feel safe during a time when everything at home seemed out of control.

I couldn't figure out why my dad left or how to stop the kids at school from calling me names but I could find the perfect cheese dome or silk ascot and, silly as it is, that made me feel in control and safe. I couldn't control the big things but I could make the details of my life shiny.

'So anyway they decided to just cremate Mr Pope,' Clams says.

'They killed the guinea pig?' I ask in horror as my feet slip off the pedals of the bike.

'No. Mr Pope passed months ago. They're fighting over what to do with the remains. Did I leave that part out?' he asks innocently.

'Yes, Uncle Clams. You did.'

'Whoopsie,' he says in a high falsetto. 'Anyway, on to more important news. The parade is less than a month away and I was thinking...'

I get off the bike. I need both feet on the ground to have this conversation again. 'I told you I'll be working the whole day. Chase is the Grand Marshall.'

'But you're the only one who knows how to make that old heap of junk run,' he says. One semester of auto repair class in high school because I had a crush on a grease monkey named Anthony DeLuca and I'm my uncle's de facto mechanic. Ever since he came out decades ago, Uncle Clams has rolled through Pride riding in a 1958 Ford Fairlane Sunliner as his alter ego, the fabulous drag queen Clams Casino. He rides perched on the back seat with his two best friends, the other members of The Giblet Triplets. They've played every gay bar from Winnipeg to Tallahassee, but The Ice Palace on Fire Island is the stage they call home.

I hate the fact that I can't drive everyone down the parade route this year. Uncle Clams is more than my mom's older brother. He's both my family and my found family, which is a powerful combination. There has got to be a way to get him to the parade this year, but with producing the live stream with Chase, the ribbon cutting and the mountain of work I have before the parade, I can't seem to make all the pieces fit.

'I have to run Uncle Clams. I'll check in later,' I say. 'Be careful on your ankle. Please.'

'The doctor said I was totally healed,' he answers back.

'He said it was on the way to completely healing. I was at the appointment with you.'

'Oh, right, which reminds me, did you ever call back that doctor? He was absolutely delicious.'

'I did not,' I say, grabbing a towel and wiping my forehead.

'I don't understand it. You're adorable. So what if your hair is more red than auburn? You're in great shape and your skin is flawless thanks to my moisturizing secrets. Any problems you do have can be worked out with a good therapist. Thirty-five doesn't last forever. Or that solid hairline.' For my uncle all of this is a compliment. He has loved me unconditionally all of my life, but his untethered desire to see me in a relationship is often more than I can handle. I'm too busy to even think about having a serious boyfriend.

'Oh look, the building next door to mine is suddenly engulfed in flames. I have to go. Stay off your ankle. I love you. Bye,' I say and hang up.

I check my phone to see if Chase has made contact. Nothing yet but I'm sure he'll be on set when I get there. He has to be.

-

An hour later it turns out he *doesn't* have to be. I'm sitting in Chase's dressing room waiting for him with a special smoothie made of all his favorite things and a few herbs that I sometimes put in to help him relax during the day. Nothing illicit, just some chamomile and mint to take the edge off. I plan to be as solicitous as possible, praise him, build him up and then get his ass on set as quickly as possible since we've already lost half a day of production and I have an important meeting later this morning.

I take out my phone and send the nicest, sweetest text I can create. Tell him how much we need him and how great he looks. That stuff just pours out of me. It's so much easier to text this stuff than to actually have the words come out of my mouth. I'm so used to spreading it all over him. I've officially crossed the line to begging. What Chase really wants to hear is how clever and smart he is. That I can't bring myself to do. It's not that it isn't true. I mean, it isn't. It's the fact that it couldn't be further from the truth. It's one thing to stretch the boundaries of truthiness but another to just surrender to it.

I stare at my phone waiting for the Bubbles of Hope. Nothing.

I wait. And wait. Nothing. Eventually the ice in the smoothie melts so the glass is filled with weird separated green layers. Once that happens, I know I'm in trouble.

A knock on the door makes me jump. For a second I'm relieved, but even Chase isn't dumb enough to knock on his own dressing room door. It's Tina.

'Have you heard anything?' she asks.

'No,' I say, unable to hide my concern. 'Maybe he overslept?' Chase has been known to sleep until noon given the opportunity. I keep trying not to think about the Hermès bag he was stuffing yesterday. He wouldn't, would he?

'Right, maybe he overslept?' Tina says, her voice climbing with each word, indicating she too thinks it's a dim possibility.

'I have to head to my meeting with Maria Luisa and if he hasn't woken up after that we'll just have to go to his apartment and wake him up.'

'To his apartment?' Tina's face freezes. The last time this happened and we woke him up he threw an entire bowl of Lucky Charms at me. Most of it landed on my face but a few of the blue marshmallows got caught in Tina's hair.

'Don't worry. Just wear something easy to clean that goes with milk and we'll be fine.'

Chapter 3

The waiting room for the network vice president's office is designed to intimidate. Blown up images from vintage hit shows like *Carol's Classroom* and *Family Time Out*, long windows with sweeping views over Central Park, and a receptionist that could make the guards on Rikers Island cry like babies. It's as much a set as any of the ones the network built for the hit shows they've produced and one day very soon it will all be mine. There are a few mountains I have to climb before that happens and one of them is seated in front of me.

'Beverly, you look amazing,' I say as soon as I walk in. 'Is that a new dress?'

She turns from her computer, looks at me with disgust and says, 'I bought this dress for my engagement party in 1987. Sit down.' Beverly is not married, so there's a story there. I sit as instructed, checking my phone nervously and praying that Chase will wake up and call me or, better yet, go directly to set.

The door to Maria Luisa's office swings open with a burst of laughter and out walks Jeremiah Jones, the producer of *Queens of the Night*, the network's second-highest rated lifestyle program. It's a glorified talk show with a rotating cast of popular celebrities. Jeremiah has an unheard-of ability to get the biggest names. There's a rumor that he's started working on having the drag queen Betsy Headaches interview Justin Trudeau. If that happens I can forget about taking over Maria Luisa's job and becoming the VP of diversity programming.

'Ethan Wells,' Jeremiah says curtly.

'Jeremiah Jones, so good to see you,' I say, hoping he knows I'm lying. I knew Jeremiah when we were both interns at *She's Talking Now*. He was assigned to the talent booker and I was technically assisting the producer of the cooking segments, but in reality we were both at the beck and call of one of the show's most temperamental host. One afternoon he 'accidentally' gave me the wrong coffee order for said host. He swears it was a mistake but he was eventually promoted and I still have a small scar from having a hot raspberry coconut latte thrown at me. Years later we're still competing with each other. I want this promotion but even more I don't want Jeremiah to get it. I'm overly competitive. Once I dated a guy who claimed to be more competitive than I am, and we actually competed to see who was more competitive in a breath-holding competition that ended with a medical intervention.

'Wonderful to see you,' he says as he shuts the door to Maria Luisa's office behind him. I know he's lying. 'I was just about to email you,' Jeremiah continues. 'I'm worried about your show. Production stopped yesterday? I really hope everything is okay.' It's been less than a day and already the rumor mill is in high gear. *Wake up*, *Chase*. *Get to set*, I scream inside my head.

'All is well. I'm so blessed because I have a real star on my show. I don't have the endless panic of worrying about a guest pulling out at the last minute. Like you do. I'm always so impressed at how you pull it off even when things go off the rails. You're a king. A real *king*.' Gayle

King canceled at the last minute two weeks ago and rumor has it Jeremiah was covered in hives for forty-eight hours. I notice he starts scratching his arm and I smile.

'She's ready for you,' Beverly says.

'Can't keep Ms Zepeda waiting,' I say, moving away from Jeremiah.

'Drinks? Soon?' he asks as he walks away.

'As soon as possible! DM me on all my socials,' I reply, knowing it will never happen.

'You got it,' he says with a Stevia smile. He leaves and the doors to Maria Luisa's office, *my future office*, open and I step inside. Her office makes the waiting room look cozy. Severe black modern chairs face her cool marble desk that looks like it took half a quarry to construct. You can see all the way to the end of Central Park from the windows behind her desk but it's hard to tear one's eyes away from the exceptional original bronze Francisco Arturo Marín sculpture of two figures embracing that she has on a pedestal next to the conference table. Apparently her family was close with the artist's family in Mexico City. It's a stunning work of art that is as beautiful as it is intimidating, not unlike Maria Luisa.

A man I don't know is seated in one of the chairs. He begins to stand up and I suddenly remember that this is a meet and greet with a new sponsor, my absolute least favorite part of my job, which is why I must have blocked it from my mind.

'Ethan, this is Michael Winthrop the Fourth,' Maria Luisa says, gesturing toward a man who looks like he might be auditioning for the role of Mr Burns in a live action film. It's a sharp contrast to the elegant silhouette created by Maria Luisa with her tight bob, round glasses and usual hand-tailored dark suit. She has hundreds of variations of the same professional uniform. They are each expertly tailored with slight variations in shade and form. I adore each one. This one I call 'Midnight in Berlin' and it has the most charming minimalist peplum at the waist. I want to tell her I am living for it but I try to remain professional.

'Hello, Mr Winthrop,' I say, smiling as I shake his hand because that is what you do when you meet a potential new sponsor. You smile and shake their hand.

'Mr Winthrop's organization is currently developing something that I think will really make an impact on our target demographics, and help the community too, of course.'

She adds that last part no matter what the product is. She would add it to a gay cigarette if you were still allowed to advertise cancerous addictions on television.

Winthrop doesn't say a word. I find it hard to believe that he's the person behind the next big gay 'it' item.

'We're so excited that Mr Winthrop has brought his product to our *lifestyle programming*.' Lifestyle programming is one of the code words for Big Homo shows. 'His research team has been developing this for a while now and I just can't be more thrilled about it. Are you ready to be wowed?' Maria Luisa asks.

'Is anyone ever really ready to be wowed?' I ask. 'I mean it seems like the kind of thing you can't really be ready for.' I make sure my snark is right on the edge but not past it. At least, I hope it isn't.

Mr Winthrop's face wrinkles and his frown stretches. Maria Luisa clears her throat. 'Mr Winthrop and a team of his engineers and marketing experts think they have really cracked the queer dollar with this.'

Cracked the queer dollar? I'm supposed to just let that comment pass. What does it even mean? I smile and nod. Smile and nod.

'It's called "Power Top Pop".' Maria Luisa grabs her tablet and shows me the screen as she sits on the edge of the desk. I look at the tablet and see four prototype bottles in four different colors but I have no idea what could be in them.

'Looks amazing,' I say. 'I love it!' There isn't really an option for another answer. 'What is it?' I have to ask.

'It's a combination energy drink *and* personal lubricant. It's both. Isn't that amazing?' Maria Luisa says with Christmas, Purim and the Fourth of July in her voice.

This would be the appropriate time to either do a spit take or throw up. Possibly both.

'Say what?' I ask, assuming what I heard can't be right. Even on an engineering level you can't have a drink and a lubricant in one bottle, can you? Mr Winthrop's expression has not changed.

'Oh, they're working out some of the kinks like the dermatitis from drinking it and the upset stomach from having contact with skin but they're this close.' Maria Luisa holds up her fingers showing me the tiniest space between them. 'I didn't even tell you the best part.'

'There's more?' I ask, grabbing the edge of the chair next to me to steady myself.

'They come in four fabulous flavors. Each one inspired by a different Golden Girl.' Maria Luisa laughs with delight.

'A personal lubricant that's also an energy drink with *Golden Girls* flavors.' I say the phrase slowly and deliberately to make sure I have it right. What beast in gay hell came up with this idea?

24

Mr Winthrop coughs to interrupt us and says, 'We've done a great deal of research on the male homosexual with our target income level and we've found that these are the three things that often motivate them to spend.' The only person who says male homosexual is someone who is not one.

'So you're telling me that one of these...' I don't know what I should call it. '...one of these things tastes like Bea Arthur.'

'Well, they're inspired by her,' Maria Luisa says. We've been in many of these meetings before so I can tell her tone is waxing annoyed. 'The flavor is bold and...' Maria Luisa is faking her way through this. I know for a fact she has never studied the Golden Girls the way I have. Once I mentioned St Olaf and she had zero reaction. She searches for another word. 'It's bold and... ah... tall.'

'It tastes tall?' I ask. 'What exactly does tall taste like?'

Maria Luisa is not amused by my response. I realize I'm overstepping my place here. I'm usually much more of a supplicant in these meetings. I think the fact that Chase is missing in action has made me unable to control myself.

'Well it sounds great. I can't imagine a better product for *Myles of Style.*' The words just come out of my mouth. It's like I'm speaking them phonetically. That's what I've been encouraged to say whenever I'm shown a new product and with so much riding on the next few weeks I have to play nice.

'Did you hear that, Mr Winthrop?'

Maria Luisa knows her job is to please the sponsors. My heart sinks a bit realizing that if I get this promotion, it will be my job too. But it also means a lot more control over everything that happens across the division. Not to mention I'll get to change all the art on the walls in this office from the imposing abstract art to something more humane like contemporary portrait photography. Still, I wonder if my desire to redecorate is enough reason to be in such a relentless pursuit of the position. Moving up is the next logical step in my career and I've spent years blindly putting one foot in front of the other. That's how you get ahead, but it makes it hard not to trip.

Maria Luisa and Mr Winthrop chat about how the details will work contractually and I tune out thinking about what I'm going to yell at Chase when I find him asleep in his apartment after this meeting.

I'm working on a list of expletives around his laziness when I hear Maria Luisa say, 'I'll make sure we have this posted to his socials in time for the launch.' Maria Luisa must be able to tell I've zoned out because her eyes give me the visual equivalent of a poke. 'Your team can get this rolling with Chase?'

I nod and smile. For a split second I think of saying, 'No, we can't,' and telling both of them that this product is the stupidest thing I've ever heard of. But I don't. I just smile and nod.

We all shake hands and Mr Winthrop leaves. Maria Luisa and I are alone. We wait to hear the ding from the elevator and then Beverly buzzes in and says, 'Elvis has left the building,' which is code that a sponsor is out of ear shot.

'Is this the stupidest product you have ever heard of in your entire life? Who wants to give a blow job that tastes like Estelle Getty?' Maria Luisa rants as she whips off her glasses. She is even more angered by the idea of it than I am. 'But the synergy of revenue is excellent. Winthrop brings a lot of other streams to the river in other areas and we currently aren't in a position to turn away sponsors with Pride a few weeks away.'

Maria Luisa has this ability to let the ridiculousness of the product roll off her back so she can focus on the bigger picture. I assume once I'm in her position it will come more naturally. I'm inching toward the door when Maria Luisa says, 'Wait, Ethan. Can you give me an update on your socials? Some sponsors called this morning. I told them you've been incredibly busy preparing the B-roll for the Pride live stream. Are you on schedule?'

'We're doing it this weekend at the apartment. Followers love to see Chase in his natural environment,' I say. What his followers don't know is that his natural environment is looking at himself in the mirror.

'Is everything okay with you two? I heard Chase was getting a bit out of control. I know you two usually find a way to make it work but we can't have any major blowups before the parade telecast. It wouldn't look right.'

One of the bigger mistakes I've made in my life was pretending that Chase and I are a couple. When we pitched the show to the network we were working with a publicist who thought the couple angle would sizzle. 'Very Portia and Ellen or Elton and David,' she said. Chase didn't think anyone would believe that someone like him would be with someone like me but the network loved the idea of 'us' and at first it seemed to make sense to perform the role of the perfect power couple for publicity events.

I've never in my life had a sexual or romantic thought about Chase. Yes, when I saw him all those years ago he struck me as incredibly attractive but a pretty face and a sexy body aren't enough for me. I need more than that and it's not always easy to find. In fact, it's never easy to find, which is why I've gotten comfortable with the arrangement. Pretending to be with Chase means I don't have to think about dating or anything like that. My dating life was a disaster. The last serious boyfriend I had quit rabbinical school right before we dated and after we dated he went back so I'm not exactly a featured profile on Grindr. Maria Luisa and the sponsors like the idea of Chase being in a relationship. Less chance of a rumor spreading about him being at some drug-fueled sex party. Good chance he'll be there, but less chance of a rumor spreading about it since I'd be able to provide an alibi. So, for now, I have to fake it and make the occasional appearance on the other side of the camera or at social events to keep up appearances. We celebrated our fake anniversary on one episode of the show and it was the highest rated of the season. People like happy couples.

Of course, Chase still gets nailed by guys morning, noon and night but he never leaves his apartment without a non-disclosure agreement in his pocket. On the surface we look content and audiences are more interested in how we are able to 'have it all' and less interested in Chase's always having a ball. Social media is a House of Mirrors with mostly jagged edges.

The publicist who suggested the cover story for the pitch quit after the first season, leaving me in charge of Chase's image on and off camera. No one at the network would work with him. Apparently she joined a geological expedition in Antarctica which still seems like a Swiss picnic compared to my job.

'Everything is fine with Chase,' I lie. 'Couldn't be better. Yes, we have our spats but you know how couples can be. Everything good with Lee? I saw them at the opening of that new musical with Sutton Foster.'

'Oh yes, Lee is marvelous.' Maria Luisa smiles and I breathe a sigh of relief that I have successfully changed the subject and evaded more suspicion. She loves to talk about Lee. They met each other in college and have been a couple for most of their lives.

After telling me about how Lee is taking a course on flower arranging she says, 'Whatever problems you two are having, work them out. More importantly, get your socials back on track.' Her tone intensifies. 'I'm really taking a chance with you doing the live remote for the Pride Parade and streaming it. All eyes will be on us. It's our chance to get some major crossover action with mainstream media and we don't want to disappoint our sponsors.'

Maria Luisa says this constantly. *We don't want to disappoint our sponsors.* I imagine them lined up like infants waiting for their warm bottle of formula and throwing a tantrum when they don't get what they want immediately. The image is not so far from the reality. 'Not to mention we need hits. Eyeballs on screen and staying on screen. That's what matters now. I know you understand that. I need buzz. How is Chase handling the pressure?' Her expertly tweezed and penciled eyebrows knit together.

'Oh, he's great,' I say, making sure my words sing across the desk so that they sound carefree and believable.

'Good to hear. I was worried it all might be too much and that Chase would leave us in a predicament. He can be a bit temperamental.'

'Ha!' I say, and then, 'Ha, ha, ha!' The sounds have no resemblance to laughter at all. It's more like an animal signaling an attack. 'Absolutely not. No, no, no. I have everything under control.' My leg starts bouncing and I have to use my hand to stop it. Maria Luisa is fully aware of the fact that Chase can be a diva. He has stormed up to this office multiple times complaining about the smallest detail until Beverly was put in charge of keeping him out. I have no idea what she did but Chase stopped visiting. Beverly could keep a Republican senator from a confirmation hearing if she wanted to.

'Good, because I plan to be running the entire studio in Shanghai by the end of the summer. I'd love to see you take over for me in this role. But it's a decision I need to make with a number of stakeholders. If it were my decision alone, I'd give the job to you right now.'

'Thank you, Maria Luisa. That means a lot to me.' I can't tell if she's being truthful or not. She's diplomatic to a fault.

'I appreciate that. It would mean a lot to me too to have someone like me in my corner. But the fact remains that *Queens of the Night* pulls in numbers and there are some who think Jeremiah is quite promotable. He's shown an amazing ability to really pull in the sponsors and make them happy. His followers are loyal and always increasing.'

Not another conversation about pleasing sponsors and increasing followers. If I'd known when I started this job how much of my life would involve 'pleasing sponsors and increasing followers' I never would have finished the three salads Chase served me all those years ago. I love working with the details, the food, the lifestyle tips and making everything look gorgeous. What I hate is finding out my perfect centerpiece needs to feature some crappy organic rainbow-colored punch bowl. Jeremiah, however, has no issues promoting any number of asinine products on his show including My Twinkle, the portable bidet, a product which he stole from my show.

'I was able to convince the team to wait until we see how everything goes with the parade and once that's a success it will be very hard for anyone to think of a better candidate than you. Still, little things like these late social media posts can be a big deal. It's the details that can prevent you from moving up.'

I catch a glimpse of myself reflected in the window. *You want this job. You want this job.* I try to implant the thought in my brain. I do. I do want this job. I think. Part of me feels like I was just crossing the street and somehow got caught up in the New York marathon without ever intending to enter but now I've started leading the pack, crossing the finish line seems like the only choice. This job would mean more money, more power and more prestige. Who am I, Joan Collins on *Dynasty*?

'I won't disappoint you,' I say, knowing that is going to be a very tall order given the circumstances. I'll be lucky if I don't embarrass her. At this point I aspire to mere disappointment.

Chapter 4

The car pulls up outside Chase's building on the Upper East Side. Last year I helped Chase decorate a stunning apartment with pre-war detail and a huge terrace a few blocks from Central Park. Most of my work was preventing Chase from bringing any of his own taste to the place. He wanted to install a stripper pole because he thought that would make the place 'classy'. We use the apartment for influencer shoots and wardrobe fittings when Chase is 'too tired' to come to set. I consider it my 'office away from office'.

Tina is waiting for me in the lobby and we get in the elevator up where I use my key to open the door. 'Chase? Chase, are you here? Wake up.'

I go immediately to the bedroom. If I wake him up and throw him in the shower I might be able to salvage the day. I open the door and his bed is a mess of twisted sheets. I was sure he was oversleeping to spite me. I pull the sheets off the bed revealing only my desperation. Maybe he got up and went to the studio and we missed him? Someone would have called to tell me if that was the case.

I sit on the edge of the bed thinking about my next step. On the nightstand next to a tangle of charging cables I see a flyer with a photo of smooth muscular torsos gyrating on a dance floor under neon-colored lights. *No, he did not*. I grab it and read the details. This weekend is the Purple Party in Miami. Chase has always been a circuit queen. He loves showing himself off on the dance floor. I've never understood the allure of these parties but they're a religious experience for him. All this BS about needing a break and being under stress. The waistband on my underwear has more tension than he does and I bought this pair in college. I remember him telling me he wanted to go. I shut it down so fast the memory of his request must have been deleted from my brain.

I take out my phone and open the popular gay hook-up app SecretSlam where you don't need a face picture to hook, just a few random images of your body parts. Each profile is geo-tagged. I only use it to keep tabs on Chase. I haven't wanted to do this yet but I don't have any other choice. I go to my Favorites tab. There's only one profile there and it features an image of a smooth bottom with suds clinging to it. I look closer and it says, 'MagicAss is 1,275 miles away.' I get up from the bed and leap to his closet. I open the door and look at the top shelf. They're gone. His special travel pillow and the eye mask with the false eyelashes sewn on it.

'Tina!' I yell from the closet door and she runs into the bedroom.

'Is he in there? Is he in the closet?'

'No, Tina, he's not in the closet. I need you to pull up the show Amex he uses and see if he...' I can barely make the words come out of my mouth. '...booked a flight to Miami.'

She doesn't ask questions. She takes out her phone, swipes through a few screens and her jaw unhinges. 'How did you know? JFK to Miami.' She looks up from her phone. 'First class. It cost more than my rent for a month. Wow.'

'Tina, I've watched enough *Law and Order* to know that what I am about to say may be used against me at some point but... I am going to *kill* him.'

Tina squirms uncomfortably and swipes on her phone. 'The return ticket is for Monday.' She squeaks the words out. 'At least he'll be back soon. I'll forward the details.'

'Monday is not soon enough. I was just in Maria Luisa's office and she made it crystal clear she wants those social media posts up *before* Monday.'

Tina lets one tear roll down her eye and then more follow. She has cried every day since I hired her. She even cried during her interview when she thought she was making a bad impression, so I hired her on the spot to cheer her up and then she cried from happiness.

'It's okay, Tina. We'll think of something.' I hate seeing her weep even after the buckets of tears I've witnessed. I don't know what to do. I can't tell Maria Luisa that I let Chase just run off. If she thinks I can't handle one temperamental star, she'll never let me be in charge of a whole division. 'Tina, I'll make you some tea to calm your nerves,' I say, since a nice hot cup might calm me down as well.

'That would be nice,' she says and plops down in the overstuffed Ralph Lauren club chair I selected for that exact spot by the bookcase.

I walk into the kitchen and put the kettle on the stove. I quickly make the tea and try to think of a solution but nothing comes to me. I'm freaking out but I need to keep my outside cool and calm. Think pretty thoughts. Expertly folded fitted sheets. An authentic mid-century Eames chair. A tart tartine with browned sugar on top. I bring the tea to Tina who is now perusing the bookcase in the living room.

'Do you want me to book us tickets to Miami? Could we do the shoot there?' she asks.

'I thought about that but we wouldn't get there until tomorrow and I've seen how he parties at these things. The sponsor is expecting their perfectly groomed gay role model, not a hungover circuit queen with little spirals for eyeballs. Chase is really screwing me over.' I don't even want to think about what the network executives will say when they find out I let our star sneak away without getting everything in the can. No one will blame Chase. Everyone will blame me and by blame, I mean fire. I can forget any possibility of being promoted to Maria Luisa's position. I pitch some ideas to Tina for excuses as to why we didn't get the posts. Flying down to Miami is looking better and better. I clear away the tea and take the tray back into the kitchen.

'He doesn't look so perfectly groomed here!' Tina says from the living room. 'Ugh, was he recovering from a coma or something?'

I walk back in and Tina brings over a framed photograph that was sitting tucked away on a shelf. 'It looks like he hasn't shaved or had a haircut in weeks. When was this?'

I look at the photo and immediately realize it isn't Chase at all. 'That's Beau. Chase's brother. Chase has an identical twin.'

'Oh my God. There are two of them!'

'I know. The very idea is terrifying. They had a huge falling-out years ago and haven't spoken since. He lives in a backwoods town upstate a few hours from here. I'm surprised he keeps that picture around. I've never met him.'

I stare at the picture for a second, amazed at how much they look alike. It's hard to tell at first because Beau has a Grizzly Adams Mountain Man beard and his hair is pure metal band, but you could never mistake those sparkling green eyes. Anyone would think he's Chase.

And then I realize: that's it. That's the solution.

'Anyone would think he *is* Chase!' I say to Tina.

Tina is sipping her tea and drying her tears with a vintage Chanel handkerchief I gave her for her birthday that's really more ornamental than functional, but I don't have time to fix that. 'Anyone would think *who* is Chase?' she asks.

'Him!' I say, pointing to the picture.

'I thought you said his name was Beau.'

'It is. For now,' I say, looking at the picture and staring right into his eyes. Chase isn't coming back until Monday. I need to have this posted before that. It's just a few pictures. How hard could it be? Even Tina thought that the picture of Beau was Chase. It's absolutely crazy but it could work and it has a slightly better chance of working than trying to pull Chase off a sweaty dance floor in Florida. We'll get a few pictures for social media. Chase will be back on Monday night and we can pick up where we left off shooting for the live stream. No one will know the difference, and by no one I mean Maria Luisa.

'Tina, didn't you say last week that you could use more overtime to help pay some of the production costs on your girlfriend's film? The one you're producing?'

'I did,' she says. My insane plan will not just help me, it will help Tina. I convince myself this is an item in the plus column.

'Do you want me to go to Miami with you? Are you going to try to find Chase?'

'Tina, if the mountain will not come to Muhammad, then Muhammad must go to the mountain... man. Pack an emergency bag and rent us a car with a full tank of gas. We're going on a field trip.'

Chapter 5

It takes over six hours of winding roads up and over mountains to get to our destination. Tina is good company. There's no satellite radio in the rental so her constant stream of consciousness narration is like listening to a Dada-inspired soundtrack. She goes from politics to pop culture to pepper grinders to her lifelong dream of visiting Paris. She treats each subject with the same seriousness of intent although she is somewhat obsessive about a few of the patisseries along the Seine she has researched. It's background noise because I'm completely focused on one thing: bringing Beau back to New York and passing him off as Chase to complete our social media obligations. Maria Luisa has been a wonderful mentor to me since I started at the network. I can't let her down and I can't let myself down. It's the only way to stay on track for the promotion. Surely this is one of the most insane plans I have ever had in my life and once in college I tried out for the soccer team just because I had a crush on a varsity player. All I know is the name of the town where Beau lives and that's where we're headed.

The aptly named Stark, New York, is like a scene from a survivalist movie produced on a budget. The center of town consists of a hardware store, a diner and something called Stark Grocery and Animal Feed Quick Mart that looks like it only sells things that have expired in the past decade.

'Let's try the Quick Mart,' I tell Tina. According to Google, it's the closest thing to a grocery store within forty miles. Even if Beau catches all his own food with his bare hands, he must at least stop in here for condiments.

'You mean go inside, and like, talk to people? I can't do that.'

'Just follow me,' I say, trying to reassure her, although I'm not so sure myself.

The parking lot is covered in black and gray melting slush despite the fact that it's the end of May. I think we have driven as many miles north as we have gained in altitude. Walking from the car to the front door is a challenge; the gale-force winds make it almost impossible to keep my balance. Maybe my suede Gucci loafers weren't the best choice for a day trip to the Siberia of America.

I open the door, and a woman sitting behind the register is smoking a cigarette. She doesn't even pretend to put it out. She just keeps smoking and staring straight ahead. 'Excuse me?' I ask. Butching it up just a little, I rub my nose with my sleeve despite the fact that it makes my insides quiver. I know when I need to protect myself.

'What?' she asks. She isn't unfriendly but her response doesn't make me want to knit her a tea cozy.

'I'm looking for someone,' I tell her, dropping my usually low voice even lower.

'Uh huh. You a cop?'

'No, not at all,' I say, losing the octave I had a second ago. A cop? I'm wearing a $1,200 Balmain black bomber jacket with an asymmetrical zipper. I decide to ignore the question. 'Do you know Beau Myles?' I ask and show her the picture I took from Chase's apartment.

'Duh? Of course I know Beau. Everyone does.'

Great. This is going to be so much easier than I thought. Get his address. Woo him with my charm. Take him back to NYC for a few pictures. FedEx him back here. Bing, bang, boom.

'If you'll just give me the address, I'll be out of your hair.' Then I remember I should buy something as a courtesy, so I grab a few packs of Slim Jims and a few containers of chewing tobacco that I'll leave outside as an offering to the people of Stark.

She looks at me suspiciously. 'Where the hell are you from?'

I don't tell her I grew up in New Jersey in a split-level home in a lower middle-class suburb surrounded by other split-level homes that looked exactly like the one I lived in. Instead I say, 'Bit south of har,' in an accent that makes it sound like I'm auditioning for a high school production of *Our Town*.

'If you're looking for Beau, you best talk to Rebus first. Over at the diner. He and his people have claim before you do I reckon.'

I've never heard anyone actually say reckon before but I suppose it's the entirely correct turn of phrase in this instance. 'Oh, I see. I don't have any claim. Nothing like that,' I say. 'I just need his address.'

'We don't like repeating ourselves around here but I'm known for being nice.' Yeah, so far it's been like chatting with Oprah. 'You talk to Rebus. Diner. Go.'

I pay for my souvenirs, give Tina a chance to use the restroom, and do as I'm told. This time I let her wait in the car.

The diner looks like an old aluminum Greyhound bus that has had the wheels cut off. From the outside it's kitsch and almost charming. I could imagine a menu full of down-home blue-ribbon specials and pies so fresh they sing as they come out of the oven. Once I open the door I see they've decorated in 'End of the World Chic'.

'Is Rebus around?' I ask. This time, I'm butching it up considerably. Like World Wrestling Federation-level butch.

A waitress wearing a stained apron over a ragged flannel yells, 'Rebus! You got someone.'

The kitchen door swings open. A man almost the size of the diner and covered in long salt and pepper hair with a beard that goes almost to his enormous belly. My first thought is *Please don't kill me*. I'm glad Tina waited in the car. She shouldn't see this.

'Yeah, who wants me?' he says, his voice like a frozen car engine barely sputtering.

'I'm looking for Beau Myles,' I say, trying to mimic his tone, hoping the subtext of my sentence is *Please don't kill me*.

'Beau Myles? That SOB? If you see him you tell him I want my money. You related to that deadbeat?'

'No way,' I say, realizing I am so in touch with my inner butch at the moment. In my head I'm singing a constant refrain of 'Please Don't Kill Me'.

'He owes my buddies down south. He knows it. And he knows I'm keeping an eye on him for 'em.' Down south? Does he mean in New York City or in Alabama? I have no idea but clearly this guy is serious. 'He don't pay by the end of the month pretty boy is gonna be missing a few things. You know, like an arm or maybe his legs.'

I don't think Rebus is indulging in expressive metaphor. I think he means he will actually break off one of Beau's limbs and use it as a toothpick or to stir some animal stew in an outdoor cauldron. 'You can go down and tell him that.'

'I would be happy to convey your message, Rebus. Can you tell me where he is?'

'Prolly at his yurt.'

'His what?'

'His yurt, his tent. Take Quarry Rock Road until it turns to dirt then walk another mile. And tell him he better have my money or he's gonna find that yurt in a heap of ashes come the end of next month.'

'Money. End of month. Broken limbs. Ashes. I'm not going to write that down. I think I got it,' I say, slowly backing out of the diner. 'It's all up here.' I tap my forehead as I make my exit. 'Thanks.'

Tina and I leave downtown Stark and she helps me find Quarry Rock Road about ten miles away. The few buildings that make up Stark quickly give way to vast expanses of wilderness. Pine trees on steroids tower over us, making the gray afternoon turn from dove to gunmetal. There is beauty in the wilderness but there's also something foreboding that makes me nervous. I'd much rather take my chances being trampled to death in Grand Central Station than being mauled by something in the forest.

The road goes from pavement to gravel to mud, at which point we have no choice but to get out of the car and walk. My wardrobe provides as much protection from the muddy forest path as a cocktail umbrella would from a hurricane.

'Tina, you've done more than your duty. I think I should do the last part on my own. Just keep the car running so you don't freeze.'

'Are you sure? I mean, you could get eaten or lost or lost and then eaten.'

'Oh sure. Be an optimist when things are looking so bleak.'

I tighten my cashmere scarf around my neck and start walking.

For the first time since we left Manhattan, my thoughts turn to Chase. He must know the predicament he has left me in. With each step I plot my revenge. I'm walking between mud, ice, slush and frozen mud which must have its own name even though I can't imagine what it is. Chase is off partying on some beach sunning his already overly tanned body while some sugar daddy pays for drinks that have Rolex watches dropped in as garnish. He thinks he can just slide back after the long weekend? Well, he can think again. I'm going to make his life hell. How I'm going to do that escapes me at the moment but the minute he's back on Monday night it starts.

After about fifteen minutes, I see smoke in the distance. I round a curve and spot what must be his yurt. There's a snowmobile, skis, and a bunch of broken mechanical parts scattered around the circular structure. As I get closer, I wonder how many visitors Beau gets and what the proper etiquette is for approaching a yurt. You can't knock on canvas and I don't see any possibility of there being a proper door. I walk closer, slowing my steps as my worries about how to approach are replaced by fear.

'Hello!' I shout from outside the structure. 'Hello. I'm looking for Beau Myles.' The yurt does have a flap that looks like a door, so I smack my hand on it like I'm playing a vertical bongo drum. 'Hello?' I hear something inside and then the flap is quickly pulled open and a man is standing in front of me.

Piercing green eyes that I feel like I've looked into before stare back at me and my heart skips a beat. An exact copy of Chase but covered in a beard, wild hair and wearing camouflage that I'm sure is not a nod to the 2016 Versace collection stands only a few feet away from me, holding a rifle.

What was I thinking? The man in front of me belongs on a show about surviving Armageddon not making irresistible crudites, though both are important life skills. There's nothing about him that makes me think I have any chance of making this work. Should I just walk away, drive back and cut my losses? I close my eyes tightly for a moment and reopen them hoping I'll be able to identify something to give me a glimmer of hope and I immediately return to the eyes. The rest of him is overgrown chaos but the eyes are clear and bright. I think maybe I can work with that and then I remember that Chase is off dancing at some circuit party so I don't have a choice.

'Rebus send you?' the unkempt one grunts. 'I have until next month to get him his money, so no sense pestering me for it now, unless you want a butt full of bullets.'

A butt full of bullets? At first I think that might be mountain talk for some kind of sexual fetish that I have yet to encounter, but Beau's face is stone cold.

'No, no, no. I'm not a debt collector. I just want to ask you...'

He cocks the gun. At least I hear the sound that makes me think that's what he's doing. Good lord, I'm a lifestyle expert. I don't know what gun cocking should really sound like. Oh, no. This is not going well at all.

'I don't treat kindly to folks who come here trying to pull one over on me,' he says. I put my hands up. His voice is rough and thick, much deeper and coarser than Chase's but there's also some warmth in it.

'Look, can we just talk?' I ask. My arms are still raised above me but I'm doing jazz hands. I realize this isn't The Broadway Dance Center but surely this move must have an international way of saying *I come in peace and in the spirit of musical theater.* 'I'm not here for trouble. I promise. I have a proposal that could help us both if you just hear me out,' I say as plainly as I can. I'm not scared of this guy. There's something in his eyes, underneath his wild hair and beard, something softer behind the light in his eyes that isn't there with Chase. 'I should tell you I know your brother, Chase.' Beau's face and entire body tightens. I can see a vein in his forehead pulse just a little. 'Don't worry,' I add quickly. 'I think he's a colossal jackass, too.'

Beau is silent, then he puts down the gun and I slowly put down my hands. 'Come in. Anyone who hates that jackass can't be all bad.' He opens the flap to the yurt and I walk inside.

An accordion-like wooden circular frame has canvas stretched across it. I was expecting the interior to be chaos, but the space is spotless. There's a small kitchen area with a portable stove and something that looks like a sink, a simple bed that has been neatly made and even a comfortable chair surrounded by a stack of books. It's not Park Avenue, but it's clear that Beau isn't an axe murderer or anything like that. I don't see any axes and I imagine if you are going on a killing spree you're less concerned about keeping your place tidy, but I'm making an assumption.

He puts an aluminum percolator on the propane burner and asks, 'How do you know Chase?'

'I'm his producer.' Beau looks at me like I said I was his wet nurse or something. 'For his show? You've seen his show,' I say. It's less of a question and more of a statement. Of course he's seen his show.

45

'Do you see anything here that looks like I would watch "a show" on it?'

I take another quick look around and he's obviously right. Still, Chase is a popular celebrity. I thought everyone knew who he was.

'Your brother Chase, the jackass,' I continue, 'is the star of a show I produce called *Myles of Style*.'

Beau pauses and then says, 'It's a show about cars?'

I laugh lightly hoping he's making a joke. 'No, no. It's Myles, like his last name. Well, your last name too. Not miles as in distance. It's a lifestyle show,' I tell him.

'A lifestyle show? How do you have a show about that? Is that a thing?'

'Oh yes, it's a thing. It's a very big thing, actually. A huge thing. We tell people what to wear, what to eat, where to eat, where to spend their vacations, how to throw parties. Things like that.'

'Because people don't know how to do that on their own?' His eyes stare right through me.

'No, they do. I mean some do I suppose but Chase tells them how to do it the right way.'

'Oh, now that sounds like my jackass brother. Telling people how to do things *his* way.' I don't tell Beau that Chase actually tells people how to do things *my* way and Chase is just the person who conveys that agenda, but we'll get to that later. He gets up to pour me a cup of coffee. With his back turned, I have a few moments to stare at his physique. Even though it's covered in a few layers of thermals, it's impossible to hide the fact that there are thick arms and muscular legs beneath that camo. He turns toward the makeshift stove and his shoulders reveal a powerful broadness that he controls with steady movement. His body is as beautiful as Chase's and seems to have the exact same dimensions, but it's clear that Beau's physique has been earned through hard work, not protein shakes and CrossFit.

Beau puts the mug in my slightly blue hands that have yet to unfreeze. I notice that his hands are a bit thicker than Chase's and certainly rougher and more calloused. 'What does any of this have to do with me?'

'Well, it's simple really,' I say. I take a fortifying gulp of hot black coffee. It's surprisingly delicious – earthy yet sweet with an unexpected tang. I wonder if there is a local roaster I should know about, but I'm not here researching a story. I'm here creating a story of my own. 'I want to take you back to Manhattan and turn you into Chase for a few promotions. It won't take very long and I'll have you back here safe and sound in a few days.' I say it as matter of fact as I can as if to convey that I have thought through all of the details, which of course I haven't. I don't have any idea how this is going to work.

Beau looks at me very seriously, like he's considering the plan, which I have to admit I laid out in a very reasonable way.

'Sure,' he says enthusiastically. 'Let me just pick up my dry cleaning and see if I can get someone to water my plants while I'm gone.' Then he folds his arms in front of his chest and looks at me like he might pick up the gun again.

I put my coffee down, stand up and walk right over to him so I'm only a few inches from his face. 'I know it's taken you years to develop your tough guy image but I didn't drive up to the middle of nowhere with an intern on the brink of a nervous breakdown to go back without you. So cut the mountain man BS and listen to me. I'm here to help you.' When you spend your childhood getting

47

stuffed into lockers by jocks who think it's fun to pick on the weakest kid you learn how to keep that anger in storage in case you need it as an adult.

'Ha!' His hot breath explodes right in my face and he smiles. He likes being challenged, or maybe he likes the little volley we started, but his energy shifts enough that I understand we are beginning negotiations. 'I don't need your help. I don't need anyone's help. You think I live out here because I'm a people person? I live alone and I like it that way.'

'Good for you. I'll make sure as soon as we get what we need you'll be right back here and you won't have to worry about that problem I heard about in town.' My little dart deflates him just enough to make him curious.

'I don't have any problem in town,' he says through clenched teeth.

'That's not what I heard. But, like I said, I'm here to help.'

'Go on,' he says, his eyes colder than the walls of the yurt but also showing a willingness to listen.

'You help me out and I'll help you out. I will, of course, pay you generously for your time.'

Beau looks down at the ground. His austere expression has changed to something significantly more vulnerable. I think maybe he's embarrassed.

'It was a difficult season. Driest in years. I got behind on some stuff I need to take care of,' he mumbles as he looks down at his feet.

'I get it,' I say. 'Bad hunting season.' I have no idea what to say to win this guy over.

'Not hunting,' he says. He looks up at me and sneers. 'I don't hunt. The gun is for safety. I would never kill an animal like that. I forage mushrooms and do some logging.

48

I don't even have bullets.' I guess I was expecting him to have the place covered in antlers and other trophies of fallen animals but when I look around there isn't a single sign of that. If he keeps a gun around just to scare people off, then he does understand the power of appearances. Maybe there's more to this guy than meets the eye.

'I'll pay cash,' I say. 'A thousand bucks. I can have my assistant send the money to whoever, however you need it,' I say, sounding like someone hiring a mafia hitman.

He snorts and rolls his eyes but then he puts his hand to his chin and I can tell he's thinking. 'That would at least cover some of it,' he says.

I wonder how much he can possibly owe. 'I just need you for forty-eight hours. That's it. I'll have you back here before you even miss... whatever all this is.'

Beau doesn't say anything. He rubs his beard with his hand. I can tell he's considering my offer. He looks down at the ground and then up toward the small skylight created in the center of the yurt. 'Why isn't my brother doing it if it's his show? Does he know about this? Is it going to piss him off?'

'He doesn't know anything about it at the moment but, yes, I think when he finds out he's going to be very pissed off.'

'Now that sounds better than any amount of money.' He sits on the edge of the bed across from me, stares right into my eyes and says, 'Keep talking.'

Chapter 6

I'm lying in bed staring at the shadows that run across the ceiling of my apartment each time a car rolls down 83rd Street. After driving up to the middle of nowhere and back, I'm exhausted, but I still can't sleep. Once Beau found out this scheme would not sit well with his brother, it was much easier to convince him. I offered him enough cash to help ameliorate his debt, though it sounds like it might only make a dent. Maybe I should have been more generous and covered the whole thing but in the end he seemed more motivated by revenge than anything else.

I had him packed and out of that yurt before either of us could really figure out the details. Now my mind is racing trying to figure out how I'm going to make this work. I have too much riding on this to fail.

Beau slept stretched across the back seat while Tina nervously chewed her hair the entire drive back. I kept stealing glances in the rearview mirror. I told myself I was trying to get a good visual on him to see if I had any chance of transforming him into his brother. His hair must have been cut with a rock, his beard makes him look like he should drive a buggy or brew his own ale in Williamsburg, and everything he's wearing will have to be burned. Despite all that, this has to work.

We dropped Beau off at Chase's apartment and got him settled. I told him to be ready in the morning.

'Got it,' he said and looked me square in the eyes without protest. His brother would have complained and asked if he could run out for a quick cocktail.

'I need you here at seven a.m. in one piece,' I said like an overbearing parent.

'When I say something, I mean it,' he said and closed the door behind him. It was the first time I believed anything that was ever said to me in that apartment.

My phone buzzes on my nightstand and I grab it in case it's either one of the Myles brothers. Beau running away or Chase coming back. It isn't.

'Hi, Ethan. It's Marguerite.'

'What's wrong? Is he okay?' Marguerite is Uncle Clams' overnight nurse on holiday weekends. A call at two a.m. is not good.

'He is now. He woke up a little disoriented. Sheila called earlier,' Marguerite says plainly.

That explains it. Poor Clams. Even after all these years he can't be himself around her. It seems to have gotten harder for both of them as he's gotten older. My cousin Sheila isn't a horrible person. When we were kids we were as close as siblings. She lived a town over with her mom but when her parents separated and Clams came out it was hard for her to accept that her dad was gay. Then when I came out I think she felt like I was choosing sides. Which I sort of was. My bond with my uncle got tighter as they grew more distant. I've done everything I can imagine not to come between them but Sheila does not make it easy. She hates anyone calling him Clams even though that's the nickname he's used for decades even when he's not performing in drag as... Clams Casino. If she hears one of the nurses use the name in her presence or on the phone she has them written up. Sheila is a few years older than me and a high school principal in Connecticut. She considers the world her troubled teenager. Clams always asks whoever was written up for the document and then turns the paper into an origami tiara, which the nurses adore. If Sheila finds out Clams has made me swear that I'll make sure he's buried in the blue suit he let her pick out *and* the gorgeous ruby-red–sequined platform pumps he wore at Wigstock in 1984, it'll be a double funeral. I'm supposed to slip them on without her noticing. Any funeral mention makes me uncomfortable but Uncle Clams has been planning it for decades and he always makes it sound like a fabulous circus in paradise.

'You doing okay?' I ask when the nurse hands him the phone.

'I just had a restless night. What are you doing home?'

'It's two a.m.,' I say, even though I know what he's going to say.

'The night is young. I'm not. But the night is. You should be out meeting guys, dancing, doing shots of tequila off muscled torsos.' Which is exactly what Chase is doing by now. It's ironic because Clams absolutely can't stand Chase. Despises him. 'You're such a handsome boy, no sense keeping it all to yourself. Go out there and let it all hang out.'

'Uncle Clams, everything hangs exactly where I want it to hang. It does not have to be on display. I can't go out tonight. I have a job.' I'm not a shut-in. I like a fake-fog dance floor with sweaty bodies just as much as the next homosexual. It's just been a while since I've exercised in my boogie shoes. 'Answer the question, are you okay?'

'I was a little restless. That's all. I'm fine. Maybe a little bored.' I don't ask about Sheila. He loves his daughter like any parent but it's complicated. I was so young when my dad left that I miss the idea of Dad more than reality. The loss of my mother right after I graduated college is a different sort of pain. Still, I'm not under any delusion that our relationship was without friction when she was alive. She was loving and supportive but we could push each other's buttons. She was thrilled that I was on my way to a high-powered career, maybe even more thrilled than I was. I think because we grew up without a lot of money it made her glad to see I was financially secure. I know Clams misses my mom every day but he doesn't talk about her much. I think it hurts too much for both of us. His lack of closeness with Sheila reminds him of what he's missing. I think maybe Clams is feeling a little lonely and a bit sad.

'Hey, you know what Clams, I had to do a road trip for work and I was thinking about that trip you took with Joan of Arse and Milk of Amnesia to do a show in Albany at Sausage and Lips or something and you stayed at a haunted Ramada Inn,' I say, knowing it will prompt Uncle Clams to begin a long monologue about his best friends, Joan and Amnesia. Amnesia was the first person Clams came out to and she's always been a mentor and confidante for him the way he is with me. She runs a hotel on Fire Island and every year I take Clams for a visit that really is more of a pilgrimage. Joan joins and they perform a reunion of The Giblet Triplets for one night only at The Ice Palace.

I've heard the story of the Albany Road Trip at least a hundred times and I'm well aware the hotel was not haunted. Rather, there was a squirrel trapped in the rain gutter but I pretend it's all new to me.

'Oh, that trip was such a hoot. Amnesia didn't know how to drive a stick and Joan said he didn't believe her considering how many hand jobs he'd seen her give after shows. Well…'

I shut my eyes, thinking I might drift off to sleep as he talks. I can't help enjoying the story and gobbling up every word. I have some major problems I'm going to have to figure out, but that's tomorrow and tonight I'm okay listening to my uncle talk about his favorite friends and found family. It makes me feel safe and loved.

Chapter 7

I've got the reinforcements I need to make some media magic scheduled to arrive and already sworn to secrecy. I can't let anyone know that Beau isn't Chase, and with the right angles, accessories and attitude I've convinced myself I can make it work for a few social media posts. I'll get everything shot today, send Beau back Monday morning and then Chase will be back later that day. How hard can this be?

I go to my kitchen to prepare an espresso when I get a text from Tina. *He's gone.*

I call her immediately. 'Please tell me you are not talking about the Wolverine from Upstate.'

'I came over exactly like you asked me to. I knocked very hard and when he didn't answer I used the key you gave me and I looked everywhere. I double checked all the closets.'

I think maybe I need to explain what 'coming out of the closet' means. Not that I even know if Beau is gay at all. I mean maybe. I hope so. Hope so? I tell myself my desire for him to be gay is simply based on the fact that it would be best for the show, although I'm not sure why. It doesn't matter anyway since I have Sasquatch wandering around the Upper East Side by himself.

I hang up with Tina, grab a Citi Bike from the corner and cycle ten blocks down to Chase's apartment. I walk in and Tina points toward the kitchen. 'He came back.'

I storm into the kitchen and he's wearing tiny running shorts, a tight tank top and his head is thrown back as he drinks a bottle of water with one arm leaning on the fridge. He looks like an ad for water or running shorts or sweat. I can't stop staring at him until I realize what he has done.

'I thought you said you wouldn't leave the apartment.'

He takes his time finishing his drink before answering. 'I told you I wouldn't leave for the night. I got up, found his sneakers and took a run. And then meditated on that hill by the museum. I'm here now like I told you I would be. Seven a.m. as ordered. What's the big deal?'

'The big deal? Someone could have recognized you!' Of course, given the way he looks at the moment, that would be almost impossible, but still, I don't like him going rogue. Then I realize he just said he mediated. Meditated? The closest his brother would ever come to meditating is medicating.

'Recognize me? Yeah, right. I haven't stepped foot in this city for years.'

So did he live in the city at some point? Did he live with Chase? What was he doing here? I have many questions but I have to make sure he follows orders. This is one situation where my habit of keeping guys at a distance is an asset.

'Don't you get it? Your brother is famous. He's a celebrity. People recognize him all the time.'

'What's he famous for? Being an idiot?' He lets out a grungy laugh. He's funny. Chase has the sense of humor of an under-ripe pineapple. I've had to explain knock-knock

56

jokes to him but this guy definitely has a bit of snark and I like it.

'It doesn't matter. I can't have anyone coming up to you and asking for a selfie or quizzing you about the show or anything like that.'

He throws the empty bottle into recycling with force and then spits out the word, 'Fine.'

He walks closer and puts his face right next to mine. 'So what exactly is your deal with my brother? I saw a bunch of pictures of the two of you around here.'

I swallow hard and say, 'We work together,' hoping that will be enough to satisfy his sudden curiosity. He doesn't need to know the whole sordid situation. We planted a bunch of photos of the two of us around the apartment to make our fake relationship believable when *Fab* magazine did a profile on power couples last year.

'I saw a picture of you both on a beach on some island. What kind of work were you doing there?'

I don't need Beau asking me questions about my situation with Chase. It's too complicated. He wouldn't understand that his brother and I only appear to be a couple in order to appease the sponsors. Sponsors love to celebrate diversity as long as the celebration fits in their neatly wrapped box of acceptable behavior. 'Don't you worry about it,' I say.

He rolls his eyes at me and says, 'Are you going to explain to me what I need to do?'

I sit at the counter in the kitchen. 'Your brother was… ah… called away and we support our show with a variety of social media products. If we don't get our promotions posted by the deadline, we lose revenue.'

Beau opens the fridge and takes out an apple from the Lucky Green farm box I have sent here every week. 'Is this Fuji organic?'

'Yes, it is. But it's a Honeycrisp.' What does this guy care about organic fruits? He looks like he has been surviving on cans of beans for years.

His mouth opens like a mechanical claw and he takes a bite. 'No it's not. It's a Fuji. See how the skin is more yellow here with red highlights.' He shows me the back of the apple before devouring the rest of it. Whatever. I'm not interested in discussing varietals of apples this morning, which is odd because that's usually something I could talk about for hours but not in this moment. But how does he know so much about apples?

'Your brother is the brand ambassador for a few products with multiple branding expressions due in the next forty-eight hours. If I don't meet the deadlines, I might as well give up on my career.'

'All this is so you don't get canned?' he asks, his mouth full of apple. I hand him a cloth napkin from the drawer.

'Well, yes, but it's not just me.' Okay. It's mostly me. That's true but not entirely. 'Dozens of people who work on the show are counting on him and millions of fans. Not to mention the brands need him as much as he needs the brands.'

He looks at me carefully. 'I'm not sure I buy any of that but it sounds like you just want me to look like him in some pictures.'

'Well...' I start thinking I'm going to have to re-explain everything since his brother usually needs things gone over at least a few times, but Beau gets it. 'Yes, exactly. Just for a few pictures.'

'Can you just Photoshop him in with a computer?' Beau asks.

'If I could, do you think I'd have driven up to get you?' I did think about doing that but sponsors want to see engagement with their product and my AI skills aren't up to the task. 'Do you think you can do it?'

'Look like him? Yeah, do you want to see my birth certificate or something?' He's mocking me but if that's what it takes he can mock as much as he wants.

'But this isn't some class picture in the yearbook; Chase is a major lifestyle influencer. It's an entire inclusive brand.' I may be stretching the importance of this and in any other milieu I would loathe hearing the phrase 'entire inclusive brand' but this guy is irritating me.

'So what? It's just some dumb stuff on social media, which is total trash.'

I gasp. 'Our show is not dumb,' I say. It's like peeking in a stroller and calling my baby ugly. How dare he? 'Our brand... our show... helps people all over the world. Every day.' I think about the products we have to shoot today like the Bluetooth ab exerciser and I feel less confident in what I'm saying.

When the show started I believed every word of it. We were going where no queer lifestyle show had gone before. We were exploring style that was outside the box. But somehow the more successful we got, the more we sold out. I kept telling myself that bigger sponsors meant bigger audiences and that was the ultimate goal – to reach people. At least I thought it was.

'How exactly do you help people? By telling them they're using the wrong fork or whatever?' He rolls his eyes.

'By empowering them to live their best lives,' I say. I realize our show doesn't examine the suppression of human rights or splice the human genome but we make a contribution.

'Fine. My point is I don't care about things like that. It's not about who may or may not be following. It's about the moment of the experience and so the rest doesn't matter.' I sort of agree with him about social media. I love staying in touch with friends and seeing pictures of their vacations but the promotional stuff is a bitter pill to swallow. I'd be much happier doing my job if I wasn't constantly worried about gaining more followers and meeting promotion deadlines.

'So where do I stand? Get out your camera and let's get started.'

He can't be serious. 'Do you think it's that simple? This is going to be a bit more than changing baseball jerseys.' Do they wear jerseys in baseball? I have no idea. 'Chase has a certain look at the moment. Yes, you're twins. You look like him. But we need to make you appear to be him and that's a bit different.' There's a knock at the front door. I hear Tina open it and a shriek of laughter erupts from the other room. My secret weapon has arrived.

Chapter 8

'Kiara Capworth, I would like you to meet…'

'No way!' she says and walks around Beau like she's judging a cow at a county fair. 'I cannot believe there are two of them.'

'There aren't. I'm my own person,' he growls and strokes his thick beard. Then he crosses his arms over his hairy muscular chest in defiance.

Kiara turns to me and says, 'He's touchy like his brother too.'

'I'm nothing like him,' he snaps. His voice is more intense. I can tell any comparison to his brother is a trigger. Kiara is, of course, fearless. Before she became a makeup artist and stylist, she was a lawyer and litigated high-profile cases. She gave up her legal career to follow her dream and open her own salon in Brooklyn just before she transitioned. I admire her for the change she made in life. We both started out with high-pressure careers at large corporations and she had the intelligence to step off the treadmill and become her own boss. I used to fantasize about quitting and opening my own cafe or maybe a shoppe with two p's. I could design every detail and make it my own. I wouldn't be beholden to bosses and sponsors every minute of the day. But once you get on the fast track, it feels like the only way to get off is to get spit out the bottom. However today is not the day to wax poetic about the choices I've made. Two roads diverge in a yellow wood and one of them leads to the hairy beast standing in front of me.

'Of course you aren't like your brother,' I say to Beau like a mother placating a child. It's a tone I always use with Chase. I wonder if I need to adjust it with Beau. 'But the reality is you're here to make everyone believe you *are* your brother and that can't happen with you looking like that,' I say plainly, hoping he will see the logic. 'We need to let Kiara work her magic.'

'I understand,' he says and unfolds his arms. It's clear he isn't happy about all of this but he won't put up a fight. 'I made a deal.'

'Kiara, what do you think?' I ask, gesturing toward Beau.

'Let me see your hands?' Kiara asks Beau before she answers. He holds them in front of her. 'These look like tree stumps that have been rotting in the woods.' She grabs the hair that's resting on his shoulder. 'This is all over-grown, damaged and tangled. Open,' she says, pointing to his mouth. He obliges. 'I'll have to whiten his teeth at least a few shades. When was the last time you trimmed your pubic hair?' she asks like she wants to know his shoe size.

'That's not really something people do, is it?' he asks and looks at me with great concern.

'They do,' I say.

'Wait,' Beau says slowly. 'Is this porn?' It's not clear if he's stating an objection or simply curious.

'It is not. You'll be wearing a Speedo for the' – I swallow hard before saying the next part and rush past the words as quickly as I can – 'the Ab Grater and if you have too much hair down there, it will stick out like a Brillo

62

pad.' My explanation seems to make sense to him. 'Kiara, the bathroom and bedroom are yours to do your magic. I have to run out to get some stuff from the offices. I won't be away long. We're doing the shoot here at the apartment instead of over there. Fewer chances anyone will see us.'

We often do the social media promotions from Chase's apartment. I designed the penthouse with the idea that we would need to use it as a prop from time to time. Chase went off to Puerto Vallarta during our summer hiatus and I had the best few months of my life. I created a gorgeous doll house for Chase to live in, not that he's grateful for any of it. I loved selecting the perfect shade of paint, finding vintage patio furniture for the terrace, and stocking the kitchen with the highest quality equipment and ingredients from around the city. I planned every detail from the tile in the entryway to the linen pillowcases on the bed. While Chase is oblivious to all of it, his fans have been commenting on the little details and each observation makes me secretly thrilled. My own apartment is a study in abject neglect but I honestly spend more time here shooting and arguing with Chase so it doesn't matter.

'Tina, can you prep the bar trolley for photography while I'm gone?' I ask, pointing to the requisite mid-century teak and gold bar that I purchased at an auction house in the Hamptons. Tina nods and I grab an umbrella since it looks like it might rain. 'Kiara, if you need anything, charge it to my personal card, not the production card. I don't want any of this extra stuff to be seen by the network. I don't need anyone producing the literal receipts for this charade. Thank you Ki.' She turns her chin up and to the side. I bend down to kiss her cheek and we both smile – a ritual we've done for years.

I give Tina a list of errands that looks like Rumpel-stiltskin created it. She may be more fragile than a cheese soufflé but she's highly competent. I thank Tina and Kiara again and go to walk out. But before I leave, I turn back to Beau.

'Thanks to you also,' I say. 'You're really helping me.'

'When do I get paid?' he asks seriously and without a hint of patience. Turns out he's more like his brother than I thought — more concerned about what's in it for him than anything else.

'You get paid when the job is complete and we put you back on a bus to where you came from. Give Tina the instructions if you need the money to go somewhere. Does that work with your financial obligations?' I ask. I know he has some kind of serious debt and I want to remind him of that fact so that he doesn't get any ideas about reneging on the deal.

'The sooner I'm back where I belong, the better,' he says. I couldn't agree more.

Chapter 9

After I shove everything I need into a giant backpack, I hop on a Citi Bike and head back to the Upper East Side from the offices in midtown. I'd take a car but the traffic is so intense, the real Chase would make it back from Florida before I'd get back to the apartment. The wind is picking up and I can feel a few drops of rain as I make my up Madison Avenue. I stop at a light on 63rd Street directly in front of Hermès. Perfect yellow and white satchels hang from invisible wire like rays of sunshine suspended mid-air. It's an elegant and clever display that makes me smile until I remember that Chase left with the Hermès bag I gave him. What a jackass. The light changes and I'm Miss Gulch biking my way uphill chasing after Toto. I can hear the classic melody in my ear with every pump of the pedals.

I enter the apartment eager to see how the makeover is going. As I walk in, Kiara is putting on her jacket.

'Finished so soon?' I ask.

She looks at me with her lips tightly drawn. 'Barely got started. His left eyebrow alone is going to take another twenty minutes. But he left.' She wraps the purple sequined scarf I got her for her birthday last year around her neck.

'He left? Why didn't you stop him?'

'I am a five-foot-one Black trans woman from Trinidad. That man is a mountain. I love you, you are my best friend and the best roommate I ever had in college, but, baby, there's a limit.'

'What happened?' I ask, not really wanting to know the answer.

Tina comes into the room; tears wait impatiently at the corners of her eyes. 'I'm sorry. I'm so sorry.'

'He said he was going to some spot in the park to chill out,' Kiara says.

'I asked if he was coming back and he didn't answer,' Tina adds. 'That's when I went in the other room to put my head between my legs.'

'That's when I started packing up my things. I don't have time to sit around if he isn't coming back.' Kiara folds her arms over her chest. She does not like to have her time wasted.

This morning when Beau went to get some fresh air, he went to Central Park. He mentioned the hill by the Met. It's my only chance.

'Kiara, please wait. I'll get him back. Just stay put. Please. I owe you big.' I give her the most pleading, pathetic look I can make show up on my face.

'Fine. You're lucky you bought Chase an espresso machine that was almost as much as my first salary out of law school. I'll make myself a latte.'

I head out the door and toward the only place where I imagine he could be.

I walk to Central Park, just past the entrance south of the Metropolitan Museum of Art where makeshift stalls are filled with various forms of art and souvenirs. I walk past the sculpture of bears and over the bridge that crosses 79th Street to Cedar Hill. At the top of the hill, sitting on a large boulder, is Beau. He has his face raised toward the sun and his arms stretched behind him for support. He's sunning himself like he hasn't a care in the world. My first instinct is to run over to him and drag him back, but I don't want to spook him so instead I approach slowly. His eyes are closed and the sun illuminates his face. I look closer and realize only one of his eyebrows has been neatly plucked into submission while the other one is a wild tangle of bristles. The effect is like some avant-garde self-portrait and I can't help staring at it.

I'm lost in thought for a moment when Beau, without opening his eyes, says, 'Please stop staring at me Ethan.'

I sit down next to him on the rock. 'How did you know I was staring?'

'I've spent years in the forest with wild animals. We are more than just a set of eyes.' Not in my world, I want to tell him. Appearance isn't everything; it's the only thing. I've spent my life making sure everything looks perfect from bangs to table settings. It's the only way I know to keep away the little voice in my head that tells me I'm not enough.

Beau sits up, opens his eyes and says, 'I don't know if I can do this. I'm sorry. Maybe I should go back. Maybe I should go someplace new.'

He isn't angry or defiant. He's quiet and reflective. For a moment I think he genuinely feels bad about not thinking he can handle it.

'Are you worried about posing in front of the camera?' I ask, knowing that I would rather chew on my own tongue than be photographed. I make sure the occasions where I need to appear on the other side of things with Chase are few and far between.

'No, I don't care about that,' he says. I want to scream at him, 'What? What? What? I can fix it.' But I don't. He looks so much like his brother, but sitting next to him in the middle of Central Park it's clear they're quite different. Something about Beau runs very deep. I can tell he's thinking something. That almost never happens with his brother. I'm struck by how similar things can be on the surface yet so different at the core.

My impulse is always to be, well, impulsive. Jump in. Fix it. Make it better and then make it perfect. But my instincts tell me that's the wrong gear entirely with Beau. I hate silence but I let the sounds of the city traffic and crowds sneak in through the grass and trees on the hill.

Eventually my patience is rewarded. 'I can't sit in a chair and be still while someone tries to make me something that I'm not.'

I assumed certain characteristics were sprinkled between and among siblings, with some getting more than others, but generally distributed. In this set, it seems Chase got no integrity and Beau got all of it. Just what I don't need.

'I understand,' I say. 'Some guys like being pampered and fawned over but…'

'But not me. I hate it. I don't like being fussed over that way.'

'I can see that,' I say, examining his half-done face. 'But we have to make you look like him or else it won't work.' I say the words as simply as I can. We are so close to making this happen.

He looks at me seriously; well, as seriously as one can look considering his face looks like it has only been rendered on one side. His eyes fixate on the dirt in front of him and he puts his hand on his beard again. Then he relaxes his shoulders, looks at me and says, 'You think I live in a yurt off the grid by accident? It's harder being here than I thought.' He points south toward the skyline of buildings lining 59th Street that are visible from where we are. I squint and look up at the skyscrapers. I'm able to make out the exact windows of Maria Luisa's office. I spent my entire childhood trying to get out of the suburbs to make it here. As a kid I would kneel on my bed and stick my head out the window. My mom would come in and ask me what I was doing. I'd tell her, 'I'm trying to smell New York.' The city has been my destination my entire life but I guess it's not for everyone.

'So you aren't a city person, so what? On Monday you'll be back where you came from.'

'I haven't been around people in this way in a long time. Years. I forgot how much of everything there is and how the energy dominates everything. I used to love it but then… it's just a lot is all.'

He used to love the city? Then how did he get from the middle of the universe to the middle of nowhere? What did he do here and did he leave or escape? The people he owes money to didn't seem like part of a civic beautification group. It's clear there was some trouble. I remind myself that this is a transactional relationship. It's none of my business. Still, I can't help but feel bad for a guy with half a plucked eyebrow who felt he needed to escape to a hill by the museum.

'I get it,' I say. 'The city can be a lot. Everything happens fast, everyone's in a hurry. It's stressful.' For example, at this very moment my insides feel like tightly wound springs ready to snap if he doesn't get back to the apartment.

'It's not just about the city. I've been thinking I should explore the world beyond my yurt again, but being in his apartment. With *his* stuff.' He emphasizes the word 'his' and that's all I need to understand what I think is really going on. 'I mean it's harder seeing his place and being in it than I thought it would be.'

Should I pry? Should I try to understand more about what happened between Beau and his brother? I'm not good at getting close to people in this way. Why can't he just be a recipe for quiche that doesn't set or an old mid-century lamp that needs to be refurbished? I'm much better with things than people. People are so complicated. Complicated and unreliable. Still, there is a genuine sadness in his eyes that opens the door so I take a tentative step in. 'I don't honestly know what happened between you and Chase, Beau. Were you close as kids?' I ask.

'We were but that was a long time ago. I was in his bedroom and I saw a picture of our mom and…'

He stops. Chase told me his parents died in a car accident not long before we first met. I don't know many details. Chase was determined to avoid the subject and I let him. I get it. I didn't like talking about my parents either. I hated the sad look people would give when I told them my dad left or that my mother died. Usually I change the subject or run to the kitchen to make an amuse-bouche but I can't do that right now.

'Do you want to talk about it?' I ask. Once the question is out of my mouth I feel a sense of relief. The hardest part for me is getting started.

'I know that living how I do, away from everyone, means that I don't have people to talk to about them, and that's what I wanted. What I thought I wanted. But seeing some of those family pictures… I'm not so sure.'

70

'I can take them down or put them away. You don't have to see them.'

'No,' he says sharply. 'Maybe. I don't really know but it's not your problem. I pushed everything so far down I thought it would never surface but seeing those photos brought it all up again.'

I get that. I don't want pictures of my mom around. I did when she was alive but after the cancer took her I couldn't bear seeing them. I consider sharing this with him but I just met this guy and I can feel him pulling away. If I share too much will that scare him off? Maybe he'll jump up and walk all the way back to the Adirondacks. I feel panic rise in my throat over the thought of him walking out. I'm not thinking and I say, 'You can't back out now. You can't leave.'

'Who said I'm backing out?' he growls.

'I'm sorry,' I say.

'I'm not quitting. I told you I would do this and I will. I need the cash but I also gave you my word. That means something. I just needed a break. Slow down, Ethan, all you do is jump around and decide what I'm thinking before I know myself.'

I do not do that but now is not the time to challenge this guy. 'If you need to chill here, I get that. Take as long as you need,' I say. I remind myself I'm not dealing with Chase at the moment. Beau seems to be a living, breathing human with thoughts and feelings. I'm not going to force anyone to do anything. Coerce, persuade, cajole? Sure, but not force. 'Is there anything I can do to make things easier?' I ask, hoping his chill time is drawing to a close.

'Yes,' he says, his tone gentle and pleading, almost childlike. 'That thing Kiara is doing with the string on my face. What is that? It's awful.'

71

'That's called eyebrow threading. She's an expert. People fly into the city just to have her do that to them.'

'It's torture. Once I almost had a finger freeze off and whatever she's doing is totally worse than that. It's like she's pulling every tiny hair off my face.'

'That's kind of the point,' I say.

'Maybe she could go slower or faster. I don't know, but it's awful.'

I've had my share of hair depilatory sessions and it's no teddy bear jamboree. 'I'll ask her but she isn't one to take direction about her art. We have to respect her process but she's always willing to meet people halfway.' That isn't exactly true but I tell these small fibs all day long – to make people feel better, to diffuse tension, to get what I want or need. Usually they have almost no impact on me, but sitting here in Central Park with Beau they actually pull at my soul a teeny-tiny bit. A television producer with a soul is like a gay sports bar. What's the point? The televisions are on but is anybody really watching? 'Scratch that,' I say. 'I'll ask her and we'll see what she says.'

My phone beeps and I look down. It's Maria Luisa with a text: *Where's the update on your socials?*

I text her back some random emojis. I have no idea what they mean or if it's even appropriate to communicate this way but it's hard to lie in emoji. At any rate she sends back a thumbs-up so I bought us some time.

When I get back to the apartment with Beau, I discreetly lock and chain the door behind me. Kiara and Tina walk in and stare at us. Kiara breaks the momentary silence and says, 'Let me get started. I'll meet you in the bathroom.' She grabs a spool of string and starts twisting it around her fingers as she walks to the bathroom and closes the door. Beau looks frightened. I hold my hand out to indicate that I will take care of it.

I walk over to the bathroom door and knock. 'Hey Kiara, do you think you could use something else instead of the thread?' I ask, praying she's in an agreeable mood.

'Fine,' she says from behind the door.

Beau puts the palms of his hands together and mouths 'thank you' but before he enters we hear a click and then a loud buzzing sound. 'I'm ready,' Kiara says from the bathroom.

'What is that noise?' Beau asks as the fear returns to his face.

'The trimmer,' I say, hoping the sound isn't too off-putting.

'Hasn't this woman heard of scissors?'

'We keep Chase's chest hair pretty trim. It'll go faster with trimmers but here's the part you may not like. It won't hurt but...'

'What?'

'We have to apply a self-tanner. I can't risk sending you out for a spray tan. Your body looks like it hasn't seen the sun for months.'

'That's because it's May. You aren't supposed to be sunburnt in May where I live.'

'Maybe not, but before we can apply the self-tanner, Kiara is going to have to shave your legs. Chase keeps his smooth to show off his calves.'

'Shave my legs? Why? Who does that? That's the stupidest thing I have ever heard. What man shaves his legs?'

I have too much riding on this and too much pressure coming from Maria Luisa to put up with his macho man routine any longer. I need him to be camera ready, looking

73

perfect, and I am not about to let whatever latent gender stereotypes that might be lurking under that amazing body speak to me that way. We only have a few hours to meet the deadline.

'Lots of men shave their legs and lots of men don't. Lots of women shave their legs and lots of women don't. In addition, there are a lot of people who identify as non-binary and in other ways, so you can take your prehistoric attitude and shove it. Now walk into that bathroom, grab a razor and make your thighs smooth like a frozen lake.'

'Prehistoric attitude? You don't know anything about my attitude,' he says.

'I know enough to know you have a bad one. I will not play tug of war with you all weekend. Either you're in or you're out. I can walk down the block to Equinox and throw a cat with my eyes blindfolded and he'd land on a guy just as built and sexy as you.' Of course, if I *could* do that I would have already. Minus the cat part. I'd never hurt a cat.

'So you think I'm sexy?' he asks.

I admired Chase's beauty but I never found him sexy. Beau has something raw and authentic about him… What am I doing fantasizing about Chase's brother? I don't even know if he's gay.

'I think you're a big pain in my ass,' I say. 'Get in the bathroom and shave. We're running out of time. We have a ton to do.' I keep thinking about my meeting with Maria Luisa and my promise to have the socials on track by the end of the weekend.

After he walks in, Kiara walks out.

'What's wrong?' I ask.

'Calm down, baby. He's lathering up. I just needed to reapply my gloss before I get started.' She grabs her purse and starts spreading a gooey shine on them. Kiara is always concerned about her lips. A few years ago we were in a minor fender bender and before she got out of the car, she did her lips.

'Ki, can I ask you a question that's sort of stupid?' I say, suddenly shy around my best friend. 'If one twin is gay does that mean...'

'Oh, no. Oh hell, no. I will pour the entire bottle of self-tanner down the sink.'

'Stop it. I don't know what you're talking about.' I know exactly what she's talking about.

'Of course you do. We just got rid of one major black hole in your life. Let's not fill the void with another void.'

Kiara hates Chase. She thinks he's an egotistical nightmare and she's right. She also thinks our fake relationship is stupid, dangerous and vomit-inducing. Those are the three adjectives she consistently uses.

'I have no intention of getting involved with Chase's brother. First, that would be super weird and second... that would be super weird. I don't even know if he's gay. What do you think?'

'If you have no intention of getting involved, why do you want to know?'

I hesitate for a second before coming up with a plausible excuse. 'Well, Chase is a queer icon and if Beau is straight, it would be very inauthentic.'

'Uhm, you're planning to convince an army of followers all over the world that he's someone he isn't and that's what you're worried about?' It's impossible to get anything past Kiara. She just stares at me knowing what I'm saying is BS.

'He hasn't mentioned a past boyfriend or girlfriend. I was hoping he would but...'

'I have an idea,' she says. 'It's a bit sneaky and very complicated but it might just work.'

'Great, what is it?' I ask.

'Hey Beau!' she screams toward the bathroom. 'What's your deal? Are you straight or gay or what?'

The sound of running water stops and my heart skips a beat. I hear him shout back, 'I'm bi.'

'Cool,' she says. 'Me too.' Then he turns the water back on.

Kiara gives me a look and asks, 'Did you get the answer you wanted?' Kiara disappears into the bathroom before I can answer. The truth is I'm beginning to realize I'm not totally sure what I want.

Chapter 10

'Are you ready?' Kiara asks from behind the bedroom door. She has been here all day and hasn't let me see the progress since the detente over the hair depilation issue. She started with the epidural layer, then moved her way outward to clothes. They spent the last twenty minutes in Chase's closet going through wardrobe, and I've been thinking about lens filters we could use that might ameliorate any differences between Chase and Beau on camera.

The door opens.

'What do you think?' Beau asks.

It is the makeover to end all makeovers.

It's so convincing my first instinct is to scream at him for running off, but as soon as I look into his eyes I know I could never truly mistake the two. I'm hoping it's something that won't read on camera.

Kiara has given him the same sharp haircut she gave Chase, a tight fade with messy bangs. She's done a rinse to make his hair a shade darker and now it has the exact violet highlights that she put in Chase's a few weeks ago. Somehow she turned that bushy mess of beard and mane into a divine topiary. His skin looks fresh, his eyebrows are two little works of art and she has even managed to make his teeth pop a bit whiter.

Beau's wearing one of the most expensive suits Chase owns. I had it custom made for an awards ceremony coming up at the end of the month. It's such a dark blue that it reads black. Kiara has paired it with a crisp white shirt and opened a few of the buttons to reveal the newly clipped chest hair and I suddenly realize how much sexier it was natural. Still, the entire effect is sensational.

'Do you think I can pass for my brother?'

I take a deep breath in. He looks exactly like the erstwhile host of the show. Feeling his presence and being in the same room with him though, there's no way I would mistake him for Chase. His energy is so different. But that doesn't matter because we just need a few shots.

'I certainly hope so,' I say to Beau. 'Kiara, you've done a fantastic job. I can't thank you enough.'

'We'll see what you say when you look at the bathroom. I took enough hair off this guy to make a third.'

'Please don't even joke about there being another one. I can barely handle two.'

We have multiple products to shoot. I decide to start with the easiest one first, a cologne and body spray that intentionally smells like a locker room. Tina has everything set up in a corner of the bedroom. She may have appeased her parents with her major but her real love is film production and she takes this part of her job very seriously. She manipulates the ring light by centimeters to make sure the composition has the right balance of shadows and light.

Tina and Kiara have been hard at it all day and with everything set up all I have to do is start clicking before writing the captions and sending everything off to the sponsors for approval. I tell them both to take a break and get some air before the rain comes back. I walk them to the door and give them my undying gratitude and some extra cash to get the artisanal latte of their dreams. I close the door and relief floods my body. My madcap plan isn't so mad at all.

But as I leave the vestibule and head toward the bedroom, I'm very aware of the fact that I'm alone with Beau in the apartment. I peek through the bedroom door without him noticing and I see him staring at the photos on the dresser. I selected the silver-plated frames but we filled them with pictures chosen by Chase. Beau picks one up. I always thought the picture was of Chase as a kid with his parents but now I think that might be Beau in that grainy color photo by the lake. I always found the photo suspect since the kid is holding a fish he just caught and I could never imagine Chase having the patience to catch anything. Beau puts the photo down and I notice him raise his hand to his face. Was he wiping a tear? I can't tell from where I'm standing but I feel like he's having a moment so I go to the kitchen to give him some privacy and make myself a doppio espresso.

When I finish I head back over to the bedroom and ask, 'Are you ready for this?' He really does look like his brother.

'I hate wearing this suit,' he says.

'Don't worry, the other shoots have considerably less wardrobe.' I pray Tina and Kiara will be back by the time we get to the body wash. I'm feeling self-conscious being alone with him and I wish I hadn't sent them away.

Kiara has left a few tie choices on the bed for us and I pick a particularly pretty lavender one with faint abstract flowers by Brunello Cucinelli. I explain to Beau that all he has to do is tie it around his neck like he's getting ready for a sexy date night and then spray some of the cologne and hold the bottle close to his face. I put the cologne on the dresser next to him and hand him the tie. He looks at it with confusion.

'I don't know how to do this,' he says.

I remind myself to stay calm. We can't afford anymore delays but this is his first time doing this type of thing so I need patience. 'You take the tie and put it on like you're going out. You don't have to say anything. I'll add music and text later. It will all just be stop-motion. Then you grab the cologne...'

'Ethan, I'm not a moron. I can remember simple instructions. I don't know how to tie a necktie.'

I've known how to tie a necktie since I was eight. I threw a tantrum when my mom bought me a clip-on for a music recital at school. I hated playing the clarinet but I loved wearing my fancy shoes for the performance so I reluctantly practiced the 'Minuet in G'. 'It's easy. Just wrap one end around the other,' I say, and he tries to follow my instructions. 'Then move one end through the loop you just made and out and over the...' Before I am even able to finish he has the entire thing in a knot under his chin. 'Stop,' I say a bit louder than I should. 'It's silk. It's the highest quality silk you can imagine. Like the worms are fed caviar and champagne to make this.' The Myles brothers have such little respect for fabric creases.

'Well, excuse me for disrespecting these incredibly well-fed worms,' he says.

I look at my watch and realize we're already behind schedule. 'Here,' I say, 'let me show you.' He hands me the tie and I smooth the fabric with my palm on the bed. Then I turn to stand directly in front of him. I swing the tie around his neck like a lasso and grab the other end. I'm standing face to face with him.

I freeze.

The space between our faces is suddenly thick with energy. His eyes lock with mine and I can feel my breath shorten. It's an awkward intimate moment that feels strangely familiar but entirely new. I've put wardrobe on Chase a hundred times but being physically close to Beau is a combination of disturbing and thrilling. I tell myself it's the fact that I'm under so much pressure to get this done that's making me feel this way.

'What's wrong?' he asks, although I wonder if he feels it too.

'Nothing. I'm just under a lot of pressure,' I say. I move as quickly as I can to finish the necktie and step away from the man. The sooner I get this done, the sooner I'll have him back on a bus to his yurt. 'I'll tie it super loose and that way you only have to straighten it for the shot. Okay?'

'Whatever you say. You're the boss.' He looks at me up and down. 'You like being the boss, don't you?' There is a mischievous cadence in his voice.

'As a matter of fact, I do,' I say, and I make the loop tighter than necessary.

'Okay, okay,' he says, putting his fingers between his neck and the tie. He pretends I'm choking him. I'm not but at least he now understands that I could at any moment.

For some reason I'm finding it hard to concentrate. It's much harder to tie a tie on someone than it is to put it on yourself. I undo the crooked knot I made but my hands are fumbling.

'Turn around,' I say, and I circle the air with my finger. Beau does as he's told and then we are both facing forward in front of the mirror. I put my hands over his shoulders and I'm very aware that the front of my body is pressed against the back of his. I work quickly and even though

I should be focusing on making the classic Windsor knot our eyes are locked on each other in the mirror.

'You know, there's only one,' he says, moving his hand over his face, pushing back his now violet and black bangs. His voice is low and even more gravely than usual.

'One what?'

'One of me. There is one of him and one of me. We look alike but we are entirely different people with entirely different personalities. I get people like to joke twins are two of a kind but that's really reductive, don't you think?'

Reductive? He has an impressive vocabulary for someone who... I don't finish that thought. I don't really know anything about Beau and if I'm not being defensive, I know he's right. I'm making a lot of assumptions and I need to stop. 'I'm sorry,' I say. 'I keep comparing you to your brother for obvious reasons but that's for the show. I know you are your own person, and until recently the only thing I knew about you was that you existed.'

'He didn't really talk about me, huh?'

I finish the last loop of the tie. 'What happened?'

'He never told you what happened after they died in the crash?' I stop fussing with the tie and look at him. There is the sadness in his eyes that I saw in the park but this time it feels more complex. His lower lip moves in front of his upper one.

'No,' I say almost in a whisper.

I catch his eyes darting over to the picture of his parents. I know he's thinking about them and the truth is I'm thinking about my mom despite trying not to. He doesn't say anything and then I decide to do something I almost never do.

'I know,' I say. 'I mean... about loss... it's hard.' The words leak out slowly at first then all at once. 'My mom battled breast cancer and I lost her right after college.' My eyes stay connected with his in the mirror.

'I'm sorry,' he says. I'm resting my hands on his shoulders and he raises his hand to touch mine. 'Thank you for telling me.' I can count on one hand the number of people I've told about my mom's cancer. Today I'll have to move to the other hand to keep count. Usually it takes me an eternity for me to open up to people but I'm glad I told him. I smile at him in the mirror just enough to let him know I appreciate his words. He smiles back.

But before I can make sense of the moment and fully take it in the door opens and Kiara and Tina walk in to find me standing directly behind Beau in front of the mirror. The intimacy of the moment must be obvious since they both appear shocked. Tina blinks like she can't believe what she's seeing and Kiara is, of course, more direct.

'What the hell is going on in here?' she asks, walking into the room.

I jump away from Beau and quickly respond. The room tone, whatever it was, changes instantly. Not in a bad way. Whatever bubble we were in bursts. 'Nothing,' I say.

Kiara's expression does not change.

'I was helping him with his tie but now that you're here I'll let you work on wardrobe and we can get started.'

Kiara looks at me as she grabs her apron with her makeup tools and pulls it over her head. Tina adjusts the iPhone we have already clipped to a tripod and we get to work quickly so I can avoid any further questions. We all snap into production mode.

Beau is awkward in front of the camera but he's passable. We keep him moving and that helps. He resists direction but eventually I get him to do the things that seem strange at first like holding the bottle of cologne up by his face so we can see it in the frame. I snap the photos; Kiara makes sure he looks perfect and Tina works magic with the filters to make everything look flawless, if not intentionally out of focus from time to time.

We move quickly from product to product. After the cologne, it's a new queer-owned coffee mug company with empowering phrases to start your day followed by an obscenely expensive sneaker and a rainbow gaming headset where he just has to sit on the couch in designer sweats and pretend he's playing. He holds the controller upside down and complains about the gratuitous violence in the game we put on but other than that we get through it. But the next product is the one I've been dreading. We have everything set up in the guest bathroom since the shower there has a stonework that will make a compelling background for the body wash. I tell Beau that his wardrobe for this product is in the bag on the bed and he goes off to get changed.

'He's not a bad guy, actually,' Kiara says to me once we're alone.

'Well, he got through most of the shoots and he's mostly behaving,' I say, not willing to surrender my judgment.

'I guess he said something to you about men and leg shaving or something and he apologized for coming off as being less than inclusive,' Kiara says as she takes out her lip gloss and recoats her already glossy lips. 'He wanted me to know that's not who he is.'

'He did?'

'Yeah, it was sweet. A bit awkward but also very genuine. We talked about being bi and he asked some really thoughtful questions about being trans. I was impressed.' I'm not sure what to make of his apology to her or his thoughtful questions.

'Did he happen to mention anything about his brother?' I ask as casually as possible. I'd share more about the intimate moment she walked in on but I don't want her jumping to conclusions, and Beau is leaving tomorrow anyway so what's the point?

'I mentioned something about Chase and he definitely had a reaction. I don't know what happened between the two of them but siblings can be family or siblings can be jerks.' Kiara has a sister who doesn't speak to her and a brother who has become a trans-activist in California. I'm an only child so it's all a mystery to me.

'Hey, Kiara, you're in charge of wardrobe, right?' Beau shouts from the guest bedroom that we have been using as a changing room.

'Yeah, baby. What's up?'

Baby? Kiara only uses that term with people who have won her hard-earned approval.

'I thought you said the wardrobe was in the blue shopping bag.'

'That's right, baby,' she says. Again with the baby.

'It's just this, uhm, I think maybe it's a headband and then there is this other part. I don't understand,' Beau says through the door.

'Beau, I'm sorry to break it to you but that's not a head band. It goes over your junk. And the other part goes with it,' I say loud enough so I'm sure he can hear me.

The door cracks open and Beau sticks his head out. 'Uhm, can I see one of you in here for a second?'

'I'll go,' I say. I knock and wait for Beau to acknowledge me before going in. He's still wearing the wardrobe from the previous shoot.

'Ethan, what the hell is…?' He points to the little blue shopping bag that holds his wardrobe.

'Ugly,' I say before he can finish. 'That metallic green thong is one of the most hideous things I've ever seen. I know. And the money print on it is garish.' I was worried about this. Chase will wear anything I tell him and loves the idea of showing off his body to anyone and everyone. In fact, it's often harder to get him to put clothes on than it is to take them off, but I was wondering if his brother might be wired differently. 'Is showing that much skin an issue?' I ask. I don't want him to do anything that feels like crossing a boundary.

'I guess not,' he says. 'I was a nude model for a few semesters at Parsons but that was different. This is having an emerald dollar sign on my dick.'

I want to find out if there are any sketches of him still circulating but I control myself.

'I'm sorry, Beau, but technically it will appear to be on Chase's private parts. To be honest with you it's not the outfit I would choose but I don't always get to decide.'

'I thought you were in charge?' he asks.

'I am but I answer to someone else who answers to someone else who answers to a board who answers to stockholders who answer to… I'm not sure who they answer to but everyone answers to someone don't they?'

'No, Ethan, as a matter fact they don't. That's something you've made up to make it easier for yourself to do what you have to do.' At least with Chase the arguing is on such a superficial level I can tune it out. Beau is making my head hurt and the fact that we connected for a moment earlier only makes me angrier. Why can't he just stay in the nice guy box I almost put him in for more than ten minutes? Any comfort I felt before gives way to frustration. So much for putting myself out there and being vulnerable.

'Easier? Do you think what I do is easy? I think you've been inhaling the smoke from the woodstove in your yurt too long. Great that you live off the grid and can do whatever you want whenever, but I still live in the real world. Maybe you've forgotten what that's like...'

'My world is real. It's realer than yours. Everything you do is fake. The products, the clothes...' He gestures to his shirt and then angrily unbuttons the front. 'This horrible tan that you made me get. It's all fake.'

I was just about to tell him that he doesn't have to wear the dumb thong and I would figure something out but he thinks he's so full of integrity. He agreed to do this and what did he think all that manscaping was for?

'You may think everything we do is fake but it's very real to me. You agreed to do a job. I know this part is a bit more challenging but that's the deal.'

He doesn't say anything. He gets up from the bed and starts taking off his clothes. He finishes unbuttoning his shirt. I should look away or at the very least not stare but his body is like a magnet for my eyes. I feel like a hormonal teenager fast-forwarding to the racy part of an R-rated movie.

'You're right. I agreed and I'm a man of my word.'

'Thank you,' I say. 'It's the final setup. After this, you'll be done and on your way back.'

'Fine,' he snaps at me.

'Fine,' I snap back. With that, he sits on the bed, kicks off his shoes and takes off his pants. Now he's standing in some no-name boxers looking incredibly hot. I'm trying to imagine his body hair kept natural and see through the stupid self-tanner we made him wear, and underneath all that is a man that takes my breath away. I've seen Chase this naked hundreds of times before and it never had any impact on me so why I am I unable to take my eyes of this guy? We're in the middle of an argument so you'd think I'd be even more disinterested but something about the heat of our exchange boils over like a risotto I once forgot to stir.

He looks in the bag.

'Do you want to bring me the other sock? I only see one,' he says.

'One will do,' I say as dryly as possible.

'You want one sock on and the other foot naked?' he asks.

'No,' I say. 'You'll be in the shower completely bare-foot. The other sock is for… ah…' I point to his groin.

'Are you kidding me?' he asks. I'm not sure if I have insulted his manhood or not.

'It's standard operating procedure on an underwear shoot. It helps makes everything look more… impressive,' I say.

'Riiiight,' he says. 'Nothing fake about what's going on here.'

'Stuff it,' I say, referring to both his mouth and thong. I walk out of the bedroom and through the living room to the guest bathroom where everything is set up.

'Is he ready?' Tina asks. 'I thought I would spray glass curtain of the shower and shoot through the water to give it a sort of *Psycho* feel.'

It's a honeysuckle and hibiscus scented raw sugar scrub called 'Daddy Me'. I'm not sure it needs a Hitchcock vibe but I'd never step on Tina's creative vision in this realm. 'Sure,' I say, faking a smile. My mind is still back with Beau, fuming over our exchange and his accusation.

The bathroom door opens.

Boom!

Beau is standing there in the black and green metallic thong with the world's luckiest dollar signs scattered about it. Other guys wear their muscles like an accessory but with Beau they're simply a part of him and that makes them even sexier. I look down to his groin in a purely professional capacity and I see that he is fully stuffed like a Thanksgiving turkey. For a second I wonder if it's too much but can you really ever have too much in that area?

Kiara fixes his eyebrows and some places where the tanner is streaking. I notice he has his hands behind his back. Tina turns on the shower and is ready to shoot.

Beau turns to me, moves his hand from behind his back and hands me the sock that was in the bag with his thong. 'Can you take care of this for me? I don't think I'll be needing it.'

'Ahh... yeah... okay,' I stammer. I look down at the rolled-up sock in my hand and he throws this sexy smile at me that's as sweet as a cupcake baked by the devil.

Chapter 11

I spend the rest of my weekend working on creating the posts for the show. Usually we have a social media intern working on this but I don't want anyone else seeing the raw footage. I like touching up the photos and finding a pleasing composition. In my role, I rarely get to work on these types of details, so even though it takes up the rest of my weekend there's a part of me that enjoys it. Before I go to sleep I upload everything to the shared drive for Maria Luisa to see and schedule the posts.

With the crisis averted I go to the sad freezer in my tiny kitchen and take out the pint of Earl Grey Van Leeuwen ice cream I've been saving for a special occasion or the end of the weekend, whichever comes first. I use a scoop I purchased at Zabar's to create a spherical globe of pale sky-colored confection and place it in the dish. A tiny drip hits the edge and I grab an Irish linen tea towel to wipe it away. I take a few seconds to admire the shape of the ice cream, the color of the plate and the way the curved lines all echo each other. Then I grab my favorite antique ice cream spoon with the fleur-de-lis handle and clamshell-shaped base and devour it before heading to bed. A well-deserved treat.

One image from the day lingers in my brain while I'm trying to sleep. It's not one I would use for social media

— a picture of the setup that happened to capture Beau looking out the window quiet in thought. He has this pensive look in his eyes staring at the New York skyline. He mentioned living here at some point and I wonder if he ever thinks about returning. There's a reason why he left and it's none of my business. I'm still surprised I told him about my mom but I couldn't let him be so vulnerable with me and just stand there. Any possibility of complications was lessened by the fact that he'll be gone by tomorrow afternoon. Maybe that made it easier to open up. Despite these thoughts rattling around my brain, I tell myself I'm tossing and turning because of eating so much sugar before bed; nothing else.

The next day I have one Myles brother on his way out and the other coming in. I'll get Beau a car service to the bus, an unglamorous but perfectly safe way to travel, and I expect Chase to land at LaGuardia some point mid-morning according to the airline reservation we discovered.

After I wake up, I stroll over to Park Avenue hoping to catch a glimpse of the tulips but the once colorful patches of plump flowers are past their bloom. Every year I try to catch the gorgeous display but with the mess Chase left I haven't had a chance. I wanted to at least snap a picture for Uncle Clams. During the summers he toured the country as the 'internationally ignored drag queen Clams Casino' and did shows at the Starlight on Fire Island, but during the year he worked as a florist. He's always loved flowers and making things beautiful.

I take a cab down to the flower district and buy armfuls of fresh white ranunculus that look like cups of whipped frosting for a wedding cake and soft white freesias that smell divine. Uncle Clams will be thrilled. I think about going over to the apartment and thanking Beau for helping me out. Maybe I could give him a tip but that would awkward. Or I could give him some of the flowers I just purchased as a display of gratitude but I can't imagine he has the appropriate vase for the arrangement in his yurt. Why do I keep trying to come up with reasons for seeing him again? He did his job. He's been paid. It's the end of the story.

I'm in a cab on the West Side Highway heading back when my phone rings and I see Maria Luisa's name. Is something wrong with the posts? Was she able to tell that it's not Chase in the images?

'Ethan, is that you? My reception is terrible. I'm on a cat—' There's the buzz of static and then nothing. Did she just say she's on a cat? 'Hello, sorry the waves are choppy.' Oh, she must be on her catamaran in Sag Harbor. That makes much more sense than being on an actual feline. But why is she calling? 'We need to talk.'

That's not good. No one calls from a catamaran with good news, ever. 'What's up?' I ask, staring at New Jersey across the Hudson from the cab's window.

'Hairlucinations is out,' she says, and I feel my stomach drop to the floor of the cab. Hairlucinations was a major sponsor for the live stream. They had their name all over the float.

'What happened?' I ask trying not to panic. Maybe this is something we can fix.

'Something with the logistics of their new seed oil conditioner. Rainforests. Profits shrinking. Blah. Blah. We've got to find a new sponsor. The hole Hairlucinations will leave is substantial. We need another national brand.' This is terrible. The entire broadcast could be at stake if we don't find a new sponsor. I reach in my pocket for an antacid.

'But here's the good news,' she says. 'I was having a cocktail at The Palm in East Hampton and found out *American Morning* had a last-minute cancel. They're looking to do something for Pride,' Maria Luisa says.

When someone says they want to 'do something for Pride' it usually means they want to slap a rainbow on something, up the price and call it a limited edition. It's nearly June so it means they forgot about Pride altogether and they need a way to overcompensate.

'I know this is last minute but they want Chase to teach Jane Trahn the Pride Pump on *American Morning*. Isn't that fantastic? It's a huge audience. National exposure that can help us pull in a new ad partner. Very different demo than we usually pull for your show but we need it, Ethan. You really need it.'

Nice job Maria Luisa going from we to you so smoothly. 'Tomorrow? Tomorrow morning?' I ask.

'Yes, Ethan. I mean "morning" is in the title. That's when it happens.' Maria Luisa has every right to be condescending considering how stupid my question is.

I start doing the math in my head. If a bus is leaving New York City for upstate this morning and a plane is leaving Miami for New York City at roughly the same time, at what point will the apartment be safe enough to *not* have the brothers meet and create an explosion? Isn't this the kind of thing that creates a riff in the space–time continuum?

Maria Luisa promises all the details in an email where everyone's team will be cc'd. She keeps talking but the reception is so bad I'm only hearing bits and pieces. Eventually the call drops completely and I hang up. Can I get even an afternoon of peace? Of not having to worry about everything falling apart for the length of an entire cab ride? I have been dreading having to do this but if we are going to be ready for tomorrow I need to start working with Chase as soon as he touches down. It's time for his little impromptu vacation to end. I loathe having to call him but I don't have any choice. To my surprise he answers on the first ring: 'Look who's decided to answer their phone.'

'Ethan, is that you? Why are you calling me? I only picked up because you had a New York City number. I thought it might be important.' I call and text him twenty times a day. How does he not have my number programmed?

'Chase, this is important. More important than the Blue Party or Silver Party or whatever color you're celebrating.'

'It was Purple Party weekend in Miami. I never miss it. You know that,' he barks into the telephone.

I bark back, 'You left me with a debacle of epic proportions this weekend. You put the show in jeopardy.'

'Blah! Blah! Blah! The show. The show. It's the same old thing with you, Ethan. I learned something about myself this weekend.' I hear announcements for flights in the background. At least he's at the airport on his way back. I wouldn't have been surprised if he was so far down a K-hole he missed his flight. 'I said, I learned something about myself.'

'What, that you're actually six foot two and not six foot three like you tell everyone?'

Chase gasps. 'I am six foot two and three quarters and you know it, Ethan.' He performs an exasperated sigh. 'I learned that I'm so much bigger than your little show.'

'Chase, stop it. You've had your fun weekend at your party and now it's time to get back to work. I'll pick you up from the airport. We have a lot to do tonight.' I hate being his chauffeur but the sooner we get started preparing for *American Morning*, the better. It took me days to teach him the dance I created for his TikTok. He'll need a refresher before going live tomorrow. It's not Alvin Ailey but it's more complicated than it looks.

'It's going to be hard to pick me up from the airport,' he says with a tone that gives me concern.

'I have your flight itinerary. The roads will be packed but that's what I do. I make sacrifices for the good of the show.' The cab swerves and I brace myself against the door.

'There you go again. You talk about The Show like it's a living, breathing thing. A monster always hiding in the closet that needs to be fed.' His analogy is not far off. Even a broken clock is right twice a day so ding-dong it's Chase o'clock. 'I'm tired of it, Ethan. I'm tired of you always telling me what to do. I have a Greek fishing tycoon who wants to fly me to Dabu Bobby to meet with some film producers and that's exactly what I'm doing. He thinks I'm wasting my time on television. He thinks I should be in blockbuster films.'

'What? Where are you going?' I ask. What is he talking about?

'Dabu. Bobby.' He says the words slowly like I'm the one who's a moron. 'It's in the Middle East somewhere.'

'You mean Abu Dhabi,' I say, trying to ignore his tantrum.

'See that? You're always correcting me. Maybe Dabu Bobby is a new hotspot that you haven't heard of. Did you ever think of that? You think you're so smart all the time and I'm just supposed to do what you say. This guy thinks I could win an Academy Award or maybe even an Oscar.'

Does he have any idea that those are the same award?

'You can't be serious, Chase. We have a ton of B-roll to film before the live stream, interviews, promos. The awards show. The Fire Island shoot. For crying out loud, you're one of the Grand Marshals of the parade, not to mention…' I don't tell him we're scheduled to appear on a national news program in less than eighteen hours or that our biggest sponsor has just pulled out, because it will only make him more defiant. I reach for the antacids in my pocket again.

'I'm serious. And that's not just the ayahuasca talking or the tycoon.' He did ayahuasca again. The last time he did the hallucinogenic he thought he was a Disney Princess living on the wrong planet. He is for the most part but that made it harder to bring him back to reality. 'I'm done with you. I'm done with your television show. Film is my future.'

'Chase. Chase! Stop being a total…' I hear the phone beep and look down as it switches from a voice to a video call.

'Here's the gate, Ethan.' He shows me a sign that says: 'Non-stop from Miami to Abu Dhabi. First Class. Now Boarding.'

'Do not. Do not get on that flight. Do you hear me, Chase? Do not. The show needs you in New York tonight.' A flight to the Middle East from Miami has got to be fourteen, maybe sixteen hours if it's non-stop. Even if he lands and turns around immediately he'll be gone for a day and a half. He cannot get on that plane.

'Chase! Do not get on that flight. The show needs you…'

'The Show is not a thing. You might need me but you aren't going to get me. I'm going to Dabu Bobby.'

He hangs up. I stare at the phone and scream 'Abu Dhabi!' so loud they might actually hear me in the United Arab Emirates.

Chapter 12

There is no time to lose and less time to think. This moment needs action. I open the partition and first apologize to the driver for all the screaming and then ask him to take me a bit further uptown to Chase's apartment. He cuts across Central Park and then up Lexington. We get to the front of the building and I see the car service I usually book parked in front of it. Maybe Beau hasn't left yet. I might still have a chance. I head straight up to the apartment and find Beau closing the door. I immediately get a flash of him wearing that ugly thong, bulge and all.

'Hi, Beau,' I say as he shuts the door. He must have just come out of the shower. His hair is wet and uncombed. He still looks almost exactly like Chase but there's a casual, unassuming quality to him that is absolutely magnetic.

'What are you doing here, Ethan? Do you need to pluck a hair that's grown back on my eyebrow?' We didn't exactly leave things on a great note after he accused me of being fake so I understand the sharp tone. 'I don't want to miss my bus,' he says and walks past me to the elevator.

'That's exactly what I want to talk to you about,' I say, standing between him and the down button. 'Your brother is on a flight...' I begin to say.

'Then I'm out of here.' He moves past me. 'I don't want to be the same room with him.'

'Don't worry about that. He's on a flight out of the country. I don't see him coming back for the foreseeable future.' Beau stops reaching for the button.

'I thought he was the drum major of the parade for the big live stream. Did you cancel that?' he asks.

'Cancel the live stream? It's the first time a national network is carrying the parade. Do you have any idea how important this is?'

'The parade is what's important. It's a chance for queer people to be themselves,' he says. 'It's a day of celebration.' Spare me the speeches on the importance of Pride. I don't recall seeing any rainbow stickers covering his yurt.

'Getting this deal was major. It means that some kid in the middle of the country that doesn't have access to any type of gay culture is going to be able to see what it's like when thousands of gay people come together.'

'Is that why you're doing it?' he asks.

'Yes,' I say without thinking, because it's the truth. There were so few gay people on TV when I was a kid. Seeing something like the parade would have had a major impact on me. It's one thing to watch clips on the news and online but another to see it treated like Thanksgiving or the Fourth of July or every other big celebration.

'Then why not get someone else to do it instead of Chase?'

'I am getting someone else. I'm getting you?'

'Nice try, Ethan. I agreed to take a few photos. Harmless. I need to get back upstate and find some work logging before all the teams are booked. I need the income. If I miss it, I'm screwed.' He picks up his bag and I take it from him and put it back down.

'How much would that pay?' I ask.

'I don't know. I guess roughly...'

'Whatever it is, I'll add 20 per cent. No, make it 25. I know I only made a dent in your debt,' I say. I see his body tense when I mention it. 'What if I erased it? Poof. I can make it disappear and send you back to your beloved yurt debt-free. Or you could get started somewhere else without any obligations.' In my head I am working out the numbers. It won't be that hard to shift some money over to a well-paid consultant without raising too many eyebrows, especially if everything is running smoothly.

He leans against the wall. He's thinking about it. Patience is not my thing but I give it a shot and wait.

'Ethan, I can't,' he says finally.

'Why not? You need the money to pay off all your debt and I can get it to you by the end of the month. A big fat check to take with you on the bus or even a sack of cash if that works better. Starbucks gift cards? Crypto? Whatever you want. And I'll pay in advance. Tomorrow. Tina will arrange it.'

'I don't mean I won't do it.' That's good. That's very good. 'I mean I don't think I *can* do it.'

'Why not? We've got the look down,' I say but I know that's only the expertly manicured tip of the iceberg.

'Yeah, I can look like him, that's easy. When we were kids our mom hated putting us in those matching outfits but we did it ourselves all the time at school. We thought it was hysterical to try and trick people and we got away with it most of the time.'

'That's good to know,' I say, thinking about how we are about to try and trick millions of viewers.

'*Most* of the time. As long as I didn't have to talk. I should let you know he was a lot better at it than me.'

'Oh,' I say, trying not to let my lip quiver.

'He could pretend anything and just make stuff up. I was never good at any of that. Someone would ask me a question and I'd answer as me right away. I always blew our cover.'

I stare straight ahead thinking about how it will only take one slip for this whole thing to blow up. He must be able to tell I'm about to descend into panic. My only option is to let him in again. Just a bit so he knows how important this is to me.

'My boss knows Chase is a flight risk. I can't let Maria Luisa know I screwed this up. Not to mention there's a promotion at the network that I'm up for. I mean, a really big promotion. If I do a good job with the parade, I'll be able to rise above the competition.'

'Oh, there's competition?'

'Yeah, this awful guy named Jeremiah Jones.'

'Why is he so awful?'

'He's always strategizing and working out how to get ahead at the network.' I get a knot in my stomach just thinking about it.

'Like you?' he asks. His truth pierces me.

'Yes… I mean no, not like me,' I protest.

'Right, you just happen to drive half a day out of the city to throw your star's twin brother in the backseat of a rental and bring him into the city so some woman could perform torture through hair removal just so you could pass him off as somebody he's not to millions of people so you can get a better job.'

'Well, when you put it that way…' I start to think I am like my nemesis but then I remember that this is not just about me. 'What you don't understand is that *Myles of Style* isn't just another lifestyle show. We're on the verge of crossing over to mainstream media. We'd be reaching so many more people. There's a big difference between being on a niche shelf in the back of the store and being on the front table when you walk in. I want our show to be front and center, displayed in the store window and not just during Pride. If I can get our show to that place, I'd be a lock for a promotion. My boss is taking a bigger job and I'd get hers.'

'Is that what you want?' Beau asks.

'It's an amazing job. Anyone would want it,' I say. The words come out of my mouth without even needing to think.

'But that's not what I asked. I didn't ask if anyone would want it. I asked if you want it.' He's not judgmental or scolding. He's straightforward and it makes answering the question evasively even more difficult.

I'm about to answer yes, but something stops me. The truth is, I never thought I would become a television executive or even hoped to become one. Sometimes you take a turn and you just keep going and you make new paths. The path I'm on is a bit different from what I thought it would be but it's something most people would die to do. I'm so far down it at this point that I can't see myself getting off.

'Do you want this promotion?' Beau repeats.

'It doesn't matter,' I firmly respond, hoping he will give up on the question. 'I know how to make you him. Chase reads the lines I write; he hits the marks on camera I set. He wears what I tell him to and he likes what I tell him to like. That's how the show works.'

Beau looks at me with his nose wrinkled. 'I guess I don't have to wonder too much about why he left.'

'What's that supposed to mean?' I ask, not liking the insinuation.

'Who wants to be ordered around and told what to do?'

'I'll tell you who. A guy who wants to make more money in a month than he can in an entire summer. That's who,' I say. As soon as the words come out of my mouth I wish that my tone was a bit softer.

'You think I'm only motivated by money? I know my brother is but it sounds like you're just as shallow as he is if you think you can throw a pot of money at me and I'll do what you say.'

How did I dive into the world's most difficult gene pool? I try to calm myself down. Swimmers who panic almost always drown. Although incredibly infuriating, he seems to have a set of ethics.

'I know this will be hard for you to believe but people look up to Chase. To be honest I find it hard to believe. But they do. He's an out gay man doing what he loves on TV.'

'Yes, he's out. I am aware of that. Very aware.' He says it like it annoys him for some reason which I don't understand. 'Well, he's doing what *you* love.'

'Yes, that true.' I've already established that this guy's currency is honesty so I mount my last appeal. 'And the truth is…' I hesitate. It's one thing to let this guy know all the behind-the-scenes drama at work with the promotion but another to let him know why it's so important to me personally and the consequences involved. 'The truth is that if you don't do it, I'll be fired. I'll have to explain to my bosses that I lost control of the show. I'll be humiliated in front of everyone I know.' As soon as the words escape my mouth I cover my eyes with my hand. I can't stomach the thought of confessing the fact that I'm a fraud. All the exquisite table settings, effortless canapes and elegant centerpieces in the world can't hide the fact that I'm barely holding on to the world I've worked so hard to create. 'No one will blame Chase,' I confess. 'Everyone will blame me and I don't know what I'll do if that happens.' I'm not pleading my case anymore. I'm telling him my honest fear. I can feel my heart beating so loudly inside my ears that I wonder if he can hear it too. Beau moves his lips together and squints a bit. I can tell he's thinking.

'Okay,' he says.

'Okay, what?'

'I'll do it. I can use the cash. I want my debt cleared but it's not just that. I know what it's like to have to pay the consequences for my brother's actions. You were honest with me. Really honest about what you need instead of just forcing me to do what you want. You need help. You'll cover my expenses so why shouldn't I help you?'

'Are you serious? Really?' I'm on the verge of jumping up and down and hugging him but I manage to control myself.

He holds out his hand. 'Let's shake on it.' I don't actually want to feel his hand in mine. It was one thing to have crazy fantasies about him when he was set to be on a bus in a few hours, but now that we're going to be working closely over the next few weeks, I'm worried the touch of his hand in mine might spark something that will need a typhoon to put out.

'Uhm, we'll need more than a handshake. I'll have to ask you to sign an NDA of course. That's a non-disclosure agreement. It will legally bind you,' I say, opting for legal intimacy over physical.

'I just told you I would do it.'

'I know, I know, but a contract will be in both our best interests. Don't worry. I'll make sure it will contain all the financial renumeration. It protects you as well as me.'

'I gave you my word. That's all you need. I trust you'll pay me. I'm not worried about that. We do it on a handshake or we don't do it at all.'

'Fine,' I say. I grab his hand and as soon as I do I know it's a mistake. I can feel something transfer from his palm to mine, an energy that is undeniable. I pull my hand away, unsure if I've just made the best or worst deal of my entire life.

Chapter 13

Beau goes on a jog to clear his mind before we get started. I start favoriting the videos of the viral dance move that I'll need to show him and then move some furniture out of the way. I saw a recipe for curried roasted chickpeas a few days ago and I head to the kitchen to see if I can scrounge up the ingredients as I wait for him to come back since cooking always calms me down. I open the cabinet door above the espresso machine and it hits me.

What am I doing? This is absolutely bonkers, a term I don't use casually. A few pictures are one thing but convincing people, live people, in-person people, that Beau is actually Chase is a level of deception that I'm not sure I'm ready for and completely sure Beau isn't ready for. The social media posts were fine. Beau looks like his brother but he acts nothing like him. They both have a powerful allure. We couldn't have built what we've built without Chase's ability to charm people when the cameras are rolling. What happens when the cameras stop is a different matter. Chase wasn't always a preening diva with selfish demands. But as his fame grew so did his ego. Now he doesn't care who he keeps waiting or who he inconveniences. Beau is super intense and stubborn in his own way but he doesn't seem to disregard the people around him the way Chase does.

After finishing the chickpeas I set a tray with small plates, a pitcher of ice water infused with lime zest, and vintage cloth napkins. I carry everything out to the terrace and set it on the cast iron table away from the edge. We're on the fifteenth floor, which is about my limit for heights outdoors. From the terrace I can see across to the Upper West Side up to Harlem and down to Midtown. It feels like the whole city is laid out in front of me waiting for my next move. Then, My Next Move comes back from his jog and pops out to the terrace. As I suspected he's covered in sweat and charisma as he stretches his calves.

'Are you sure you're ready for this?' I ask. 'If you changed your mind while you were out I'd understand.' I don't want to force him to do anything.

He looks at the tray I have prepared and grabs a few chickpeas from the bowl and stuffs them in his mouth.

'There are plates,' I say, pointing to the elegant vintage Johnson Brothers dishes I have laid out. 'And napkins.' He ignores me and grabs another handful. 'Thank you again for doing this,' I say.

'Why shouldn't I help you out of a jam? This seems really important to you. Why else would you be so tightly wound? It's like you're going to explode.'

'I'm not tightly wound,' I say, stomping my foot the exact way someone who is tightly wound would do.

'Right,' he says with a laugh, but it's not like he's laughing at me at all and it makes me laugh at myself.

'Okay, fine. Maybe I am tightly wound. I can accept that.'

'Well, that's the first step,' he says, pouring himself some ice water.

'Toward what?' I ask.

He finishes his drink and puts the glass back on the tray. He puts his hands on the front of my shoulders and stares directly into my eyes before saying very seriously, 'Toward getting you unwound.' His eyes linger on mine, waiting for the words to sink in, and they do. He releases his stare and heads toward the terrace doors but turns around before he opens them. 'These need salt and maybe cumin. Just FYI.' He smiles and exits.

The nerve. The absolute nerve. I bypass spooning a serving onto a plate and directly toss a few chickpeas in my mouth. I take a second to absorb the creaminess of the legume and the sweetness of the curry and then it hits me. They need more salt. And maybe cumin.

He changes his clothes; I season the snack. We get started in the dining room. There is a whole schedule to explain including remote locations, our Fire Island shoot, the ribbon cutting on the day of the parade and a kaleidoscope of promotional events including an awards show ceremony, but I'll get to all that later. Right now we need to focus on the most pressing issue.

'Tomorrow, we have you, or rather Chase, or you. I...' I'm so confused about things at this point I can't keep it straight. 'Tomorrow's segment features the viral sensation the Pride Pump to SeanSeanSean's "OutNout".'

Beau shows no reaction. Zero. He just stares at me. 'I don't really even know what any of that means.'

I grab my phone to show him all the viral videos of Chase and people doing the dance that they think Chase created. The fact is for a week I worked on the moves with a choreographer that I knew from my days waiting tables. As soon as we posted it the dance started racking up views and then other people started doing it and tagging Chase and the show and then celebrities were doing it. I show Beau the footage of Chase dancing in Times Square with random people who recognized him or the dance or both.

'You want me to show these videos on TV?' Beau asks.

'No, I want you to teach this dance, the Pride Pump, to Jane Trahn. She's the host of the show. *American Morning*. You'll dance it together.'

'Dance? You want me to dance? With music? Like moving my... and music... and stuff...' He stands up and runs his hand over his newly coiffed hair, nervously making the top smoother. I think there might be sweat just above his lip and I try to remember if I locked the door. 'No,' he says. 'I'm not good at that. Not good at all.' His usual deep and resonant voice is higher than I've heard it before and with a definite tremble. 'Can't we start with something easier?'

It's the first time I've seen him have this kind of reaction to anything. I know he's nervous about convincing people that he's Chase but I can prepare him. 'I'll tell you exactly what to do and what to say.'

'But what about the dancing? Do I actually have to do the dance?'

'It's really not that hard a dance,' I lie. It is in fact a challenging combination. It took Chase a full week to learn it and he's actually pretty good with that kind of stuff. 'I can break it down for you step by step. It's Boom. Pop. Cha, cha, cha. Swizzle. Swizzle. Sha-blam. Slaaaay.' I show the moves associated with each word. I've done this viral dance so many times I don't even think about it. It's not that I could do it in my sleep. I have done it in my sleep. I practiced it so long I couldn't get my brain to shut down in bed.

'Boom, chop, swizzle, zizzle? Those are dance moves? People dance those words? Like with their bodies? I'm not a dancer. Not at all. Maybe I could decorate something or cook something or wear something. Don't you do that kind of stuff too?'

'Yes, we do and you'll be doing plenty of that. We have a ton of segments to shoot before the parade but this is for tomorrow. *Tomorrow* as in a dozen or so hours,' I say, slowly emphasizing each word. 'Let's go slow and start with the first move. It's just one arm up and one arm down, like this,' I continue and show him the move. He sort of does it but with the wrong arms and more like the Tin Man after a week of rain. I do it again with a bit more flow and he still does the wrong arm. I move to stand directly in front of him and say, 'Just pretend I'm a mirror. Look at me and do what I do.' I'll have to do everything in reverse but that's easy enough. I'm standing just a few inches in front of him to show him the moves, but our eyes lock quickly. The intensity of it startles me, and I struggle to try to stay focused.

'I'm trying. I really am,' he says.

'I know. It just takes practice.'

I keep moving my arms up and down for the first beats and it takes a while but he finally does the correct move. I move on to the syncopated hip sways. I demonstrate the move, then ask him to repeat it but his hips shake up and down like a jackhammer instead of swaying.

'Think side to side,' I say. 'Let me slow it down. Watch.'

His eyes drop to my waist and I start moving the center of my body slowly from side to side. I'm not doing anything overtly sexual but having Beau study my body so acutely makes me aroused in a way that I'm sure will become noticeable quickly. He moves his hips in the wrong direction again and without thinking I just put my hands on them.

'Is this okay?' I ask and take my hands off. I don't want to do anything that makes him uncomfortable.

He looks me in the eye and takes my hands in his and places them back on his hips. 'I want to get this right tomorrow, so yes, this is okay.' Maybe he wants to learn this dance because I'm paying him or maybe he doesn't want to be embarrassed or maybe he just knows how important it is to me. It feels like a combination of all those things.

Having his hands over my hands on his hips is more intimate than I was calculating. I feel the strength of his body as it pushes back and forth. He's solid and connected to the ground. I take my hands and use my strength to move his hips from side to side. Handling his body this way makes it impossible for me to hide what's happening in my pants a second longer. I jump back from him.

'What's wrong?' he asks. 'I thought I was finally getting it.' He looks confused and he should be. He was getting it. The problem is I was getting it too and a little too obviously.

'Nothing's wrong. Here, keep studying this video.' I grab my iPad and scroll to the video and let it play on repeat. 'I think maybe it's easier if you learn the basics from watching the video. It's too complicated to have me do it also. You practice. I'm going to the bedroom to pull some looks for tomorrow. I'll be back in a minute or maybe an hour. Doesn't matter. You practice.' I leave him in the living room and run to the bedroom where I study the production budget to find a less arousing task and seriously consider taking a cold shower.

I let Beau practice on his own for a while before I return with a much more hands-off approach. Three hours and thousands of replays of the video later Beau has gone from completely awful to mostly terrible. He hesitates before each move as a flash of panic streaks across his face like a robber caught during a burglary. It's a disaster but at this point I'm out of options. We have to be at the *American Morning* studios in a few hours.

My phone buzzes. I look down and see a text from the night nurse. '*Clams in the hospital.*' I can feel the blood drain from my face; my entire body is suddenly still. I've been here before and I know how to stop the flood of emotions with action.

'I'm sorry, I have to go,' I say calmly, despite the explosion of feelings I'm keeping at bay.

'Don't you want to stay here and keep practicing?' Beau asks.

'That was my uncle's nurse. They had to take him to the hospital. I'm not sure what's going on. He has diabetes and sometimes… he loses…'

'Oh no. I'm sorry,' he says and walks over to the coat rack. He opens my jacket for me to put on. I walk over and put my arms through each sleeve. Then he grabs his coat.

'Beau, this isn't part of the deal. You don't have to go with me. You should stay here and practice or sleep or whatever. I'll be back. I can get you in the morning or send a car or…' My mind is racing. I'm barely able to make sense of anything or figure out what I need to do next.

'Ethan,' he says, looking me in the eyes. 'I can tell this hit you hard. If you want to call Kiara or someone else to go with you I understand, but I'm here now and I know what it's like to be in this situation. I'll sit outside or go in with you but you need someone with you.' He puts on his jacket and that's that. It's not an argument or a directive. It's just a simple statement of fact and it somehow makes me feel better. We walk outside and before I can even open an app Beau somehow has the door of a cab open for me.

Chapter 14

'He's fine. He's stable,' the nurse says. I feel the relief flood my body. She explains that Clams was simply having a reaction to a new medication which they have now changed and he'll be fine, better in fact since this was apparently the root of some lethargy he's been having. They even had a chance to look at his ankle.

I thank the nurse and call Sheila to let her know what's going on with her dad. I'm clearly waking her up and she panics when she hears the news but I tell her what the doctor said and promise to call her after I see him.

'I told them not to call you,' Clams says as soon as I walk into the room where they're treating him. He's awake but clearly a little shaken. He's lost some of his color and his eyes are a bit droopy.

'Uncle Clams. The nurses have strict instructions to call me at any time day or night if you need me.' He has an IV in and even though I know they just want to make sure he's well-hydrated the sight of it makes me dash to his bedside and hug him.

'Oh crap. I'm dying,' he says.

'Wait. What? You are? You're dying?'

I'm about to lose it and then he says. 'I mean, I don't think so but if you're coming here and giving me a hug without any cajoling then something must be wrong with me. Ethan, darling, you're a wonderful boy but you aren't a hugger. What did they tell you?'

He's right. I'm not a hugger. But the stress of the weekend and seeing him like this makes me want to squeeze him tightly and never let go. I wrap my arms around as much of his stocky frame as I can with him lying in bed. It reminds me of when I would come home from school upset and he was visiting and he'd hug me and tell me everything gets better.

'You aren't dying. In fact, I spoke with your physician and with this new medication you'll be as good as new. They also think your ankle is doing very well.'

'I told you I was fine. You're such a worry wart,' he says, putting on his glasses to look carefully at his nails. He may have chipped one. 'I've been in this room too long. I need to get some fresh air,' he says and starts to get out of the bed to try and walk.

'Let's start with the wheelchair if you want to go out. Are you sure you want to?'

'Yes, and grab that purple turban from my bag. My hair is a mess and I don't want any of the cute night nurses to see me like this. Have you met Guillermo? He's gorgeous and the right height and age for you. He says he's a top but if you believe that…'

'Uncle Clams, you cannot go around asking the nurses about their preferred sexual positions.' I hunt around in his bag past fashion magazines, a jar of onion salt and a few packages of fake nails until I find his turban.

'It's not like they're expecting me to perform any of them. Anyway I thought you might get his number and see if you can meet him after work. And wear something snug that fits you tightly. You might as well show off what you got. Oh and something bright. You wear too many dark colors. You aren't a Beatnik.'

Uncle Clams knows my relationship with Chase is fake so he's desperate for me to have a 'real' boyfriend. I thought it might make things easier if I let him think I was involved with Chase but he saw through that immediately. He does whatever he can to set me up with someone new every single chance he gets. He's relentless.

Despite the late hour Clams is, of course, able to convince the nurses to let him get some air. I help him get into a wheelchair and we head out to the terrace. We walk through the waiting room so I can let Beau know what's going on and I see an attendant has her arm around him, snapping a selfie. She's giddy as the flash on her phone goes off.

'Thank you, Chase. I'll be watching *American Morning*,' the attendant says as she leaves, staring at the image she took on her phone.

'What was that all about?' I ask.

'Someone who works here said she watches *Myles of Style* and she wanted a selfie.' Yes. It worked. It's working. It is going to work. A sudden rush of relief about my uncle, the situation with Beau and my life in general rushes over me. Maybe this isn't going to be as hard as I thought it might be.

'Excuse me,' my uncle says, looking at Beau like he's the food ingredient label he can't read on a jar of sauce. 'Why would she want a selfie with you?'

'Uncle Clams, you know Chase,' I say, realizing this is a much harder test than a random nurse. 'He's getting more famous by the day. He's going to be on *American Morning* with Jane Trahn.'

'Ethan, my turban may be missing a few sequins and it may be the middle of the night, but I know this is not Chase.'

I stare at Beau and then at Clams. I'm not sure what to do but Beau comes to the rescue.

'Hello, I'm Chase's brother, Beau. I'm so sorry to hear you're having a hard time. I know diabetes can be hard to manage. I didn't want Ethan to have to get here on his own. I hope you don't mind me being with you.' He lowers his head and nods gently. He's so polite and thoughtful and the way his voice glides through the air is quite intoxicating. How did this man share a womb with the biggest idiot I know?

Clams scrutinizes him. 'His brother? There are two of them?'

'There are not two of them,' I say and out of the corner of my eye I see Beau's lips rise. 'Beau is his own person. Period. He's just helping me out until after the parade.'

My uncle looks at Beau and then looks at me. He raises his eyebrows and says, 'This ought to be good. I want to hear everything.' He points his free hand over his head toward the terrace where I explain the disaster movie that is currently my life.

Chapter 15

'Get on board the Pride Pump. Woo hoo! Can't wait for our segment this this morning, Chase,' Jane Trahn, the host of the show, says with the bright sunshine she usually sprays all over the morning telecast. She has stepped off set during the commercial break. The ground-floor studio has the usual crowd of tourists watching through the soundproofed windows. 'Hello, Ethan, sweetie!' She air kisses me so as not to mess her makeup.

'Hey Zany-Janey. You look great. I hear your ratings are through the roof. Thanks so much for having us.' I kiss the air next to her face.

'Of course. Happy to do it. It's a big deal doing the live event for Pride and I know any exposure you get can help. Word around here is you're up for a big promotion. You know I owe you for the rest of my life, so this is nothing. I put in a good word with Maria Luisa when I saw her in the Hamptons.'

I thought Jane might be behind all this. She and I met when we were starting out at a small network station. I was an assistant to the assistant for the food and restaurant reviewer and Jane worked at the news desk. We bonded quickly. I loved dreaming up crazy things for us to do to impress our bosses and she loved executing them. One day the local anchor broke her nose playing volleyball. I suggested Jane fill-in. I never thought anyone would take me seriously, we were both just kids at the time, but the managing producer did and it was the start of her career. She's always been very grateful and very successful.

'Jane, we're back on in fifteen,' a stage manager says, tapping her on the shoulder.

'Chase is on right after this segment on bio-terrorism.' She goes to walk back to set but stops and turns back to me. 'By the way he looks even more delicious than usual. You're a lucky man.'

'That's me, Mr Lucky,' I say through clenched teeth, and she walks back to set.

I head over to the makeup area expecting to see Beau sitting in a chair getting his cheeks powdered so they don't shine on camera. Instead, I see Blaine, the makeup artist, in the chair and Beau standing next to him. Blaine has his eyes closed and it looks like Beau is whispering something is in his ear. I leave this guy alone for half a second and he's screwing up already.

'What's going on here?' I ask.

'Shh. Ethan, you're ruining it,' Beau says.

'Ruining what?' I ask.

Blaine gets out of the chair and grabs a pallet of brushes from the makeup counter. 'Sorry Ethan. I was telling Chase how I've been stressed out and he was helping me do a guided meditation.'

'He was what?' I ask in shock. I've been so focused on this stupid viral dance I forgot that I also needed to instruct Beau in his brother's horrible attitude.

'Thanks a lot Chase,' Blaine says. 'I was nervous about seeing you again since the last time at that photoshoot you…'

'Last time I what?' Beau asks. I remember the incident vividly. Blaine used the wrong color base on Chase and he was so angry he yelled at Blaine and made him cry. I should have remembered this history and prepped Beau but the fact is after doing the Pride Pump on repeat yesterday and then going to see my uncle, I'm not exactly on top of my game.

'Thanks, Blaine. It's always great to see you, and love your blouse. Is that fuchsia or magenta? I always confuse those two,' I say, grabbing Beau by the arm and yanking him away. 'Great work on *Chase*. We have to get *Chase* to set.' I make sure I sprinkle his name liberally like some kind of hypnotic suggestion.

'Remember, exhale longer than you inhale. That helps short-circuit your nervous system and creates more opportunity for relaxation,' Beau says as we walk away. I barely let him get the words out.

'Would you please remember that your brother is a callous, self-centered diva?' I whisper sharply in Beau's ear once no one is close enough to hear. 'Chase does not go around helping people with relaxation techniques. If there's anyone who needs help relaxing it's me.'

'You take terrible care of yourself,' he says.

What's that supposed to mean? I haven't had my own eyebrows threaded or my skin exfoliated in a few weeks. I run my hand across my stubble. I admit I could use some maintenance. 'I've been very busy with the show. My personal appearance has had to take a back seat.'

'No, not there. Here,' he says and puts his large hand on the upper part of my chest indicating my heart, or maybe that's where my pancreas is. I have no idea. I'm not great with anatomy. 'I'd be happy to give you a massage tonight to help you de-stress. I think you'd like Reiki.'

'You what?' I ask and look at him. The thought of his big strong hands all over me in a candlelit room with soft music playing makes my heart almost skip a beat. A PA taps me on the shoulder. 'We need him on set.' Saved by a production assistant in a baseball hat. I shake my head, erasing the last thought and say, 'Are you ready for this?'

'No,' he says plainly. For the first time today a flash of panic crosses his face. It's clear Beau's default mode is set to extreme chill. He's handled everything I've thrown at him the past few days. However, it's one thing to practice the dance at the apartment, but the set is a beehive of activity with so many moving pieces a Carmelite nun would be on edge. He's staring at the cameras.

'Just ignore all the chaos. Jane is a pro. You're just having a conversation with one person.'

'This isn't the apartment living room. This is thousands of people watching.'

'Actually millions but it doesn't matter, it's just you and Jane.' And my entire career, reputation and dignity on the line I remind myself, but I try not to let my panic feed his. 'You have this down. Our last run-through was pretty good. You even got the sha-blam.'

'I did, didn't I?' The panic seems to ebb, and I notice he takes a long breath out and a short breath in like he was doing with Blaine. I guess his relaxation techniques work.

'Chase, this is going to be so much fun,' Jane says, the natural warmth and enthusiasm that has made her so successful oozing out. She puts her hand on his arm and gently squeezes. I imagine it's something she does for all of her guests to make them feel comfortable and it seems to be working.

'You can do it,' I say, putting my arm on his shoulder and squeezing gently. I can feel him breathing. He smiles and they head to set. For the first time this morning I feel like this might work, but then I spot something on set that I don't like. Something I don't like at all. I walk over to the source of my concern and grab the stage manager. 'What are those?'

'They're the new Summer Seashell ornaments from Swansenstein Crystals.'

'What are they doing on set during our segment? And why are there so many of them?' I ask, trying to imagine how Beau's massive frame is going to fit between Jane and the shimmering artificial ocean of ornaments hanging from fishing wire.

'They're part of our Summer by the Sea giveaway. We choose a new winner at the end of every show. We call them live. It's a whole thing. Last week this woman in Lawrence, Kansas won and she almost fainted. They're a pain in my ass but the sponsor wants them on camera,' he says, and walks away. I'm all too familiar with the contractual obligations to sponsors so I don't even try to suggest moving them.

I watch as they bring in more dangling ornaments on two stands with so many strings it looks like a marionette workshop. Should I warn Beau about these fragile booby traps or will that make him more self-conscious?

'Here we go,' Jane says, whizzing past me with Beau in tow. They stand among the glittering landmines and the show's theme music starts, bright cheerful strings with upbeat bells and a peppy choir singing, 'Let's wake up with a cup of *American Morning*.' How you have a cup of a show I have no idea.

In a matter of seconds the set transforms from chaos to polished enthusiasm. Jane and Beau smile. He's convincing for the moment. He's not nervous or self-conscious. I'm impressed.

'Welcome back America. I'm standing with the Swansenstein Crystals glittering Summer Seashells.' She glances from side to side. 'Aren't these decorations so elegant?' She nods as if to answer her own question. 'We have a special treat for you now. The gorgeous and talented star of *Myles of Style*, Chase Myles. Welcome Chase.'

'Thank you, Jane,' Beau says, remaining cool and totally in character. His eyes twinkle just a bit and his attitude is aloof and the tiniest bit bored, just like his brother. Good job, Beau, and good job, Kiara. He looks spot-on. I'm maintaining my optimism.

'I know you have a big live stream of the Pride Parade for your show this year and you're cutting the ribbon. Are you more nervous or excited or both?'

'Oh, I would definitely say both,' he says, and I wonder if his voice will crack.

Jane laughs her patented morning show cackle. 'Nothing to worry about. You'll be great. Just remember the most important thing is that love is love,' Jane says.

'That's true...' He pauses for a second and then adds, 'But it's also important to vote for candidates who...' What's he doing? I shake my head frantically from behind the camera. This is about teaching a trendy dance to a wacky newscaster. This is not an opportunity for him to get political, although truth be told I hate the way people sticker over marriage equality issues with endless 'love is love' comments. Love is love but if your right to express that love is taken away, we need more than stickers. Luckily Jane is a professional. She knows to steer things toward the light and frothy. Maybe no one noticed.

'Now, speaking of Pride, do you think I can learn the Pride Pump? I mean this move has gone viral. Everyone is doing it and I want to learn.'

'Absolutely. It's really just a combination of different moves and it ends with the slay,' Beau says, like it didn't take us hours and hours to get him to remember the entire combination. 'First I'll break it down,' he says, exactly as I instructed him.

I've been holding my breath since the segment started; I remember to let air out so I can let air in. Beau goes over each move and I'm just off camera mimicking each one in case he forgets, though he doesn't even glance my way. He's really focused on teaching and his connection with Jane. Maybe too focused on her and not enough on the moves. The Chase-like attitude begins to fade a bit and it makes me nervous. They say the camera can pick up on this type of thing, the relationship between two people. Usually when Chase is on camera it's like a gorgeous robot spitting things out but Beau is really talking to Jane about each move. If he's still nervous he sure isn't showing it. Jane thrives on having a connection with her guests and she's so comfortable it seems to make him more comfortable and easy-going, which would be nice if this were a high school dance. But it isn't. Comfortable and go-with-the-flow are not part of the Chase Myles brand, so while this isn't horrible, it isn't exactly headed in the right direction.

When Jane gets stuck Beau helps her and they laugh together, which is something Chase has never done on camera. Jane is known for her morning chuckle but Beau brings out a softer, less constrained side of Jane. During a segment like this the behind-camera crew would be totally checked out but they aren't. Everyone is watching and some people are trying to hold back laughing since Jane is not known for her dancing. They're enjoying the segment. I'm hoping the chemistry they have on camera is helping hide the fact that Beau is nowhere near as graceful as Chase. Beau has the grace of a pile of mud.

'Wait, do I swing to the left or the right after the arms and before the bounce?'

In my head I am screaming, 'Left! Swing to the left!'

Beau looks confused. I can tell he can't remember and he says, 'Oh, it doesn't matter. Just do whatever feels right. It's more about enjoying yourself than how you look. The most important thing is to make it your own. You don't have to be perfect; you just have to be yourself.'

Oh, hell no.

Chase would never, ever say that and anyone who has ever seen a second of the show would know that. Appearances matter. Details matter. Style matters. Perfection is what keeps viewers watching. They can be themselves on their own social media feeds. They come to *Myles of Style* to be inspired. Jane even looks a bit shocked. Is she on to us? 'You don't have to be perfect; you just have to be yourself.' No one is ever going to believe those words came out of Chase's mouth.

'Oh, okay. You're the expert. Should we try it up to speed?'

The music starts blasting and everyone expects Beau to jump into the move but he freezes. Jane is such a professional that she covers for him.

'Wait, wait,' she says. 'I wasn't ready. Let's try it again. What do you think, Chase?' she says and gently taps him on the arm to break whatever spell has come over him. I am wildly gyrating my hips trying to show him what he should be doing to remind him of the moves we practiced.

The music starts again and a look of panic crosses over Beau's face. I catch his eye and move my arms up and down for the first move and he catches it a beat before that part starts. Jane is doing the same thing and then I go to do the second move, sweeping my arms from side to side, and Beau begins the same move but the studio space is much smaller than where we practiced in the apartment.

Beau does a shuffle to the left when he's supposed to go to the right, which is the direction Jane is going and they bump into each other, which makes them both laugh. They keep laughing and doing the move but instead of facing the camera they face each other, which I immediately understand to be a terrible mistake.

I wave my arms frantically like I'm signaling to a ship from a deserted island, trying to indicate they should turn toward the camera but it's too late. Beau starts the next move by bending over slightly and sticking his ample behind in the air for the drop to the ground. As he sticks out his butt, it hits the display of crystal seashells causing them to teeter back and forth. Jane sees this and goes over to stop the crash, but as she does she gets tangled in the web of strings. He tries to untangle her and instead he winds up attaching himself until they are wrapped together, covered in crystals. They teeter for a second and then fall to the ground.

The director pulls the camera person with the hand-held to cover the pair on the floor. At first I'm worried one of them is hurt but I'm too far away to tell. I look at the monitor and Jane is laughing so hard she's crying. It's not TV laughter either. It's actually human laughter which has a totally different sound. Once everyone on set figures out she is amused by the situation they all start laughing, which makes Beau laugh, so everyone is laughing.

Except me.

This has been the most un-Chase like segment that could ever have happened. Chase is more likely to fly a jet fighter over Manhattan than laugh at himself on television. He has a cool, aspirational attitude that keeps viewers striving to achieve their best.

Jane is on the floor with Chase next to her. She looks around at the destruction and laughs. The glitter sea of shells has been flattened by a tornado with purple bangs.

'Chase,' Jane says, 'if your live stream of the parade is anything like this, I *know* it's going to be a smash.' She rises to her knees, adjusts her skirt, looks right into the camera and says, 'We'll be back with our ongoing series on how the water you're drinking is killing you after these messages.'

I look down at my phone and see a text from Maria Luisa. '*Come to my office. Now.*'

Chapter 16

When I get to Maria Luisa's office Beverly points to the uncomfortable chair next to her desk and tells me to sit. 'She's still on the phone with her nanny.' I know this is Beverly's way of letting me know where I am in the pecking order.

'To think Maria Luisa needs a nanny at her age,' I say, hoping my awful attempt at a joke will allow Beverly to crack a smile. It doesn't. She rolls her eyes, acknowledging that I have spoken, and then turns back to her computer. Without looking at me she says, 'I said sit. I did not say speak.' That's Beverly, sunshine all the way. My foot taps and I clench my jaw, anxious about what awaits me on the other side of that door. Does she know? Did she figure it out? She's going to be furious I risked the program's reputation by trying to trick everyone and lying about it. It must have been so obvious that it wasn't Chase. No one seemed to notice in the studio and I've been way too anxious to check the socials. All I can see in my mind is Beau on the floor covered in crystals next to America's favorite morning anchor.

This was a bridge too far. I'll just explain that it was a silly misunderstanding. I accidentally rented a car and drove up and found my star's twin and he fell into the back seat. Once my heart rate reaches an uncomfortable level, Beverly tells me Maria Luisa is ready. She smiles a bit, which only means she must know something about the horrible fate I'm about to meet.

I walk into Maria Luisa's office and try to focus on not crying when she inevitably fires me. That would be unprofessional. She's wearing my least favorite black suit. That's not a good sign. She looks at me and says, 'So Ethan, tell me, who is this guy you have standing in for Chase?'

Maybe a confession will help ease my punishment. I'd get on my knees but that might seem a tad dramatic. Appropriate, but dramatic nonetheless.

'Maria Luisa, I can explain everything. You see...'

'I don't care what the explanation is.' She's right. There is no excuse for what I've done. I wince and prepare for the worst. 'Keep doing what you're doing.'

I have no idea what she's talking about, but I'm not stupid enough to keep talking for once. 'This brand-new version of Chase is amazing. The way he was with Jane. Relaxed and easy-going, not so uptight. People are loving it. I don't know what you said to him, but it's working. Have you seen the socials? He's a meme already. He's had a substantial gain in followers this morning and we are talking key demographics. Have you seen this one?'

She holds up her tablet to show me a picture of Beau smiling his gorgeous smile, on the floor covered in crystals. Over the image it says: 'You don't have to be perfect. You just have to be yourself.'

Maria Luisa looks at the screen and grins. I guess she finds this charming or refreshing. I have no idea. 'We need to lean into that this week,' she says. 'Everyone wants to see him after he almost destroyed the *American Morning* set. I have sponsors calling me telling me they want in on this new Chase and that means ka-ching.'

I'm so confused. This morning was a disaster. I was sure this was going to be my comeuppance, but here Maria Luisa is telling me this is a success and booking us on more promotional events. Normally this is something I would be thrilled about, but this morning was awful, not to mention how long it took to prep Beau. I don't see how we could ever pull off taping the segments we need to get in the can before the parade and prepare for more live segments.

'Those sounds like great opportunities, but there are only so many hours in a day and we have our shoot on Fire Island coming up and...'

'Ethan, I know you'll work it out,' Maria Luisa says, uninterested in the challenges she is presenting.

'Thanks,' I say. Now I have to create someone who looks like Chase and acts like Beau pretending to be Chase, or is it Chase pretending to be Beau or Chase pretending to be Chase? My mind is a salad of confusion. I have no idea. I get ready to walk out of her office and wonder if I should turn around and just walk out the window.

'One more thing,' Maria Luisa says, and I freeze. Will she add, 'You're fired,' leaving her prank until the very last moment? I turn back to face her.

'I know you have a lot on your plate but Lee saw Chase on TV this morning, and they got it into their head to have one of their famous game nights.' Lee is Maria Luisa's spouse. They're famous for hosting these elaborate game nights with the most important people in media. It's almost exclusively couples, which is super annoying and super exclusive in a very bad way, but I'm not unaware that our whole fake boyfriend situation makes us eligible. 'It would be wonderful if you and Chase could join us. I hope everything is still okay with you two?' she asks, her mellifluous contralto snaking toward me.

'As good as it's ever been,' I say through clenched teeth.

'I'm so glad to hear that. You know what the media can do with gay couples who have any dirty laundry to air. They can be absolutely savage with the bad press and we want to avoid that as much as possible during this important, shall we say, potential transition.' She nods with a sly smile. I like the way 'potential transition' sounds so I block out all of the other stuff for at least a second and a half.

'I understand. Sounds super fun. See you then.' I walk out of Maria Luisa's office and past the sneering Beverly in a haze of confusion and stress.

I press the button for the elevator but consider taking the stairs down the forty-four floors. It might destroy my knees but it would give me time to think. It's one thing to teach Beau to style a centerpiece or mix a signature cocktail, it's another to have him hold my hand as we walk into my boss's apartment. Everyone will want to see the couple that we created on social media. It was hard enough to get Chase to be my fake boyfriend. I've only asked Beau to pretend to be his brother on camera. Now I have to convince him to pretend to be my fake-fake boyfriend. I feel a throbbing pain begin to pulse around my forehead, and then my phone buzzes. I look down and see an international number from Dabu Bobby.

Chapter 17

I immediately hit ignore and hop into the elevator. I check on MagicAss in the SecretSlam app and it says he is 6,840 miles away. I silence my phone. He's made his choice and now he has to suffer the consequences, although at the moment the suffering seems to be all mine. Did Chase hear about his brother filling in? Is it possible the *American Morning* segment made it to the Middle East that quickly? He's barely landed. Chase is so out of it, even if he did see it I wouldn't be surprised if he thought it was pre-taped and that it was actually him teaching Jane the moves. More likely he wants me to go to the apartment and send him his favorite swimsuit or wire him some extra cash. Whatever he's selling, I'm not buying.

I'm alone in the elevator as it glides down the floors and I let out a tiny laugh thinking about Jane and Beau wrapped up in the crystals. But I push it out of my head. I don't want anyone laughing. *Myles of Style* is a serious show about... well, maybe not a serious show but I want it to be taken seriously. I know we aren't curing diseases but I don't want the show to be laughed at. It's not a joke. Growing up I had enough of people laughing at me to last a lifetime. When you're a kid who worships Martha Stewart and sets a table with flatware and cloth napkins in the school cafeteria, you learn to eat alone and to put up with the snickering.

But that wasn't the same laughter I heard today. Everyone was laughing *with* Beau, not at him. There's a difference but I have to admit I'm not exactly sure what it is and I don't have time to figure it out today. I have to get to the studio, get through an entire day of shooting, prepare Beau for more publicity and then break it to him that he also has to pretend to be my fake-fake boyfriend.

I hop in the car that's waiting to take me to set and take out my phone but I can't deal with Chase. I don't care if he's seen the segment on *American Morning* or not. I bet he wants me to beg him to come back. He'll make me video chat on my knees telling him that I can't possibly do it without him. That I'm lost without him. Well, I'm not. I don't need him. Just thinking that feels good. I've spent too many years catering to his every whim. Begging him to do the social media and make the sponsors happy. What was I thinking? I find the number that called me at the elevator and swipe through the screens to block it. That is the end of that.

I reach into my jacket pocket again without even thinking. First my hand just rests on the small square to make sure it's there like a portable security blanket. Then my fingers gently touch the wrapper. Of course, the inside of my jacket is nowhere near the proper temperature at which it should be stored but I'm an iconoclast when it comes to my chocolate. The car makes its way to the FDR and I can see the studios across the river anchoring the Long Island City skyline. I take out the small square I've prepared for the day in case of emergency. I had no doubt I would need it today; I just didn't think I'd need it before noon.

Each tiny bar of To'ak chocolate costs more than a good pair of shoes but the pleasure of the experience is

worth it. I can taste the cognac notes from the fermenta-
tion process. I place the square under my tongue and my
phone vibrates.

'What have you done?' Kiara whispers into the phone.
'Don't say anything. I still have my law license. If you
decided it would be easier to work with Beau and you
have the real Chase tied up somewhere… as your lawyer
it would be better if I don't know where. As your best
friend, I'm curious but really, don't tell me.'

'I do not have anyone tied up anywhere. How did you
know that wasn't Chase? We seem to have the rest of the
world fooled.'

'Honestly, I did such a good job with the makeover
even I was fooled at first. I bet you had Blaine today at
American Morning. I love what he's doing with pressed
powder these days but there's no way Chase would say
that stuff about not being perfect. No way. That's total
Beau-talk.' She laughs.

'It's not funny,' I say although it is kind of funny. 'I just
got out of a meeting with Maria Luisa and it turns out
she *loves* this new Chase. Only this isn't a new Chase, it's
old Beau. Chase is in Abu Dhabi on some yacht. He met
some fishing tycoon who claims to be a casting director
and he's giving up TV for film. I'm on my way to the
studio.'

I let the chocolate melt in my mouth as I update Kiara
on the events of the last twelve hours or so. By the time
we get to the studio there isn't a single morsel left in my
mouth or pocket.

I wanted to be present when we introduced the fake
Chase to the staff and crew but Maria Luisa called so
that was impossible. I gave Tina explicit instructions to
bring Beau directly to the studio, get him into wardrobe,

lock him in his dressing room and tell everyone Chase has refused to come out until I get there. She's to instruct them we had an argument or whatever it takes to keep him out of sight except when he has to be on camera. I walk in and plan to make a beeline for the dressing room but instead of finding everyone hiding in fear of one of Chase's tantrums I find the exact opposite.

The entire crew from camera operators to food stylists are lying on various mats and towels around the set. If Chase were here I would assume it was an act of civil disobedience after being unable to put up with his tantrums everyone laid down in protest. Instead I see Beau walking between each person and cooing soft words of encouragement. 'You are enough, you are enough...' he repeats and then instructs everyone to breathe in deeply. The group takes a long collective sigh and I swear every gram of that To'ak chocolate I've swallowed is about to spew.

I'm about to scream, 'Beau!' But I catch myself and shout, 'Chase!' I scream his name a lot at work but this one might be an all-time best. Everyone on the floor pops up. 'What the hell is going on here?' I ask.

'Sometimes a dark cloud floats by but that doesn't mean there aren't sunny skies on the other side of it. Stay focused. You can ignore the darkness,' Beau continues. He looks at me when he says the words 'dark cloud'. Everyone knows he's the dark cloud, not me. I mean, they know Chase is. Not me. But with Beau here I certainly feel like the dark cloud of the day.

Beau walks over to me and then says, 'This will only take a few more minutes to find our internal center and then go back to what we were all doing. We will be clearer and more efficient in this work if we are calm. Isn't that right, Ethan?'

'Of course,' I say, faking calm as much as I can. 'As long as finding our center doesn't take more than 120 seconds.' He nods and I wait as he brings the meditation, relaxation, pep rally to a close. I'm like a Dr Frankenstein who can't get it right. With one brother I release a preening poser and with the other a Zen master.

He finishes and everyone gets up, smiling and chatting. Mike, the camera person who usually stays as far away from Chase as possible, walks right over to Beau and says, 'Thanks Chase, that was a great way to start my day. You were so fun on *American Morning.*'

'Aw, thanks Mike. No problem.' Mike looks at him with his face twisted and I worry that this might be the point when it all explodes.

'You called me Mike,' Mike says and my pulse quickens. It's the details that can sink me.

'Yeah, that's your name, right?' Beau looks either confused or maybe a bit nervous like he got the name wrong, which he did but he doesn't know that.

'Sure is, Chase, thanks. Sure is.' Mike walks away and I march toward the dressing room with Beau in tow. My hands are in a tight fist and my fingernails are digging into my palms.

I shut the door behind me and as soon as we're alone I explode. 'What is wrong with you? You called Mike, Mike. Why would you do that?'

'That's his name, isn't it? I went on LinkedIn and got the org chart for the production and memorized everyone's name. Isn't that Mike? I mean there's another Mike but he's a wardrobe assistant and went to Tulane.'

Beau raises his hands above him and bends to the side in a stretch.

'There is?' I respond. I didn't know there was another Mike on set. Is that the name of the guy who always has a needle and thread in his hands? Maybe I don't know everyone as well as I thought I did. Still, I can't believe he took the time to learn everyone's names, something Chase would never do. 'That's not the point. The point is Chase does not know Mike's name. Chase calls Mike, Chuck.'

'Chuck? Chuck is like twenty pounds heavier, ten years older and commutes from Five Towns. Why would he call him Chuck?' Beau stretches to center, takes a deep breath and then bends to the other side.

'I don't know and I don't care,' I say. That's not true. I've spoken to Chase multiple times about how disrespectful it is to call people by the wrong name. 'Chase doesn't know anyone's name so that means you don't either.'

'Ethan, no, that's rude. Fine, I'll be Chase but I'm not going to be a jerk to people just because my brother is. I won't do it.'

He has a point but what else can we do? I can't let anyone find out I'm passing off a fake. Maybe I should have told the staff and crew about the plan but the fact is it's too late. I already passed him off on *American Morning* so I can only move forward. Kiara, Clams and Tina know. I can't let the circle get much bigger. If someone like Jeremiah found out he'd quickly leak it to his friends in the media.

'I get it. I hate the way he treats them, too,' I say. I'm speaking from the heart which feels strange since I rarely do that in this dressing room. I'm always figuring out what

I need to say in order to get Chase to do what I want. 'Everyone has to believe that you are Chase and if you can't be the jerk he is that's fine. I get it. But it doesn't mean that you can also lead yoga retreats between takes.'

'I wasn't doing that,' Beau says.

'What exactly did I walk in on with everyone on their backs?'

'It was just another guided meditation,' he says matter-of-factly.

'Wait a minute. I thought you hated being around people. Isn't that what you said in Central Park?'

'I said I hated being around people who were fussing over me. Being around people in general isn't as bad as I remember. Maybe I missed it. Maybe I don't hate it as much any more. I don't know. Have you ever noticed how on edge everyone is here?'

'Yes, that's called television. Television is just another word for stress. We have a ton of shooting to finish before Pride. Of course everyone is tense.'

'That's ridiculous. If there's anything I learned upstate it's that finding your personal calm is essential. No one should be that stressed all the time.'

He's got a point. The amount of stress we endure on this production is through the roof. I used to think it was all Chase's doing with his bad attitude. But with him gone, the tension remains, so it makes me wonder if I'm responsible. Am I pushing people too hard?

There's a knock on the door. 'Yes?' I call out.

'It's Tina. Tina Wong.'

'Yes, I know,' I say, trying to be a little nicer than I usually am. Is this guy rubbing off on me?

'We need Chase on set now. Is Chase in there with you? Is that Chase?' She adds his name to each sentence, emphasizing it.

'Thank you, Tina,' I say and I hear her head back to set.

'We need to get started on the "Choosing an Elegant Lawn Chair for your Pride Picnic" segment. Are you ready for this?' I ask, expecting him to be nervous or at the very least unsure of himself.

'I got it. Tina went over all the stuff you prepared. Bro, you know a lot about lawn chairs.'

'Having the wrong lawn chair can ruin a party. The vintage ones are fun but you have to know how to repair them if you don't want to have your guests bust through the bottom or get tetanus.'

'Ethan, calm down. I was kidding. I'm ready. I know how to weave the webbing and use that stuff to get rid of rust. Tina showed me the finished one. It looks great.'

I spent a full weekend last month refinishing a vintage lawn chair with fresh webbing. I could have sent it out or had someone on staff do it but I really wanted to complete the project from start to finish. Chase never compliments me on any of the content, so when Beau does it I'm surprised but also annoyed. The whole point of bringing him into the dressing room was to remind him to be *more* like Chase. It takes me a second to figure out how to say it.

'Beau, I know you can do this but I need something from you that might be hard. Unfortunately, it's the only way we can really pull this off.'

'What is it? I can do whatever you want.'

'That's the problem.' Maria Luisa may want a kinder, gentler Chase and that might work on camera but not here on set. 'The staff and crew are used to a certain rhythm with production and a certain, shall we say, environment. Did I mention that Chase once threw an entire head of lettuce at Alan because he thought he made his pores look too large in a tight close-up?'

'Alan? The war vet with the dog named Chainsaw?'

'Alan has a dog named Chainsaw?' I ask, shocked that Beau could uncover this detail in the short time that he has had on set. I've been on the production for years and I didn't know that. 'Anyway, yes that Alan.'

'I'm not going to throw anything at Alan, or anyone for that matter. Not even you.'

'No, I don't want you to hit me but I do need you to throw something... a tantrum. At some point I need you to storm off.' If Chase doesn't go into a rage and walk off I'll have to make up some story about a weekend lobotomy.

'Ethan, maybe that is the source of the tension. Have you ever considered maybe running things differently?'

'Every single day of my life. But we've never, in the history of the show, gone an entire day without Chase having a meltdown. The stress of waiting is worse than the actual storm in some ways so can you at least yell at someone?'

'No, I will not yell at anyone.' I'm about to make another plea but then he adds, 'But I'll argue with you.' He folds his arms in front of his chest and gives me a sly smile. 'If that's what you want.'

'Yes, please,' I say with relief. I feel like I'm in a bondage video begging for a spanking, which is maybe exactly what I'm doing. 'That's all I am asking for. At some point today I need us to have a disagreement. You and I. Thank you.'

Chapter 18

The rest of the morning runs like *The Good Ship Lollipop* when it should be the SS *Titanic*. Beau goes through each shot without so much as a fumble. We do very few takes and when our director, Lauren, gives Beau a note he listens and adjusts his performance accordingly. In other words, it's a disaster. As soon as we break for lunch Tina walks over to me and says, 'Can I talk to you privately?' She points to the door leading outside.

The sharp contrast from the dim studio to afternoon sun makes my eyes tear so I put on my pair of Tom Ford aviator sunglasses. Tina is also wearing sunglasses, a pair of Vintage Dior I bought for her birthday that are the size of airplane windows, but she's been wearing them inside as well. She has completely taken to her new counter-espionage role. She's a cross between Mata Hari and Carmen Sandiego. 'I don't want to alarm you but people are talking,' Tina says while looking both ways down the empty alley.

'What's wrong?' I ask, moving us further away from the door in case anyone comes out.

'Some people think you've drugged Chase for him to be acting this way and other people think he's hit his head and had a concussion.'

'Okay, I can work with either of those,' I say, nodding. Both rumors at least don't involve a double so that's something.

'But there is a third contingent that doesn't accept either explanation. They don't believe he can become this nice overnight. And you know Marlene?'

'The food stylist with the baggy army fatigues from Vero Beach Florida?' I know the team just as well as anyone. Take that, Beau.

'Right. She said maybe it's his non-evil twin. Which everyone thinks is funny but maybe that's still not a good thing.'

As soon as I hear that old pathetic twin trope idea I bristle. 'That's a very shallow way of looking at a monozygotic pregnancy,' I say, revealing that I might have done a bit of research after Beau chastised me for being reductive.

'Anyway, that made someone else say that he remembered there was a rumor at one point that Chase had a twin.'

'That's not good. Not good at all.' I was hoping no one would remember that he had a brother. Chase almost never mentions him but I suppose there was always a chance that someone might have heard something.

'I'm sorry,' Tina says, and I sense her lip about to quiver. I'm moments away from seeing tears run behind her over-sized frames.

'Don't worry. I know exactly how to stop this.' We head back inside and I'm ready to squash any and all rumors.

The one segment on the schedule that made Beau groan when I went over it with him was a device that involved a complex series of facial exercises to help shape the structure of the face. Beau has been going along with everything but he hasn't always kept his opinion to himself. He thought the segments on exercises you can do anywhere using a chair and two bottles of water would be useful for people who don't have access to a gym. But this might be enough to make him snap.

I think about giving him another talking-to in the dressing room but the more I push him to be a jerk the more he turns on the charm. 'Moving on to the facial exercises segment,' I yell as we return to set knowing that this will be the thing that makes the volcano blow. 'Will someone bring the Chisel–it materials to set?'

Three small silicone cubes arrive next to Beau on a tray. For weeks I've tried to eliminate this segment but Chisel-it is a huge sponsor and Maria Luisa was so enthusiastic about including them I couldn't say no. When I explained how they worked to Beau I thought he was going to get up and leave, but he went along with it.

'Do we really have to do this part?' Beau asks and I can feel trouble brewing. I'm glad he's playing along.

'Yes, Chase. I told you,' I say, awaiting more pushback, but instead he turns his attention to the tray and indicates that he's ready. Beau and the director briefly go over the lines for the segment and the general flow. Then they start rolling. I sneak by craft services and grab a handful of M&M's, casually trying to overhear snippets of conversations. As I suspect, I begin to hear two PAs talking about how they can't believe Chase has been behaving all day. Not good at all but I suspect that's about to change.

Lauren starts rolling. I should have told Beau that it's more cost efficient to argue before the cameras begin but I'll take what I can get. He has an uncanny ability to remember the lines. It's remarkable. He's able to read a script once and commit it to memory. I've never seen anything like it. Chase uses cue cards to remember his name.

I usually stay out of Lauren's way while she's working, although I'm not sure she would agree with that statement. They go through the first shot without any outburst. What's wrong with this guy? He loves to disagree with me off camera but once everyone is around, he's the Barack Obama of television. I quickly come up with an idea.

'Hey, Lauren I was just texting with Maria Luisa and it turns out they really want to see the Chisel-it in action rather than just laying on a platter. People really need to see how to use it,' I say, knowing this will get to Beau. He made it very clear that he did not want to put that thing in his mouth.

Lauren says, 'No problem,' and chats with the assistant director briefly. Lauren always says 'no problem' no matter what I ask her to do. Once we needed an aerial shot of a raspberry Pavlova and she literally had someone hang upside down from a rafter to get it without any complaint.

Once Lauren is ready to shoot again, I say to Beau, 'Remember to open wide so you can get the whole thing in your mouth.' The premise of the Chisel-it is that you exercise the muscles in your jawline so that they grow and create sharper definition. Neither Beau nor Chase has any issue in this area. You could sew hemlines with their jaws but there are millions of people across the country who must suffer from weak jaws or else the product wouldn't be advertising with us.

'Ethan, can we talk about this?' Beau says. I see my attempt to instigate didn't exactly land like the assassination of Archduke Franz Ferdinand but at least it's a start.

I notice people pause what they're working on and turn their attention to the potential fireworks.

'No, Chase,' I say. 'We don't have time for one of your tantrums. Just recite the script as written.' I say this a lot on set. So much so that the words just roll off my tongue.

'No seriously, Ethan. I just want to talk about this.'

What's he doing? This is very un-Chase-like. 'We're already behind schedule. I don't need you screaming... or yelling... or crying.' I say the words screaming, yelling and crying with great emphasis while nodding my head to indicate what I actually want Beau to do. Then I repeat them. 'No screaming, yelling or crying,' I say, making intense eye contact.

'I have no intention of doing any of those things,' he says politely.

I want to shout out, 'Oh, yes you do,' but instead I ask, 'What's going on?'

'I understand an exercise segment about stretching and building stamina. That's important for health. Everyone needs to be at their healthiest physical state.' I look around and everyone on set looks as confused as I am. Albeit for different reasons.

'Yes, Chase. What's your point? We need to get back on schedule.' I discreetly tap my finger to my eye and let the tip run down the side of my face. I'm hoping I'm secretly indicating to him that he should start crying. Tap. Tap. Why won't he get the signal?

'I understand, Ethan. I do and I want to be mindful of everyone's time here and their contributions but...'

Okay. Now he is the anti-Chase. What is he talking about? Mindful of everyone's time? Chase has never been mindful of anyone's anything. I look around and everyone

145

is watching but I can tell no one is sure what they're seeing is real.

'But I think we should consider the ethics involved in promoting facial exercisers.' He gestures to the tray of colorful mouth cubes. I walk on set making sure I'm not disrupting any of the marks or set pieces. I pass through the shadow of the world behind the camera and enter the overly bright universe in front of the camera.

'We aren't making anyone do anything they don't want to do,' I say. I squint a bit to look out beyond the cameras and we have an audience. Everyone is watching, waiting to see what will happen next. They are waiting for a scene and I have every intention of giving it to them.

'Maybe not,' Beau says, his voice even and not nearly as shrill as I would like it to be in this moment. 'No one is being forced to do anything but I think it's an artificial standard used to exploit the other. Don't you?' he asks calmly.

'I… ah…' I have no idea what to say. I'm simply trying to get the job done today, save people's jobs, not get fired myself. Is that so wrong? I continue to stammer, not sure how I'm going to explain why Beau is speaking like a Humanities professor.

'My concern,' Beau continues, both his voice and tone gentle and sweet, 'is that we are implicitly promoting a standard of excellence that's impossible for the viewer to attain. By suggesting that only a certain type of jawline is beautiful it also suggests that those who don't fit the standard are therefore less-than when that's certainly not the case. For example, Ethan, your face is beautiful but your jawline isn't overly developed.'

Everyone on set gasps. One person drops a cup of coffee. But is it due to the fact that he just called me

146

beautiful, something that Chase would never ever do, or the fact that he also threw some serious shade, something Chase totally would do? At least we're getting closer to our goal. I turn away from the cameras and the audience that has formed and discreetly whisper to Beau. 'Keep it up with the insults. Come on, just go at me. We need this,' I say, my voice desperate and insistent but quiet and low.

'What we need,' Beau says loudly, facing the group that has gathered behind the cameras, 'are some other opinions. You and I as host and producer are in positions of privilege that prevent us from understanding. Hey, Madison.' Beau shields his eyes with his hand so he can look above us toward the lighting booth.

'Yeah,' she answers. He knows the name of the person running the lightboard. I wasn't even sure who was on it.

'Could you turn off the set lights and turn up the studio lights? I think we need everyone in on this.'

What's he doing? I look at my watch. We were doing well, really well. We were almost only half a day behind but with this impromptu sharing circle we will never get back on track.

'Come on, everyone,' he says, waving his arm and pulling everyone over.

'What are you doing?' I ask, not even trying to whisper. He knows that I've instructed him to argue with me.

'Exactly what you asked. Aren't we disagreeing?' he asks.

'Yes, but...' He's right. We are disagreeing but we aren't fighting. Everyone is expecting fireworks, not a sing-along. Before I can figure out how to turn this around Beau has everyone gathered on set like he's running for student body president.

'What do you all think? Do you think these jaw exercisers are promoting an unattainable standard of beauty? Or is this just part of the landscape of the culture?' he asks thoughtfully. Everyone must think Chase has had a brain transplant to be speaking like this. I try to not reveal the depths of my internal cringe.

As if in unison everyone turns to look at me. Their eyes seem to ask me if it's okay to answer. Beau is holding an inclusive dialogue and it's not exactly what we need at the moment but I'm not going to stop it. I shrug my shoulders and say, 'Go ahead. Speak your mind. I'm listening.' I prepare myself for everyone to call me out as a liar and Beau as a fraud.

'Can I ask something?' Lucian, a short non-binary recent graduate from FIT asks.

'Go ahead,' I say. Bless you Lucian. Maybe we can end this entire charade. Call me out and I'll confess and go home and eat an entire pound of chocolate. 'I mean, I don't think I would ever use a jaw exerciser but not because I don't want the results. It's more because they're super expensive.'

'Great point, Lucian,' Beau says. Does he know every single person's name in the entire New York Metro area? 'This isn't just about lookism,' Beau says. 'It's also about class.'

How did I get here? I just wanted to make canapes and teach people how to create elegant place cards and now I'm hosting a queer revolution, which is fine but I always thought I'd be doing the catering, not supplying the microphone. 'Does anyone else have anything to say?' I ask.

More people speak and it's a mixed bag for and against the jaw exercises. Some people think it's a personal choice and others are unsure about the standard of beauty they promote. To be honest I had no idea so many people felt so strongly. I'm not thrilled we're getting so far behind but it's nice to see that everyone cares so much about what we do. As Beau facilitates, he encourages each person to speak their mind and I start to forget how behind schedule we are and just start listening. I don't want to hurt anyone. I don't want to promote impossible standards of beauty.

We take a short break and the writers start to huddle and come up with some alternative copy for the segment. Shanice, a woman who used to work in serious news and covered the Gulf War, reads the new copy to the group. 'What do you both think? Chase? Ethan?'

The writers have added a disclaimer explaining that beauty comes in all shapes and sizes and that jaw exercises might be one way to reach a goal, if that's your goal. If it's not it doesn't mean anything. You still deserve to be loved. It's sweet and kind and totally off-brand but I think about what Maria Luisa said to me this morning. She wanted a kinder and gentler Chase so maybe there's nothing wrong with this. I certainly agree with the sentiment, so why not?

Beau is nodding as they read but once they finish he turns to me. 'Ethan, you're in charge,' he says. It's like he has learned only to say the exact opposite of what his brother would say in any given situation. 'What do you think?'

'I think it's great,' I say and hear everyone mumble expressions of relief and approval. It is great. It's not something I ever thought would be part of the show, but why not? This is my favorite part of the job. When we're all working together toward the same thing. It's been a while since it's been like this but it feels good to get back on track. 'Louise, can you get it all on the cue cards, and Shania, can you set up the shots so we can wrap all of this before lunch? Everyone else, you know what to do. Let's get back up and rolling in no more than fifteen,' I say. A low hum of activity rapidly spreads across the set but it's broken by the sound of one person clapping. I turn around and see Keegan Ellis slowly slapping his hands together.

'Well done, Mr Producer. That was quite something to witness. I suppose rumors of trouble on set have been greatly exaggerated.'

'Keegan, darling, what are you doing here?' We air kiss, which is what homosexuals who hate each other often do. Keegan and I both freelanced for a popular nightlife website many years ago competing for the same material although he was more gossip oriented and I was more focused on trends. His best friend is Jeremiah from *Queens of the Night* and since Jeremiah is my mortal enemy that makes Keegan my mortal enemy as well. Not to mention Keegan's situation with Chase.

'Didn't Maria Luisa tell you? I'm doing a big piece on the Pride Parade for *Mediapedia*. Maria Luisa said to stop by set and talk to you about Chase's availability.'

'Oh, she did, did she?' I laugh a mindless chuckle that's really just a way to give me time to think about how to stop this. Keegan writes for a major media empire and including Chase in a piece would be great but having the two of them spend time together is out of the question. Even if I could fill Beau in on all the sordid details of Chase's past with Keegan, I…

'Ethan, we're ready…' Beau says, walking over to us. Keegan eyes Beau up and down and since he knows Chase so intimately. I wonder if this is the moment when everything will explode. Then as if to strike the match before it lands in the gasoline Beau extends his hand and says, 'Hi, Chase Myles, nice to meet you.'

I laugh as loud as I can. I'm so loud that a few people turn to see if I'm okay. Keegan looks at Beau like he's an amnesia victim, which he would have to be to have forgotten their complicated past. I keep laughing and move my hands across my eyes to wipe away pretend tears, only they aren't pretend. My eyes are definitely watering. Is that a sign of stress or desperation?

'Keegan, you know how funny Chase can be. Stop it, Chase,' I say and playfully hit him on the arm. He looks confused so I repeat myself. 'Really Chase, stop it.' This time my voice is stronger and my slap might create a bruise. 'Who could ever forget you, Keegan?' I ask, throwing just enough shade to cover the flub.

Keegan lets out a nervous titter since this exchange is so painfully awkward. 'Anyway, Chase, just wanted to get your answers to some questions instead of emailing them. That can be so impersonal,' Keegan says and then adds, 'and you know how much I like keeping things personal. Maybe I can stop by your place later. Much later.'

'Sure,' Beau says, missing Keegan's shameless inuendo. There is no way I can allow the two of them to be alone. I know exactly what Keegan will expect and Beau's not ready for that, and neither am I for that matter.

'Chase, you forgot we need to go over those recipes this week so they look great on camera,' I say.

'Oh,' Beau says, finally realizing that the situation is more complicated than it seems. 'Whatever Ethan wants,' he adds, trying to be a nice guy, or maybe he really is a nice guy. I have no idea at this point. What I do know is that he's dangerously close to blowing his cover.

'Did you just say, whatever Ethan wants? I guess word on the street is right. Things really have changed here at *Myles of Style*,' Keegan says. Rumors spread like warm cream cheese on an everything bagel in this industry. Beau looks at me knowing he did something wrong but his face is sort of pleading like he doesn't know how to fix it.

'I better head back to set. Talk soon,' Beau says, sensing something is off. Keegan's eyes drop to a few feet above the ground, clearly focused on Beau's back end.

'His eyes are up there,' I say, pointing to the back of Beau's head.

'More jokes? Dear me, it's like walking into The Giggle Hut today at *Myles of Style*. You don't mind if I just stick around and observe? I want to get a feel for the new look and tone of the show.'

'Keegan, you know I'd love to have you here but it isn't possible today. We just had a rewrite and we got a teeny-weeny bit behind schedule.' I make sure to hold up my fingers showing the smallest possible length of a penis, hoping he knows I'm throwing shade.

'What are you hiding?' he asks, and I can tell he has caught a whiff of something. 'Maria Luisa said I could have unfettered access to make my deadline for *Mediapedia*.'

'And you can. Completely. Just not right now.' My eyes narrow and I smile tightly to show I'm not messing around with him today. 'Tina!' I yell and she appears from the mist.

'Yes, Ethan,' she says and identifies Keegan immediately. 'Uh oh.'

'Good, you remember Keegan. I have to run to set. Would you see Mr Ellis to the door and get his schedule so we can figure out how to get him what he wants?' I walk away but turn back before I'm out of earshot.

'Within reason of course.' Tina takes Keegan away. I've either found my way around this obstacle or just felt the first breeze of the storm that will eventually sink my ship.

Chapter 19

At the end of the week I'm ready to collapse on the studio floor. I've managed to put a halt to Keegan's requests and keep the production marching. But I've been putting off the one task I'm dreading the most. I need to find the energy and the opportunity to break the news to Beau that I need him to be his brother both on and off camera. He only agreed to play Chase for the filming. I never thought about having to get him to pass as Chase socially at Maria Luisa's or worse, eventually dealing with Keegan. It's time to deal with life beyond the camera lens.

I knock on Chase's dressing room door and Beau answers. 'Come in.'

I gasp slightly. Beau is naked. Well, not completely naked. He's wearing socks and boxer briefs but it doesn't take a lot of imagination to think of him naked, and my imagination is going at it. He has one leg up on a chair and he's rubbing a washcloth on his thigh like Lady Macbeth.

'What are you doing?' I ask, ignoring the casual nakedness.

'Trying to get the self-tanner off. We're done with those shots, right? I know Kiara said it was organic but I don't like it.' Now he's rubbing the area below his knee but it has little impact.

'We are. I'm sorry about that. But everything needed to match and it would look strange if you're three shades paler when we cut back and forth. You should try using some distilled vinegar.'

'Why do you do that?' he asks and stops rubbing. 'Why do you try to fix things that aren't a problem?'

'I don't know what you're talking about,' I say. I'm only trying to help him. 'Let me get you a bottle of vinegar. Sometimes that can...'

'Ethan, you don't have to do anything. It's nice that you're showing concern. I like that,' he says and sits down. 'But you don't have to fix everything all the time or explain away any discomfort. It's okay for me not to like the tanner and it's okay for me to be stuck with it until... until I grow a new layer of skin I guess.' He rubs his hands over his arms and chest. He's not trying to turn me on but there's no better way to turn me on than by doing exactly what he's doing. I spot a robe hanging on a hook and walk over to it and hand it to him hoping to douse whatever flame is being ignited. He slips it on without comment. Everything he does is so matter-of-fact. Every gesture, every expression comes from who he is, not how he wants people to see him. I've never met anyone like him, which is odd to say since he looks exactly like the person I see every day.

I do try to fix things too much but right now everything around me is broken and combusting into flames, and not even yellow ones. More like those lavender colors at the base of the flame that are super-hot. When my mom would come home crying after a day of working two jobs to fill the gaping hole left by my father, I felt responsible for making her feel better. I'd create some scrumptious appetizer using a box of mac and cheese and serve it like it was cracked crab. It made me feel good to help her, to fix things that were so broken.

'This is a lot. You must be exhausted,' I say, trying to be nice.

He shrugs. 'It's mostly just standing around. It's not like I was searching for a water source in below-freezing temperatures.'

'No... I suppose not.' I can't get the image out of my mind. 'Is that something you really do?'

'Did you see plumbing in my yurt? How else am I supposed to get water? Hope my place is okay. I left a note for a buddy to keep an eye on it while I'm gone.' Instead of pursuing this topic I press on.

'There are a couple of loose ends I need to go over with you tonight.' The recipe for the cooking segment is complicated. A sponsor insisted we do a beef Wellington for Pride. In June? Nothing says summer like a slab of meat covered in pastry with savory dressing. At least I was able to develop a recipe that I think will work. It's a bit fussy but manageable.

'After I take a run, my night is totally yours Ethan.' Charm oozes out of him like jelly from an over-stuffed doughnut.

'Good. There are a couple of things we need to go over in addition to the recipe,' I add, looking around the dressing room hoping to cover my anxiety. How can I tell this guy he has to be my fake-fake boyfriend in public?

'Like what?' he asks.

'Weekend after next we have a big shoot on Fire Island coming up. Have you heard of Fire Island?' I ask, avoiding the more challenging topic.

'Ethan, I've been living in a yurt upstate. Not another planet. Anything else?'

'Odd and ends, I don't want to ruin the surprise,' I say coyly. He probably thinks I'm flirting and maybe I am.

My mouth needs a rewind button. 'See you tonight at the apartment,' I say and scurry out of his dressing room.

–

With only three weeks until Pride, I need as much time as I can get with Beau. There's so much we need to go over; I can barely fathom it all. There's the cooking segment, the fashion segment on location and then the location shoot on Fire Island, not to mention all of the promotional opportunities we still have to do. Still, nothing could keep me from my engagement tonight at the foot of the Brooklyn Bridge in Dumbo.

The sun has just begun to set across the river over Manhattan and a pleasant breeze with a slightly salty scent comes up from the water. I spot a table with streamers and cake just in the grassy area just beyond the antique carousel. Kiara is fastening decorations to the table and her wife, Nisha, is pouring water into a bowl for their stunningly handsome Affenpinscher named Otto. He barks to announce my arrival.

'I wish you would let me be the party planner. Next year?' I ask when I reach the table and bend down to pet Otto.

'Brooke is turning seven,' Nisha says. 'I think an Ethan Wells Extravaganza would be lost on her.' She fans her hands across the sky as she says my name and I like it.

'You don't know that,' I say. 'At nine I had my own subscription to *Martha Stewart Living* and I was proficient in using this,' I say, holding up an exquisitely wrapped box with lime green, aqua and candy apple red ribbons. A color combination I wouldn't normally approve, but when your favorite seven-year-old requests a specific palette you respect her choices.

'Is that...?' Kiara asks.

I nod.

'I'm sure you paid way too much,' Nisha says, pushing back her long black hair.

'I paid way too much and then paid way too much for express shipping but it was down to the wire and I couldn't disappoint Brooke. She wanted an original Easy-Bake Oven and now she has one.' I dig out some organic treats from a dog bakery in Soho from my pocket for Otto. I sneak him a few without either of the women noticing. Otto puts them in his mouth and moves under the table to devour them.

'Where did you finally find it?' Kiara asks as she sets the picnic table with plastic forks. There is never an occasion for plastic forks but it's a celebration so I shut my mouth and answer her question.

'Uncle Clams helped me search. We finally found it at an antiques store in New Hope, Pennsylvania called The Beautiful Things Shoppe. Super nice guy and his husband run it. They said it was in mint condition.'

'Brooke is going to lose her mind,' Kiara says, smiling.

'I wish Clams could be here tonight,' Nisha says.

'Me too. His ankle is doing better but I told him he needs to stay off it a bit longer if he wants to perform on Fire Island. Even he understands that dancing in heels will take all his strength. He sends his love.'

'And we send ours back,' Kiara says.

I take a seat at the bench they have set up for the party. I look underneath and see Otto's little black tail wagging. 'I plan to teach Brooke the basics of creating your own recipes. The way Uncle Clams taught me. Sifting, creaming, precise measurements. But most importantly presentation.'

'She'll love it,' Nisha says. I help her take the cake out of the box. It's Brooke's favorite from Costco but I treat it like she picked it up at Lady M on 78th Street.

'I hope so,' I say and watch her on the exquisite turn-of-the-century carousel with the other kids and parents. Brooke is beaming as her brown palomino gallops up and down. As a kid I loved the pastoral paintings above the carousel more than anything else – peaceful, romantic landscapes where everything was artfully arranged. I'd stare at them for hours. It's clear Brooke loves the motion and the energy of the ride. 'Look at her. She doesn't have a care in the world.'

'But it looks like you do,' Kiara says.

I don't say anything. I bend from the waist and put my head on the picnic table in surrender.

'Is Chase acting like Chase again?' Nisha asks.

'You didn't tell her?' I ask.

'You swore me to secrecy on my favorite makeup brush,' Kiara says. 'I love my wife but a makeup brush like that only comes along once in a lifetime. I love you baby,' Kiara says to Nisha and blows a kiss to her. They get each other's humor.

'Let me explain. The problem is Chase isn't acting like Chase,' I say.

'Now I'm confused,' Nisha says.

I take a deep breath and explain everything to Nisha about the switcheroo.

'The problem is he's being nice to everyone?' Nisha asks once everyone is up to speed. She's a counselor for a school in Bensonhurst. She's very good at asking questions that reflect back a neutral reality.

'Yes, exactly.'

'What an awful person,' she says and even though I know she's being sarcastic I pretend I miss that part.

'Oh,' Kiara says. 'I don't think Ethan thinks he's awful at all.'

'I do,' I say. 'He's as bad as his brother. Maybe worse.'

Kiara and Nisha just look at me. They both have this way of not saying a word but conveying everything they're feeling with their eyes. They both would've been great in silent films. Kiara breaks the silence and says, 'Tina and I came back and we found him with his arms around Beau. Can you explain that again?'

'My arms were not wrapped around him. I told you; I was helping him with his tie. That's all.'

Kiara nods. She doesn't believe a word and I'm not sure I do either.

'Uncle Ethan. Uncle Ethan,' Brooke shouts as she jumps off the carousel and runs toward me.

I pick her up in my arms and give her a big hug. 'Happy Birthday!' I put her down and she looks from side to side. There has been a rumor of an Easy-Bake Oven for months now so I assume she is looking for her present, but she looks up at me and says, 'Where's your new boyfriend? The one Moms say looks like that other guy on the TV?'

It's my turn to look at them and convey everything with a look.

Chapter 20

The plan tonight is to teach Beau how to prepare my special beef Wellington so he can do it on camera. I get in a cab to head back to Manhattan. I instruct the driver on my bridge preferences and start going over the lists of details for tonight's cooking lesson. I'm sure Beau has almost zero cooking experience. It's going to be torture watching him struggle through the recipes I've so painstakingly developed.

As soon as the elevator doors open I smell something extraordinary. One of the neighbors must be having a dinner party. Roasting garlic and simmering onions with a definite savory undertone fill the hall. Now I wish I had ordered something before I arrived since the aroma is making me hungry despite stuffing my face with birthday cake shortly before leaving the party. As I get to the apartment door the smell gets stronger. I knock. The door opens and I'm blown over by the aroma as it becomes richer and stronger.

'Oh, no,' I say and run to the kitchen. 'No. No, no.'

'Hello to you too Ethan,' Beau says as I rush past him.

Lobel's must have sent the wrong order. I wanted all of the ingredients for beef Wellington and they must have sent one of the finished pre-made ready-to-cook meals. I'll never be able to show Beau how to make it for the camera next week. But when I get to the kitchen I notice

161

something is off. I've eaten the Lobel's meal a hundred times, and from the scent I can tell this one has some distinct differences. I open the oven and see that Beau has transferred the entire meal to the correct shape of Le Creuset Dutch oven. That alone impresses me. I take a tasting spoon from the drawer and lift the foil cover so I can dip into the brown sauce. A small pearl onion drops into the spoon and I pop it all in my mouth. Delicious but different from their usual recipe. They must have changed it. This version has more aromatics or something. I'd have to sit down and really study it to see what makes it an improvement over their usual recipe and, dare I say, over my own.

Beau walks in.

'I'm going to have to call Lobel's and see if they can correct this mistake.'

'What mistake?'

'I need to teach you to make the meal from my recipe, from scratch for the camera. I can't do that if that's already done,' I say.

'Ethan, please don't do that,' Beau says.

'I'm sorry Beau, but we need to make it look like you know what you're doing on camera and...'

'No, I mean leave the foil on the casserole.' He brushes past me to grab the aluminum foil I left on the counter. He opens the oven and carefully seals the edges of the dish. I suddenly notice that over his gym shorts and tank top he's wearing the apron I keep here that has Warhol's portrait of Liza Minnelli plastered across it. Liza has a few puffs of flour on her so it looks like she's had a rough night at Studio 54.

'I don't want the crust to be too brown on my Wellington.'

'Your Wellington? What's going on here? I specifically asked for all the ingredients so *I* could show *you* how to make *my* Wellington.' I take out my phone and begin to dial the butcher shop but I'm beginning to think that's not the issue. Maybe this is one of those problems that doesn't need to be fixed, as Beau pointedly suggested.

'Hang up. That's exactly what they did. Except this is not your beef Wellington. It's my vegan Wellington.'

I look through the kitchen to the dining room and see the stunning reclaimed wood table I selected is set for two. He's found the vintage blue willow plates that are a bit too on the nose but precious nonetheless. He must have washed and polished the stemware and there's a bottle of something that looks delightful chilling in a crystal wine bucket.

I'm totally lost. 'Okay, Beau. What exactly is going on here? Did you have Tina do this?' I ask as I walk back into the kitchen.

'I do not boss Tina around the way you do. I would never make her do this.'

'What? I do not boss Tina around.' I'm about to explain to him the lavish end-of-season bonus and gift I am planning for her, but I need to figure out what has happened so I can correct it. 'Beau,' I say calmly, 'where are the ingredients for the beef Wellington and the chilled carrot soup?' I had forgotten about the chilled carrot soup myself but seeing there are soup bowls on the table I suddenly remember.

'You've already disturbed the browning of the crust so you've seen the ingredients.' He gingerly opens the oven door to check on the meal. 'Well, all of them except the beef. How anyone can consider not converting to a plant-based diet at this point is beyond me. I'll donate the

163

beef tomorrow but for now I put it in the freezer. My Wellington uses a savory lentil mixture and I don't know why your recipe calls for so many dried herbs. Who wants to eat dust? Fresh herbs are so much more aromatic.'

'I agree but sometimes our viewers don't want to go out and buy an entire...' I start to explain and then realize the man who I found in a yurt with a gun has a point of view about marjoram. 'Wait a minute. You took the ingredients I had delivered and made this using my recipe.'

'Well not really with *your* recipe. I mean I started with that but, Ethan... there are a lot of problems with that recipe and it's not just the use of meat or dried herbs. Refrigerated dough? Do you have any idea how many preservatives and chemicals are in that? All you need to make dough is...'

'I know how to make dough,' I say, irritated that he's dissing my recipe and even more confused about how he knows all this. The dough maker is the sponsor and the whole reason we're making this dish. He goes back to the refrigerator and takes out a pan of roasted carrots. Even experienced home cooks struggle with dough so this is more than knowing one's way around a kitchen. 'The question is how do *you* know how to make it?'

He gathers the carrots into a bowl and then moves to a chopping board where he has a few sprigs of fresh rosemary waiting. He picks up a knife and says, 'Culinary school.' He starts chopping like his statement is no big deal when it is a huge freaking deal.

'You went to culinary school? How? When? Where?' Is there anything this guy hasn't done? I wonder if he's flown the space shuttle or knows how to shear sheep.

'You didn't know?' He moves the blade through the rosemary with the finesse of a professional chef. 'Didn't Chase tell you anything about me?'

'As a matter of fact he didn't.'

'I guess that doesn't surprise me. Yeah, I went to culinary school. When? When I was in my twenties. Where? École de Cuisine Alain Ducasse.' He says the name of the famous cooking school in France like a native Parisienne.

I put my elbows on the counter and cover my face with my hands. This guy has studied cooking in Paris and might speak fluent French.

Beau's opening and closing cabinets and finally asks, 'Where's the blender?'

'Bottom cabinet left of the sink,' I say without thinking. I know this kitchen better than I know my own. I developed most of my recipes here since my own cooking area is actually a kitchenette, which is an adorable way of saying 'no counter space'. Beau finds the blender and plugs it in.

'Can you please wait a minute?' I plead. I need a second to take this all in.

Beau doesn't stop. He glides from the prepped ingredients to the appliances. There is no doubt he's telling the truth. 'So before escaping the world and moving to Stark, New York you lived in Paris, France and studied with Alain Ducasse?' I ask although that's not really the question. The Ducasse school is for serious chefs. How could he let all that training and study go to waste? I'm stumped but if there's anything I've learned about Beau it's that he doesn't like to answer personal questions about how he got to Stark. I've been assuming that he had a childhood

165

similar to Chase's in Wisconsin, but they certainly wound up in different places.

'Yes, I studied with Monsieur Ducasse. Now that we've got that cleared up,' he says with a tone that expresses how annoyed he is with my inquiry, 'I want to go over some problems I found in your recipe.'

'There are no problems in my recipe,' I say.

'First off, beef? Ethan, moving to a plant-based diet is easy, delicious and it makes sense for the planet.' He's good. I should get a pen and write down what he just said. It would make great copy, but no one criticizes my recipes. No one. 'This carrot soup has way too much dairy. If you use a blender to emulsify...'

'It's a cream of carrot soup. Where do you expect the cream to come from?' I ask as he scoops the roasted carrots into the blender, puts the lid on and presses the button.

'That's where you need a good brand of cold-pressed coconut oil and coconut creamer. You'll get all the smoothness without any of the dairy.' He raises his voice so I can hear him over the roar of the blender.

'Stop it,' I say. 'I have everything planned out. I don't want any changes to the recipe.'

'What?' he asks. The blender is so loud he can't hear me so I stop it and repeat what I said. He barely acknowledges me. He goes on cooking, removing the lid, stirring the bright orange concoction in the blender and mixing it a bit more.

'Beau. Did you hear me?' He's moved to the cutting board to chop some scallions.

'Yes, I heard you. I get it but why don't we talk about it over dinner. Just try what I've made.' He checks the oven and then goes back to the soup. He may have heard me but he isn't listening. I'm so frustrated right now that I can't even think. We have so much to do and he has spoilt the ingredients, changed everything I've worked so hard to set up and is plowing along in the direction of his choosing. He knows how to cook. I'm impressed. But that doesn't mean I'm going to let him do it however he wants. The show has an editorial voice we have to follow or viewers will be confused.

'Ethan, have a seat and I'll…'

I don't want to hear him talk anymore. I'd rather go back to the roar of the blender so I hit the button that makes it spin. Click. In a flash the blender starts but I forgot that Beau has taken off the lid. A bright neon orange tornado gyrates up the sides of the blender and out to the furthest reaches of the kitchen covering both Beau and me in carrot mess. I quickly hit one of the buttons but since they're covered in carrot I hit the one that makes it spin faster and we are seasoned with another layer of soup. Beau pulls the cord from the wall and the entire things stops. Poor Liza. His apron looks like she has had a terrible reaction to some medication across her face.

I laugh. Slowly at first and then almost uncontrollably. Beau laughs too. I must look as ridiculous as Liza does covered in soup. I'm laughing so hard tears appear in the corners of my eyes. It takes me a few seconds to gain control and when I do I wipe some soup off my cheek and taste it.

'Well, what do you think?' Beau asks.

'Not bad,' I say. The coconut is just underneath the sweet carrot and he's added some ginger to balance everything out. It's a nice touch. I'm sure it would taste even better in a bowl than it does being rubbed off my face.

Chapter 21

I wanted to lie. I tried to lie. But I couldn't. I'm sure the expression on my face gave me away. Beau's vegan Wellington was absolutely delicious. Devout carnivores would fall in love with it. I never believed you could make creamy soup without dairy but what was left in the blender was exquisite. I volunteer to clean up but Beau insists on helping me with the dishes.

I'm wiping down the counter and finally decide I have to ask him. 'So what's the deal… with the crust. How do you get it that flaky without butter? I have to know.' On the show we'll need to use the refrigerated dough since the sponsor has paid a great deal for the promotion but it doesn't mean I'd serve something out of a can at a dinner party of my own.

'So you admit you liked it?'

Of course I liked it. I ate more than my share although I claimed each mouthful was only for research purposes. 'I admit nothing.' Not about to give into him so easily.

'Fine, but you have zero poker face. I just need to look in your eyes to see what you're really thinking.' My eyes. He's been looking into my eyes? The thought of it makes me suddenly shy. I turn away and wipe down the counter furiously.

'You have to be gentle,' he says. At first, I think he's talking about wiping down the counter but then he adds, 'with the dough.'

'I see,' I say, not looking up. I'm scared about what my eyes might give away.

'Some people think you need to really beat it and knead it under your knuckles, but that doesn't work. With a mix of vegetable shortening and coconut oil, you have to help everything bloom and you can't do that by force. Let everything find its own way.'

I don't know who I expected Beau to be or what I expected of him. My first thought was that he would be a copy of his brother. That went away almost immediately. Then I thought he would be this rough mountain man ready to use an axe to divide a sandwich. He isn't that either.

I think about how he is on set – gentle and patient. I'm always making sure we meet deadlines and don't go over budget. I think about Chase and how I order him around. I have to acknowledge my part in Chase's departure. Maybe I never gave him a chance to bloom. I'm beginning to regret that.

I finish wiping down the counter and realize I have to tell Beau about the party at Maria Luisa's and the role he needs to play at it. A little alcohol might make this conversation easier.

'How do you feel about wheat beers?' I ask. The fruit flavor is not appealing to everyone.

'I feel like they get a bad rap for being too fruity but the right ones are excellent,' he says.

I reach in the back of the fridge where I know I have some hiding from Chase. I put the bottles on the counter and go to get a pair of glasses, but when I open the cabinet above the sink where the glasses for wheat beer are kept I only see coffee mugs and wine stems.

'I guess he broke the pilsner glasses. Let me see if there's something else in the liquor cabinet.'

'Just use the mug or the goblet,' Beau says. He opens the cabinet I just closed and grabs one mug and one goblet. I stare at the counter. He might as well have pulled out a dead rodent.

'Beau, I'm not putting one of the finest craft wheat beers in a goblet and please let's pretend the mug isn't even here. I can't. I just can't.'

'What's the big deal?' he asks.

'You went to culinary school. Surely your training has taught you to use the proper glass for the proper drink. A wheat bear needs a vase-shaped glass or at the very least a pilsner glass so the bubbles don't break the surface too easily.'

'Well there's an easy way to solve this glass problem,' he says. He holds the beer bottle up.

'I swear if you try to open that bottle with your mouth and need reconstructive dental surgery this weekend I will...' He puts the bottle down and opens a drawer to find a bottle opener. He opens one bottle and hands it to me and then opens the other one for himself.

'Do you have a problem drinking out of the bottle?'

I look down at the brown rim. I can't remember the last time I drank out of a bottle. Maybe in college. Who am I kidding? I would never have done that in college. I must have been an infant.

It's the first warm evening of the summer so we head back out to the terrace. Central Park is quiet and only a few lights puncture the inky dark. We are high enough up to clear most of the short brownstones before the park but not too high up that my nerves get the better of me. The further away from the edge of the terrace the better. That way, I don't get that sinking feeling at the base of my back.

'Is that one the Dakota? With the long balcony? Or is that the San Remo?' Beau asks. I look out across the night sky with him.

'You're right. The San Remo has rounder edges here,' I say, tracing my finger in the sky. How does he know the Dakota from the San Remo? What part of town did he live in? Why did he leave? It surprises me how little I know about him and how much I want to know more. I can't help it. We stand next to each other studying the buildings. A gentle summer breeze blows across and I watch lights in apartments randomly turn off or on reminding me that each square is really a whole life.

'How does someone become a person who can get so worked up about glassware?' he asks. He doesn't look at me. He keeps staring out at the view and I think he knows it will be easier to get a real answer out of me without the intense eye contact.

'My Uncle Frank, you know, Uncle Clams, he was a florist at this high-end place not far from here. I loved visiting him in the city and being at the shop. A lot goes into a flower arrangement. Not just the greens but the structure that supports it and the vessel, and Clams could make an arrangement out of dandelions and poison ivy look beautiful.'

Beau gives a soft chuckle but he keeps his eyes on the horizon so I keep going.

'Sometimes when I stayed with him in the city I'd help deliver the flowers to these catered banquets, lavish parties with fine china and the most elegant clothing and fancy food. Then at home I'd obsess over magazines like *Architectural Digest* or *GQ*... oh and *Martha Stewart Living* was my bible. I've always liked making things look nice.'

'So you liked the good life?'

I shake my head. 'No, not like you're maybe thinking.' He's making a fair assessment and usually I might just agree and go along with it but I want to be clear with him. 'It's not about the price tag or even the luxury. It's about finding the best way to do something. My dad wasn't around and there wasn't a lot of money but my mom behaved like we were the most elegant family on the block. On Fridays while other families were having pizza, we'd dress up for dinner. I loved it. I can't explain it but those dinners made me feel normal, although there's nothing normal about a nine-year-old boy in a bowtie eating a dinner of Dented Can Casserole with his mom in a gold-sequin evening gown.' I smile thinking about how my mom would wear a long dress some nights and then I laugh wondering if those actually came from Uncle Clams. I never made the connection before.

'Something about knowing the right way to do things always made me feel safe and when the show came along, I thought I could share that with people.'

'So you didn't always want to be a television mogul?'

'Never actually.'

'But you do now?' he asks. It's a logical question and one I should be able to answer quickly and easily but it takes a second for me to locate the desire and then pull it to the surface. It's almost there when I decide I should just change the subject.

'Yes, I guess so,' I say, getting the words out quickly. 'But how does someone go from Paris to Stark, New York? That's really the question.'

'That's easy to answer. You screw things up so bad you don't have a choice.' He takes a swig of beer and is quiet for a few moments. 'That and some bad luck. Bad choices too. That'll do it. But thanks to you and your payday a lot of that's in the past. At least the financial part.'

'I'm glad. Sounds like it was a tough time,' I say and bring my bottle up to my mouth. I'm always terrible at this part of conversation.

'In the end. It was good for me. I always loved cooking and making food but I didn't think I could make it a career. After college I did a bunch of odd jobs. Trying things on. Eventually I started to realize I couldn't *not* go to cooking school. But after I made it my job it got harder. Cooking became about instant gratification. Pleasing people. Not the long term. I was obsessed with reviews. I'd read a bad review online and it would destroy me. I'd fixate on it.'

'Don't read the reviews,' I say. It's a mantra in any type of creative work.

'I know. But I put my entire self into my food so when people were saying mean things, that was rough. I read every bad one. I couldn't help it. You make something and you want to know what people think. The good ones made me feel so good but the bad ones hit me really hard. I get that it can be part of the job but I'm still human. It hurts.'

Reviews can be brutal. I avoid them as much as possible but I get where he's coming from. If you're sensitive it can be harsh. I'm sorry he had to endure that.

'I had to know what people thought. I was running a small business. They live and die by reviews. There were a lot of good ones, and bad ones that were critical but kind. But some of them were pretty toxic. You cook someone a

173

risotto and they feel like they get the right to say whatever they want to you. It made me think about what I put in my mind and my body. When I got upstate, I focused on not connecting with anything toxic, people or food.'

'Thus a more plant-rich diet?' I suggest.

'Exactly. Learning to be more inside myself and learning to relax and not let external pressure control me. You should try it,' he says.

'I might be able to pencil that in for a few minutes next month. Would that work?' He laughs at my joke and I appreciate the fact that he isn't preachy or judgmental. The beer is making me feel a little buzzed so I decide it's time to tick off my next agenda item. 'Beau, I want to thank you for agreeing to all this on-camera stuff and the promotional events. You've been great all week.'

During dinner we were able to get through the logistics of the next few days, what we'll be filming, and what he's supposed to say and do. All of the basic stuff but I haven't had the courage to ask him for the stuff that goes above and beyond.

'You've been great and I appreciate it but we have a couple additional wrinkles that we need to iron out so everything goes smoothly. Let's go inside and chat,' I say. I'm not sure I can stomach being that high up with what I need to ask.

I take a seat on the couch in the living room. For a second I think he's going to sit right next to me and I can feel my heartbeat but then he sits in the chair. A safe distance. 'What wrinkles?'

I look at him and take a deep breath. Before I tell him about the party with Maria Luisa next week, I have to explain the situation with his brother.

'Your brother and I... we...' I stop. The words get a bit stuck so I have to push them out. 'We are sort of... it appears... dating but...' I can't go any further at the moment.

He doesn't say anything and his expression is unchanged. I'm not sure what reaction I was expecting but I was at least expecting some kind of reaction.

'I'm not surprised,' he says finally. 'You're exactly the kind of guy he likes to get attention from.' His tone is suddenly sharper. There's an edge to it I don't like.

'What's that supposed to mean? Do not put me in a box. It's not like that. You don't know what you're talking about...' I'm about to lose my temper but yelling at him isn't going to help the situation, and he's also done a lot for me so far. He doesn't deserve that. I just don't like being associated with Chase in that way.

'All I'm saying is that I know my brother has a type. Smart, handsome red heads with dimples who are...'

'Oh,' I say, not stopping the direction the conversation is going.

'Incredibly bossy,' he adds.

'Hey,' I say, my balloon deflated. Focus. Get out what I need to get out. 'It's more complicated than it seems on the surface. The issue is that we, meaning Chase and I, have been invited to a game night at my boss's place.'

'Is this the boss that you're trying to impress so you can get that fancy new promotion that I get the sense you don't really want?' he asks like he has me all figured out. He doesn't. Not at all. Well, maybe a tiny bit.

'Yes, that boss. She invited me and insisted I bring Chase. I couldn't very well tell her that the person she thinks is Chase...'

'Is actually his better-looking twin brother.'

'You do realize you're identical. You're equally good-looking or not. That's the identical part.'

'So you say.'

'Right,' I say, passing by the comment. 'The thing is Maria Luisa will expect us to act like a couple.'

'So how long have you and my brother been dating?'

'You know...' I hesitate to avoid the question. Our arrangement is a professional one and he doesn't need to know all the details. How can I explain to him that in front of Maria Luisa we faked our relationship so she, the other network executives and the sponsors could see a perfectly partnered gay couple? It was good for ratings and happy couples always have the most followers and the biggest sponsors. It made sense at the time but I'm embarrassed to admit all of this to Beau. If I tell him it was all fake with his brother that might be the final straw for him. He has so much integrity. I'm beginning to feel ashamed that I ever agreed to the whole fake boyfriend thing. I decide not to tell him everything in order to save some of my dignity.

'Can I count on you to go to this game party social thing with me as Chase?' I ask. I can feel my knee bouncing up and down from nerves.

He doesn't say anything. He just grins like he's enjoying watching me sweat over this, which he probably is.

'I mean, I'm being him all day at work. Do you want me to be your boyfriend?' he asks. Slowly his grin pushes out to become a smile.

'Yes,' I say, not taking my eyes off his lips. 'I want you' – I take a breath in sharply – 'I want you to be my boyfriend.' As soon as the words leave my mouth I realize what I have said. 'For the night!' I add quickly and in a panic. 'Just for the night, I mean.'

Beau gets up from his chair and starts walking around the apartment. 'So that means you want me to do things like casually grab your hand as we roll the dice on the game board or whatever, maybe a kiss on the cheek with some sweet endearment or...' He walks back toward me and this time instead of sitting on the chair he sits on the couch just inches away. 'Or making sure everyone sees me looking at you like you're the most important person in the world, like I can't wait to get you home and make love to you all night and make breakfast for you in the morning. Look at you... like this.'

His face turns toward me and his eyes zoom into mine and lock there. There's even smoldering. I guess it's fake smoldering but it feels like smoldering from where I'm sitting. I don't know if this is real or if he's faking and I don't care. I know Chase would never do any of those things and anyone witnessing him behaving like this would know Beau is an imposter but instead of telling him not to do any of that I stay connected to his eyes and say, 'Yes, I want you to do that. Do all of that.'

Chapter 22

'Eggs in Purgatory, with double the chorizo and make the polenta extra crispy, please, the orange brioche and...' Tina pauses her order and turns from the server to me. 'Are you sure this is all right? I mean, it's a lot.'

'I want you to order whatever you'd like. What happens once it enters your body is between you and a good gastroenterologist.' I have no idea how someone can eat their weight in pastry before eight o'clock in the morning but Tina has no problem doing it. She's told me that eating an enormous breakfast is one of her biggest guilty pleasures, and she's been so amazing helping me with everything the past week and a half. It's the least I can do for her. Once this mess is behind us and the parade is over, I'll find a way to really thank her.

'Okay,' she continues. 'Where was I? The orange blossom brioche and a palmier. Thank you.' She turns to me and says, 'There's a patisserie in the third arrondissement that I've read does amazing things with citrus rind and brioche.' I nod politely. I've heard about her love for this bakery in Paris for quite some time. She hands the server her menu.

'Just black coffee, thanks,' I say over my sunglasses and peek around to see if I recognize anyone. Breakfast service at Balthasar in Soho tends to be crawling with a potpourri of minor and major media moguls. Large, intentionally antiqued mirrors dominate the walls of the dining room. The look and feel is an updated version of the Cafe Les Deux Magots on the Rive Gauche in Paris, which is appropriate because at the dawn of the last century that cafe hosted the rising intelligentsia of gay society. And at the start of this century, I know for a fact the queer version of *Love Island* was sold three booths away from me. Not exactly *Giovanni's Room* but the comparison is still apt.

'I was able to get the guest list for Game Night at Maria Luisa's,' Tina says, scrolling her screens. 'The good news is Jamie Bautista will be there with his boyfriend, Jamie Gomez.' Jamie B appeared on a popular WB drama and occasionally wore a shirt, although even then it was never buttoned. He came out halfway through the filming and sort of gave up acting to focus on activism. His partner is also an actor but he tends to appear in cerebral crime dramas. They are both super-darling and every time I see them I have a good time. I used to wish I could find a relationship like the one they have. They always seem connected and supportive of each other.

'The bad news, well I really shouldn't call it bad news because there is worse news after that…'

'Tina, is this the type of training in conflict resolution they taught you at NYU?'

'I guess.' She shrugs. My snarkiness is unable to penetrate her sweetness. It's one of the things I love about her. 'Do you want the bad news or the awful news first?'

'I'll take Bad for 500 please.'

'Keegan is going to be at the Game Night,' she says as the waiter begins to unload a tray of food onto the table. Plates jockey for space as a vein in my forehead begins to pulse.

'What's he doing there? I thought those events were couples only?'

'Me too,' she says, tearing off a piece of the orange brioche completely consumed by the banquet in front of her. 'He's working on that story on Beau.' She takes a sip of her cappuccino and then stops. 'Or is it a story on Chase? Should I call him Chase or Beau when we are alone? Or maybe we should have a code name. I could call him Base or maybe Cheau?'

'Let's just call Beau, Beau when we are alone?'

'Beau-Beau?'

'Yes,' I say trying to prevent this from becoming an Abbott and Costello routine. At some point today I need to explain the whole Keegan situation to Beau. I ran out of time the other night; or did I chicken out? Either way I did not fill him in.

'Ethan, how are you?' I hear from behind me.

'Please tell me that is not who I think it is,' I plead to Tina.

'I don't think I can do that,' she says, stuffing her mouth with a forkful of eggs.

I turn and see Jeremiah dressed in his usual jacket, vest and bowtie. Today's palette is lavender and lime green with a seersucker vest that I recognize from Barney's spring collection since I have the same one in my closet. I make a mental note to burn it this weekend. 'Jeremiah, aren't you an early bird this morning?'

'Hello,' Tina says, hiding behind her croissant. Tina is terrified of Jeremiah. She's got good instincts. Jeremiah looks at the plates of food covering our table.

'Hmm. A breakfast banquet? I hope Ethan isn't buttering you up so you'll work even harder than you do, you poor thing.' Jeremiah grins.

'Well, actually he is——' she starts, and I shoot her a look.

'Jeremiah, treating one's team with respect and gratitude is simply standard operating procedure at *Myles*. You know that,' I say, cutting Tina off.

'Do I?' His grin widens. 'Anyway, I can't tarry.' Good lord, who in the world says 'tarry'? Who does he think he is, Charles Dickens? 'I'm meeting... Oh, I shouldn't really say.'

'Well, if you shouldn't, then you shouldn't,' I say, hoping he will leave.

'But I'm among friends. I would hate for this to get out. I'm headed to one of the private rooms for a breakfast meeting with Alexandra Petras.' He whispers her name like it's a life-threatening disease.

I would do a spit take if I had enough coffee in my mouth. Alexandra is the head of international programming. She works directly with Maria Luisa. Is she interviewing him for the job I want? Has Jeremiah already been given the job? Maria Luisa told me they hadn't made a decision yet. Still, this is not good news.

'I don't want to keep Ms Petras waiting. She's off to the coast this afternoon. So nice to see you both,' he says and slides off.

'Why would Jeremiah be meeting with Alexandra? Isn't she above Maria Luisa?' Tina asks.

'She is,' I say, still glaring at Jeremiah's back as he leaves the main dining room. Tina knows I want the promotion but maybe she doesn't realize Jeremiah wants it just as much as I do. 'Who cares why he's here? He's gone now. That's all that matters. Are you sure you don't want some brioche with jam?'

Tina pushes her lips to one side as she considers the idea. 'Sure. If you don't mind.'

We review the rest of the schedule including the trip to Fire Island and everything we'll be shooting there, the beach locations, the pieces in town and at the pier. The day of the parade itself is constantly on our agenda and I review the action items still pending, including writing the speech for Chase for the ribbon cutting to start the parade and making sure the remaining sponsors stay on board after the Hairlucinations debacle. Finally I ask, 'What else is there you need to tell me? I can't put it off any longer.'

Tina keeps packing away her breakfast with glee. I'm enjoying seeing how much she relishes eating. 'Today's schedule involves the on-location shoot at *that place*. You told me not to mention it until the day of the shoot and today is that day so, I'm mentioning it.'

'That's today?' I ask. Why wouldn't it be today?

'I'm afraid so. It's on the schedule but I deleted it from yours because you don't want to think about it.'

Back before everything started unraveling, this shoot was the one big source of stress I had in my life. I would have thought that with all the other sources of stress in my life begging for attention this would fade into the background, but it doesn't. I remember exactly what's on the schedule for today and my heart starts racing. 'Tina, hand over your pastry.'

Tina pushes her plate over to me. I rip off a small piece of the golden brown *kouign-amann* she ordered, leave it on the plate and shove the rest of it in my mouth.

Chapter 23

There are some problems pastries can't solve — very few, honestly, but some issues are pastry-resistant like some horrible strains of bacteria are to antibiotics. When we had originally planned this location, I thought I would, at the very most, watch remotely. The director and crew wouldn't have any issues doing it on their own but with Beau taking over for Chase I can't risk any slipups, which means I need to be there. In person and on location.

We grab a cab on Spring Street and head uptown.

'You can do it Ethan,' Tina says, holding the box of pastries we've brought as a security blanket. 'It's just an issue of mind over matter,' she says, and I wonder if that is yet another one of the helpful phrases she learned at NYU. The cab arrives at 42nd Street and Lex. The sidewalk is crowded with tourists and locals in equal proportions. I get out of the taxi and look up... and up... and up. My heart drops to my feet. Months ago, I thought the Chrysler Building would make a fantastic backdrop for our art deco-inspired Pride eve cocktail party fashion segments. The over-the-top details fit our theme like a charm and it's just a bit off center of the usual locations. The gleaming chrome tower comes to a point with dazzling triangular windows forming a crown at the top. Most people would think the Empire State Building or even Rock Center, but the Chrysler Building surpasses everything else in New York.

My stupid idea was to have Chase walk the deck on the 61st floor like a runway. We'd capture Manhattan's skyline and feature our fashion picks with some of the building's ornamentation as a delicious backdrop. It was a great idea when Chase was around and I didn't need to be attached to him. But now I need to be there and that means I need to be up there. I look down and wonder where on the sidewalk my body would land if I fell over the railing.

We are about to enter the building but my feet won't let me take the final step. I look up again and expect to see the Wicked Witch on her broomstick writing across the sky: 'Surrender Dorothy.' It's not a bad idea.

'Tina, I don't think I can...' I start to say when Kiara comes out of the lobby. She's wearing her usual stylist armor — an apron that she sewed herself, with pockets for brushes, combs and styling products. At first I'm not sure what she's doing here but then I remember I booked her freelance talents for the day.

'Get your skinny ass in here,' she says, holding open the entrance next to the revolving door. She knows revolving doors are on the list of things that terrify me. Once I was caught in one as a child and just kept going around until my mother pulled me out. Still, I have overcome that terror. My fear of heights is another thing entirely. In theory you could go around in a swinging door for days. Falling off the 61st floor has a definite end point and that alone is enough to keep me hugging sea level.

I slip into the lobby and I'm able to put my trepidation aside and focus on the beauty and grandeur of the location. I'm suddenly in a Fitzgerald novel — all elegance and decadence. Illuminated geometric panels with angles that move the eye sharply around the walls mix with chrome details reminiscent of hubcaps and hood ornaments. Maybe we don't even need to go any higher than the lobby. So what if we spent months getting permission from both the building and the city to film on the observation deck that's been closed to the public for decades? So what if we rented an external crew to help build a runway? Then I imagine Maria Luisa reviewing the line budget and not seeing anything that reflects the need for the expense.

The curtain to the makeshift dressing room in the lobby opens and Beau appears perfectly groomed and camera ready.

'What do you think?' Beau asks.

The first outfit is a vintage Yves Saint Laurent black pant with a tightly tailored black Prada dress shirt. His trousers have a sharp pleat down the front and break just before his shiny black wingtips. Kiara has slicked back his hair and I can't help staring at him. *What do I think? I think you look like a superhero who's about to host the world's most elegant dinner party and I want to smother you with kisses from head to toe.*

'You look fine. This will work,' I say coolly to counterbalance my actual reaction.

Ha-Joon, who is directing today's shoot, comes over to us. 'That black is going to look marvelous against the blue in the sky this morning and all that steely metal up there. Marvelous.' She points above him indicating our setup on the observation deck. 'Shall we head up? The light is really stunning up there right now with all that marvelous chrome. I don't want to miss it.'

'Sure,' I say and swallow hard. Ha-Joon begins gathering everyone for the migration to the 61st floor and leaves me standing where I am.

'You okay, Ethan?' Beau asks as everyone starts packing up.

'Yes, fine,' I say without moving.

Now he's the one staring at me. His eyes move over my body, taking it in carefully. 'Are you sure? Your breathing seems shallow and your posture is trapping all your energy here.' He takes his finger and taps the left side of my chest. 'Did something happen?'

'No,' I say quickly. 'I just have to focus on getting myself up there.'

Kiara comes over. She must sense I'm not doing well. 'You okay, baby?' she asks. 'You don't have to do this if you can't.'

'I can do it,' I say. 'Go up ahead. You need to get everything set. We'll be up right after.'

'Are you sure?' she asks, grabbing my hands and looking into my eyes. I can tell she is trying to transfer some of her natural confidence. I nod and point to the elevator, unable to make words. She heads up with everyone else.

Only Beau and I remain in the lobby.

'I take it you are not a fan of heights?' he asks. There isn't any judgment in his voice; it's just an inquiry.

'I am not,' I confess. 'I max out around twenty floors up. Once the people start looking like ants, I know I know I've reached my limit.'

No one here, except Kiara, Tina and now Beau, knows about my issue with heights. I'm the leader. The one who is supposed to have everything under control. If I let everyone think I can't do this it will start rumors and

186

those rumors might lead to sniffing around Beau and I can't let that happen. I look at my watch. I have to start moving.

'Let's go,' I say, marching toward the elevator, instructing my feet to walk. The doors of each lift are decorated in concentric rows of triangles echoing the design of the spire. I try to focus on the beauty of the architecture and not tumbling hundreds of feet to my death. Once I'm standing in front of the elevator, I freeze again. I know I should push the button but I can't.

'Would you mind?' I ask Beau, nodding toward the button.

'Are you sure?' he asks. I nod.

A sharp ding and then the doors to the car open. Inside is a glittering cage of gold and brass ornamentation. It's certainly a pretty way to die, I think. Beau walks in first and then turns around to face me. I know I just need to take two steps in and the rest will simply happen. My left foot advances into the car and then my right foot. I'm in but I can't do much else. I nod to Beau who presses the button for the observation deck. The doors close and the elevator begins to ascend.

I feel my pulse racing. My breathing accelerates and a feeling of doom overcomes me. I want to pull the emergency stop but that only means I'll be stuck in this gilded deathbed for longer. Then I hear: 'Keep breathing in through your nose and out through your mouth. I'm here. I'm here. I'm with you. I'm standing right next to you and we are here and we're together and we are both just breathing in this moment.'

Beau's voice is soft and kind. He's cooing to me like a dove, but it may be too late. My body tenses as I watch the floor numbers tick higher and higher. I undo the buttons on my shirt near my neck. Am I having a panic attack? The dread feels almost uncontrollable now. What's going on? Is it the height or the stress or a combination of both? I've had strong reactions to heights before but this feels different. More intense; less in my control.

'I'm here. I'm with you. I'm standing right next to you and we are in this moment together,' Beau repeats. His voice is even softer this time but I can't help staring at the numbers as they rise. Forty-six, forty-seven. Forty-eight. We arrive at the observation deck on the 61st floor and the doors open. I force myself to step out into what is called a 'sky lobby', a title so terrifying it could be in nightmares. Everyone is waiting for us. I just need to get over my initial fear, I think.

'Are you okay?' Beau asks.

'Not exactly,' I say. I close my eyes and just walk a few steps toward the doors to the observation deck to get my momentum going. I locomote and push open the doors where everyone is waiting. Beau is right behind me.

Once I'm actually outside I can see the Manhattan skyline and feel the wind. My heart starts pounding like it's going to jump out of my chest and run down all the stairs back to the ground floor. Everyone starts asking me questions at once. 'Do you want the runway longer? Is the order of looks the same? Can we do a light check? Where do you want this? Where do you want that?' It's a cacophony that I can't handle. I look back at Beau and his eyes connect with mine. I feel him sensing what's going on inside me. I feel helpless and unable to take control of the situation. My eyes plead with him for a solution.

'Ethan. Absolutely not!' he yells in a voice I haven't heard before. It's higher and more shrill. Much more Chase than Beau. All of the questions stop. 'I told you

in the elevator I will not wear that shade of purple. It's…
vulgar!'

Am I hallucinating or having a memory lapse? What
shade of purple is he talking about? I look at the crowd
of production assistants and they're focused on Beau,
thinking they're witnessing the start of one of his tantrums.

'I need to speak to you in private,' he shouts and then
gently guides me to the other side of the deck where we
can be alone and away from everyone. He finds a bench
where we can sit down as far away from the edge of the
building as possible. 'Just keep breathing. Do you want to
go back down? I can make an excuse.' His voice is in sharp
contrast to the one he used in front of the crew.

My chest feels tight and the sense of doom feels like a
rock I'll never be able to lift off my chest. I'm in way over
my head with this – with everything. I rub my chest with
my hand hoping to relieve the pressure but it just sits there
weighing on my body and spirit.

Beau doesn't push me. 'Do this,' he suggests calmly. 'Sit
with your legs a bit more open and see if you can bend
forward like this.' He demonstrates and without thinking
I do what he's doing. Then he grabs my hand and puts it
over his chest. 'Try to empty your mind and just follow
my breathing. In and out. In and out until you can do it
on your own.'

My mind is flooded with images of all the stress
weighing down on me. I think about deceiving everyone,
wondering if Chase will come back, having to explain
Keegan to Beau, losing Hairlucinations as the float
sponsor, disappointing Clams and The Giblet Triplets on
Pride. I even see images of my father walking out and
childhood things that still upset me like being shoved into
a locker for no reason and being laughed at.

'I can't,' I say, and my hand starts to pull away from Beau. I don't feel in control of my body, my breathing or anything.

'I'm here. I'm with you. You are safe. You are safe,' he says, and my hand stops pulling away and stays with him and his breathing. His chest rises and falls. Up and down. Up and down. I try to let my mind stay there. I stay with the small motion of his chest and let it melt from his body to mine.

It takes a few minutes but eventually my breathing matches his and I'm able to do it on my own. I keep my head between my legs for a minute until whatever sensation it was that felt like it was taking over my body abates and I feel more in control. I stare at the sleeve of Beau's shirt as he speaks calming words. Then I get there, to a place where the panic is contained, at least for now. I'm still stressed but I'm not so deep under it all that I'm terrified.

'I'm sorry,' I say. 'I'm really sorry. I don't know what came over me. I've always had a fear of heights but I've been able to control it. I've never had quite this reaction before. I mean, I'm not thrilled to be up here but I feel like I can manage at least. For now, that is. I don't know why that happened.'

'Sometimes when we're in a very stressful situation, an old lingering fear can crop up and the two can sort of create an irrational explosion. You're under a lot of stress. It makes sense that confronting this fear might lead to something like a panic attack.'

That's what stepping out of the elevator felt like, a panic attack. I think I had one when my mom died and maybe once or twice growing up. I'm not sure but it felt uncontrollable and like the entire world was closing in on me, but it doesn't feel that intense now and I'm so grateful.

'How do you know so much about this?' I ask. Did he study Psychology before or after cooking school? There is so much about this guy I don't know. So much I'm realizing I want to know.

'Experience. I've suffered from panic attacks my whole life. Since I was kid really. I suppose I still do but now I have a technique for getting through them. They got really bad when I was living here and running the restaurant. That's why I practice mediation and try to be aware of my breathing. I thought being back in a city would reignite them for me but that hasn't happened. I think whatever tools I've been practicing seem to have created new pathways in my brain. When I looked in your eyes, I thought you might be having one or something similar, so I pretended we were having an argument, or rather that you and Chase were having an argument.'

It was not just smart of him to figure all that out, but kind and thoughtful too. I try to stay calm and not spin out in any direction good or bad. 'Is it over? How can you tell when the attack is over?' I ask. I'm so grateful for his help and knowledge.

'I'm not a doctor but your pupils seem to have returned to their normal state.' His smile widens and it comforts me. 'Of course, your normal state is more like a headless chicken than a sleeping panda bear but it's all about stasis rather than nirvana.' He smiles at me and strokes my arm gently.

There is a dig in there but I don't care. It actually makes me feel even better because it means he thinks we're out of the crisis and back to where we can playfully jab. I take another deep breath and check in on myself. I'm doing okay. The darkest layer has lifted. For now. Another breath and this time I decide to look up from my feet and take in the view. Another breath and I look out in front of me. I'm okay.

'You're doing great,' Beau says, and he's right. I look across the sky and slowly observe the skyline. I feel the sensation shift from frantic nerves to a nervous excitement. I peek beyond the platform and lower Manhattan glimmers in the late morning sun as large clouds float toward us. Bits of sunlight reflecting on the windows create pops of gold and orange across the otherwise monochromatic scene. I'm able to look out and enjoy the view just a tiny bit. The wind rips around the corner and I shiver.

'How are you feeling?' Beau asks.

'Better,' I say. 'A lot better. I'm sorry you suffer from panic attacks.'

'Thanks,' he says. 'I can handle it now. I couldn't then. Being a twin means you can get a lot of unwanted attention. Chase seemed to soak it up but I could never get comfortable with it.'

'I'm sorry I'm making you do all this,' I say. 'I hope it isn't a trigger.'

'Nope. It's fine and you aren't making me do anything. It's my choice. In fact, I wasn't going to admit it but I think it's been good for me. You've been good for me.'

'Oh,' I say, unsure if I heard him correctly.

'I mean, the way you've made me engage with people again. I'm grateful for that. I didn't think I was ready, but I am.'

I can hear the crew around the corner. Everyone is waiting. I can feel the pressure enter my body and as it does I realize that stress is the reason I had such a severe reaction. Beau's right about the intersection of stress, fear and control. It's a dangerous combination.

I take a breath and try to find the words to explain when Tina comes over.

'Ethan, there's a storm coming in and Ha-Joon says we have to start shooting now to get everything before the weather changes.'

'Are you sure you're okay?' Beau whispers to me, and I nod before checking my watch and turning my attention to Tina.

'Let's go. Tina, can you tell hair and makeup to get ready for touch-ups? I'll do a final wardrobe review and then walk through some of the shots with everyone so we're getting exactly what I want.'

Tina heads back to set, leaving me with Beau.

'That sounds more like the insane person who showed up at my yurt and started ordering me around. Welcome back,' he says.

'Thank you. And to be honest you don't sound anything like the grumpy misanthrope I found in that yurt.' He helps me up and I watch him walk toward the runway. No one has ever taken care of me the way he did. I feel like I'm on top of the world, but it doesn't have anything to do with the height of the building.

Chapter 24

I think Beau might cry. The man I found holding a shotgun in a yurt might actually be broken by a fashion shoot at the top of the Chrysler Building. I thought I would be the one in a pile of tears clinging to a hand railing, but Beau got me past that and now he's the one struggling. He was so patient and kind with me when I was freaking out, so I'm trying to return the favor, but I can't seem to get him to understand how to do what we need him to do.

Ha-Joon is losing it. She's one of the most talented high-fashion photographers working today. She has an unparalleled eye for editorial but her patience is wearing thin. I'm trying to balance helping Beau understand what he needs to do and not having Ha-Joon take the elevator down to the lobby to walk out. Ha-Joon and Chase had a way of working together. Ha-Joon loves taking beautiful photos and Chase loved being beautiful. It worked. But the dynamic between Ha-Joon and Beau for this segment is not working at all and I'm worried Ha-Joon might be getting suspicious.

'Ethan, can I talk to you?' she asks. I wonder if this is the moment when it all blows up. Ha-Joon has an incredible attention to detail but the fact is she could be orbiting the earth in a SpaceX starship and she'd notice something is wrong down here.

'Everyone take ten,' I announce, and Tina starts the clock. Kiara and her team pounce on Beau to fix any flaws in his appearance although I am sure they are hard to find. The issue isn't his appearance.

Ha-Joon and I walk from the runway we constructed on the observation deck to an area just inside the doors where we can be alone. Even though I'm no longer terrified of being outside, it still feels better to be inside.

'Ethan, this is *not* marvelous. What is going on with him?' Ha-Joon asks. 'He isn't acting like himself at all. I've photographed Chase enough to know that something is off. Is he feeling okay?'

I pretend I have no idea what she's talking about. 'What do you mean?' I ask, making sure I sound very sincere.

'I mean he can't find the light. He's not using his eyes at all. His body is at every wrong angle imaginable and he's letting me shoot the side of his face he himself calls "The Forbidden Zone".' Ha-Joon sighs as she rests her camera on her hip.

Beau has been able to handle everything I've thrown at him so far. I never thought modelling would be the thing to break him but he's seriously struggling. So much so that people on set are beginning to wonder what's going on.

'Look at these,' Ha-Joon says, leading me over to the laptop she has connected to her camera. She clicks around, showing me some of what she has shot so far. Each picture is worse than the one before. Beau looks scared, awkward and completely uncomfortable.

I make a face like Lucille Ball tasting sour milk and say, 'Eww.'

'I know, and those are the best we have so far. If I didn't know better I wouldn't even recognize Chase in these shots. It's like he's been replaced by a robot that just looks like him.'

'Ha! Ha! Ha!' I almost shout the laughs at her. 'A robot? You are so funny. That's hysterical. He's not a robot. Not at all. He's a real human. I mean, where would we even plug in a robot?'

'Sure,' Ha-Joon says. She backs away from me a bit. I'm sure she's wondering if I'm a robot.

'Let me talk to him again,' I say in the most lifelike way I know how.

'You'd better hurry. We're losing light.' I look across the sky and see clouds approaching. The forecast predicted a storm in the afternoon so we have to get something we can use soon.

I walk back to set and approach Kiara who is fixing Beau's hair. 'Can I steal him for a minute?' I ask. She looks at me with a worried expression.

'You okay, baby?' she asks and rubs my arm with her hand for comfort.

'Just when I get over one obstacle another one pops up. Promise me that once the parade is over, I can book us a weekend at that spa we love in Ojai.'

'The one with that spearmint and honey massage oil I adore? Oh, baby you must be stressed. I'll even do the couples salt scrub with you.'

The last time we were there I was dying to do their famous salt scrub treatment, but they only had slots open for couples and Kiara wasn't up for it. She has an aversion to grit. I always thought I'd go back there one day as part of a *real* couple. For a second I daydream about the private outdoor Jacuzzis attached to each suite and I get this crazy idea that it would be fun to go with Beau. I shake my head to erase the thought. As soon as the parade is over, he'll be back upstate.

'Beau, can we have a chat?' I ask.

'Ethan, I'm sorry. I know I'm screwing this up.' I walk Beau over to a spot where we can be alone.

'What's going on?' I ask, trying to be calm and gentle. It's my turn to play counselor, I guess.

'Ethan, this is so much harder than I thought it would be.'

'But we took all those pictures back at the apartment for the socials just two weeks ago and those were great.'

Can it be only two weeks ago? It seems impossible. I feel like in some ways I know Beau better than I've ever known his brother despite spending years with him. Chase has been a part of the show since the beginning, but it's never really felt like we were in tandem. Chase was the star, and I did everything else. We had the common goal of making him look like sheer perfection on screen but we came at it from opposite corners. Beau makes me feel like we're doing this together. Sure, it's been a roller coaster but one where we're seated next to each other. With Chase I'm at the back of the ride trying not to get thrown up on.

'Back at the apartment. That was different. This is actual modelling. Before I was doing stuff as you took pictures. It was *stupid* stuff I was doing but at least I was doing something. This is just me and these fancy clothes and I don't know what to do with my hands or my legs or my arms...' Beau wrings his hands as if he is trying to squeeze out all the nervous energy. 'Ha-Joon keeps telling me things to do that don't make any sense.'

'Like what?' I ask.

'Relax my eyes. What does that mean? The eye is not a muscle. You cannot relax an eyeball.' He points a stiff finger at the space above his nose. 'Then she wants me to look one way and then face another. How does that even happen? Am I missing some anatomical secret? The whole time she's telling me, 'Find the light. Find the light.' There is a lampshade thing as big as a cow pointed directly at me. How can I find something that is about to swallow me whole?'

'I get it. It's hard. Sometimes the things that look easy are the exact opposite.' Then I remember what he said about his experience with panic attacks growing up. I wonder if he could be having one. 'Are you okay? Do you think you might be having a panic—'

'I'm fine and no, I'm not having a panic attack. I know what those feel like and this isn't that. But thank you for asking. It's sweet of you.'

I feel my face flush and can't help a smile from appearing across my face. I look down at my feet to make sure he doesn't see it.

'Ha-Joon is annoyed and she has every right to be. I'm just feeling frustrated. Incredibly frustrated and I don't want to mess things up for you,' he says.

Now he's the one being sweet and it makes me melt just a little inside, but I have to ignore it and press on.

'You're doing great,' I say, although that's a big lie so it has almost no impact on him. He always seems to respond when I'm open and honest about things so I figure I might as well give it a try. 'I don't think I've really told you how much I appreciate you doing all this. It's a lot and it's hard and you've been spectacular about it.'

'You really think so?'

'Yes, I do. The fact is I was starting to really hate work, hate the show and everything to do with Chase, and since you've been here I don't totally feel that way. I mean, most of my contempt has been replaced by panic but that's a step in the right direction, isn't it?'

'Only you would think that, Ethan,' Beau says, and he smiles a natural open smile.

'It's the truth,' I say. Two weeks without Chase is like being on hiatus for a year in terms of my nerves. But I'm beginning to realize it isn't just the fact that Chase isn't here to annoy me; it's also the fact that Beau is here to help me. Even though I'm holding on to my job and everything I've built by the tiniest thread, the fact is I haven't felt this engaged with everything for a long time. Part of it is seeing it all through Beau's eyes and part of it is just Beau's eyes.

Then behind me I hear a camera snapping. Ha-Joon has picked up her DSLR camera and started taking pictures.

'That's it,' she says. 'Marvelous. That's what I need in front of the camera.'

'I'm not doing anything. I'm just talking to Ethan,' Beau says.

'Then don't do anything. Your face is relaxed, you're in the light. This is stuff I can use. You two keep talking,' she says, and she leads Beau back to the runway we have set up.

Of course, now I don't know what to say to him but then I ask, 'What were the spices you used in the vegan Wellington? Did you braise the lentils or just do a rapid boil?'

I remember he loved talking about food and I do too. I did want to know more about the secret to those lentils and it seems to be a great question because he starts talking about the food market at the Place d'Aligre in Paris. 'There was this wonderful woman there who sold the most unusual variety of lentils…' He starts talking about this woman and the market and the lentils and he seems to immediately forget that the camera is there. All I have to do is keep talking with him and keep him relaxed and we can clear another obstacle. We start talking about our favorite food markets in Europe and with me out of frame Ha-Joon keeps snapping away, so she must be getting some good stuff, but before I know it, I've forgotten that she's there as well. It just feels like it's me and Beau chatting about the things we both love.

'Marvelous. Marvelous,' Ha-Joon says between camera snaps, and I must agree. It feels marvelous.

Chapter 25

Maria Luisa lives on the opposite end of the earth: the West Village. It takes longer to get to her brownstone on Jane Street from the Upper East Side than it would to fly to DC, but I use the time in the back of the cab to go over some last-minute prep with Beau. After our morning at the Chrysler Building, we spent the afternoon working on some of the food segments, which went surprisingly well. We were able to make some plant-based options including the newly named 'Vegan Vellington' using the same sponsored dough. Most of the camera work was covering close-ups so there was barely an opportunity for anyone to figure out that Beau isn't Chase. Earlier in the week was filled with some publicity events with canned question and answer so it was easy enough to get through. It's surprising how much people believe what they want to believe. Tonight however is different and the stakes are higher. If one of the grips suspects something is off the consequences can be contained. Not so much with Maria Luisa. If she finds out I've been lying to her, the entire network and our loyal viewership the last few weeks, she won't shrug it off.

We arrive at their brownstone. A vibrant coral honey-suckle vine winds around the short brick building creating a dramatic sweep of color. Lee greets us at the door. They are wearing an ivory kaftan and a statement necklace whose statement is 'Look at me! I used to be a doorknob and piece of fencing!'

'Come in, come in. *Kumasta*,' they say. Lee often peppers their sentences with Tagalog.

'Hello,' I say.

Then I hear Beau say, '*Masaya akong nandito ako*.'

My eyes immediately begin to roll back in my head but I catch them so it must look like I'm in a trance. We've been here all of three seconds and Beau is already making everyone suspicious. Lee looks a bit startled but also pleased. They say, 'It's nice to have you here. Let me get someone to help you with your coats.' A hint of confusion lingers in their voice.

I slap Beau on the arm. 'Stop it,' I admonish.

'What? I was just saying to them, "I'm glad I'm here."'

'But you did it in Tagalog. You speak Tagalog?'

'Not fluently but I picked up enough during my travels in Southeast Asia.'

Of course he did. Yet another piece of the Beau Myles mystery puzzle. 'Your brother does not speak Tagalog. He's barely able to conjugate a verb in English so cut it out,' I jab in a sharp whisper.

We enter their game room – modern minimalist decor designed to enhance conversation. Charcoal walls with glossy black trim and various poufs and comfy chairs are scattered throughout. My studio is half the size of this room alone. An elegant mid-century bar has an equally elegant early millennial bartender. 'Can I go get you something to drink?' Beau asks.

'Sure,' I say. 'Something easy like a gin and tonic but make sure the ice goes in first, then the gin and then the tonic. If you put the ice in last it scares the gin. They should rub a lemon peel over the rim but not put the lemon peel in the drink or the lemon oil will overpower the gin. Ask them to skewer the peel and then place it over the glass. Make sure there's no pith on it. And absolutely no lemon carcass in the glass. Thanks.'

'Ethan, that's as easy as nuclear fission. I'll be back,' he says, and I watch him as he walks across the room, smiling and pretending to know the people who are waving to him. So far, so good. No one is screaming at the top of their lungs and pointing at him for being an imposter. Scattered about the room are the glitterati of television media. There are various producers, executives and on-air talent. No one seems to notice that in this evening's performance the role of Chase Myles will be played by Beau Myles. I imagine those little inserts they stick in the Playbill when an understudy is performing scattered about the apartment.

I see the two Jamies and wave. I'm about to go over to them when someone taps me on the shoulder. I turn around.

'Keegan,' I say with a mix of surprise and annoyance. 'What are you doing here?' I pretend I wasn't briefed on his attendance.

'Nice to see you too Ethan,' he says with a short huff. 'Didn't Maria Luisa tell you I'd be here? I'm still waiting for Tina to give me time when I can get Chase alone.' Keegan is like a Disney Villainess somewhere between Ursula and Cruella de Vil. He's wearing red and purple culottes that flow down to his ankles and a black severely fitted vintage marching band jacket with a brooch that looks like a bejeweled bagel from where I'm standing.

'Keegan, this is a social event. Chase is off the clock. I don't really want anything said here to make its way into your article.' I wrinkle my nose playfully, hoping he will think this is closer to friendly banter than a warning.

'Ethan, you have to relax. Seriously. Tonight is only to get background. Everyone says you've been so weird lately. I'm beginning to wonder why.'

Who is everyone? What have people been saying? Of course I've been acting weirdly lately but I don't want him to know that. Keegan looks me up and down. His eyes squint a bit and then he frowns.

'Something is up with the two of you. The investigative reporter in me feels it right here.' He pats his chest with his hand although my hunch is he should have tapped much lower.

'I don't know what you're talking about,' I say. I can feel my armpits sweating. I'll look like a gym teacher by the end of the night at this rate.

'I was looking for Chase on SecretSlam the other night and he was nowhere to be found.' In this moment I'm grateful that Keegan is either hot enough or his standards low enough that he doesn't need to pay for a premium membership. I checked with my upgraded subscription last night and Chase is still somewhere in the desert.

'As I said, we're super busy.'

'You can cut it with the "we" talk. We're alone,' Keegan says. He rolls his eyes and twists his face. When Keegan figured out Chase and I were faking it he agreed to keep it out of the media since it meant he and Chase could continue whatever arrangement they had. I wouldn't call it blackmail but I can't think of another word for it. 'Ethan, you might as well tell me what's going on now because you know I'll find out and when I do…'

'Welcome, welcome,' Lee says, coming over to us and cutting off Keegan. I have no idea how much longer I can keep Keegan neutralized.

'Where are the girls tonight? I hope they'll make an appearance,' I say. I swear those kids belong in some creepy movie about toddlers who use their evil powers to destroy others. I don't just think that because one of them threw up on me at a company holiday party. The younger one has the potential to be a criminal mastermind.

'They're at a sleepover, my little darlings. It's strictly adults tonight.' They put the Jonathan Adler bowl they're holding in front of us. It's filled with tiny pieces of paper. 'Here, pick your team.'

'I thought we were doing a couples Trivial Pursuit.' I've been planning on playing with Beau to help ease any awkwardness.

'Change of plans. Baby Equity found the Trivial Pursuit game and had an accident on it. Whoopsie.' I'm sure that kid has a bigger plot in mind that's beyond anything I can understand. 'We're playing Celebrity and you get to pick your partner from the bowl.' They mix the bowl with their hand and jumble the paper.

Celebrity? I was completely prepared for Trivial Pursuit. Last time Chase thought Charles Dickens wrote *Romeo and Juliet*. All Beau had to do was get everything wrong. But the one thing in the world Chase knows backwards and forwards is who is hot and who is not. Everyone knows he can rattle off the hottest singers and most popular YouTube stars. I do not believe for a moment that Beau can name a single Kardashian.

Keegan pulls a piece of paper out of the bowl. *Please not Beau. Please not Beau.* He slowly unfolds the piece, looks at it, laughs and then opens it so I can see. 'How funny.'

Keegan says. 'I got Chase. Oh, this is going to be fun.' I never got the courage to brief Beau about Keegan. The last thing this is going to be is fun.

I look around the room, scanning to see if there is anyone I should be hoping for or anyone I should wish away. I see the one person I do not want to be with. The one person who can actually make the night worse than it's already going to be. I dig my hand in the bowl. There have to be at least a dozen pieces so there's no chance I will pull her name. I grab, unfold and read the worst possible name I could read. 'Delilah Kaufman!' I say and I suddenly feel her eyes dart across the room and land on me like a sniper through an eyepiece. She sees me. She does not wave. She rolls her eyes and shakes her head. I go to put the piece back in the bowl, hoping for a do-over, but Lee stops me. 'No give-backs,' they say, smiling.

I'm going to be spending this entire night on damage control so I might as well start. I walk over to Delilah. 'Hey, Dee. How have you been?' I ask, all smiles and cheerfulness.

She moves her trademark bouncy blonde hair to the side of her head. 'Don't you, "Hey Dee" me, Ethan. I don't know how I got stuck with you again.' She lets out a frustrated puff of air. Delilah takes her game playing seriously. She may be a beloved actor and game show host but try being her partner in charades at a company picnic and not knowing her one action movie *Do Not Pass Go* and you'll see a different side of 'Darling Dee' as the media calls her. She looks me dead in the eye and says, 'I'm sure that little demon-baby Equity had something to do with it.'

'I know, right? That kid is terrifying. Lee told me...' I hope we can heal the past and bond over our fear of that toddler, but she cuts me off.

'Pfft,' she says and snaps her fingers closed to indicate what I should do with my mouth.

'Got it,' I say, and she walks away to chat with that woman who subs the evening news sometimes. I can't remember her name.

I scan the room and find Beau chatting it up with a popular morning show host and one of the reality housewives known for her tantrums, which I realize could be all of them. I walk directly over to them and when I arrive Beau slides his arm around my waist. He pulls me in tightly and my nerves about the evening suddenly ease. It feels like we are in this together and it's a nice feeling. I never felt that way with Chase. It was always two solos rather than a duet.

'I was thinking Hamptons,' the morning show host says.

'That's been done to death. Have it at my estate in the Berkshires,' the housewife says.

Oh, no. This is exactly what I didn't want to happen. Not like this. Not here and not with them. Tell me they are discussing something other than what I think they're discussing.

'Well, darling, what do you think? I told them it was your decision,' Beau says. He's as cool as a bowl of gazpacho laced with garlic and strychnine.

'What?' I ask in a gale of nervous laughter.

'The wedding, of course,' Housewife says. 'I think a spring wedding is ideal. Everything is so beautiful in Massachusetts, maybe late April.'

'That's very generous and something to think about,' I say, hoping to end the conversation. Months ago Maria Luisa was going on about wanting to do a show featuring a celebrity wedding. She asked me to consider it and I gave a vague answer suggesting it would be impossible. I thought that was the end of it but I was clearly wrong.

'Ethan and I have a lot to talk about. A lot,' Beau says and it's clear I should have been more transparent about some things with Chase, but it's too late now.

'Hi everyone,' Maria Luisa says as she makes her way through the guests. 'Thank you so much for coming,'

All three of us start a chorus of ass-kissing with coos, thank yous and 'You look fabulous. No, you look fabulous.' Beau simply smiles.

'We were just discussing their wedding. Do you think Hamptons or my estate?' Housewife asks.

'Actually, I was thinking Paris,' Maria Luisa says. The small group oohhs and aahhs. 'Mind if I steal him?' she asks, and then she pulls me by the elbow toward the bookcase nook so we can be alone.

'I'm working on a deal with a European network and they are looking for something queer, something romantic, something cool and I pitched them a special reality wedding show featuring a gay style icon and his supportive behind-the-scenes husband.'

'Wow,' I say because I don't know what to say. It's a tremendously horrible idea but I can't say that to Maria Luisa; at least not right now, or ever really.

I figured once I was able to leave the show, Chase and I could have a public breakup. I'd be free of him and there would even be some added publicity for *Myles of Style* as I moved up to the executive suite. A win-win. But adding a reality show to the mix means committing to the fraud at a grander level. Sure, everyone loves to see reality stars break up, but I'd have to actually go through with the planning and the ceremony. I never wanted to let any of it get that far.

'That is quite an idea,' I say since I don't really know what to say.

'Isn't it?' Maria Luisa says, pleased with herself. 'I knew you'd love it. I've already been kicking it around upstairs and everyone is so impressed with your commitment to the network.' That's code for 'Do this and your promotion is in the bag'.

'Well, yes, I'm... ah... committed.' What I am thinking is that I should *be* committed. Some institution in the country where they make the bed with tight hospital corners.

'I think this whole couples-angle is playing well. I have a serious bite for replacing Hairlucinations,' she says. I try not to get too excited since this is supposed to be a social event but I want to jump up and down. I've been so focused on passing off Beau as Chase that I almost forgot about the gaping hole with our sponsors.

'Who?' I ask. I'm hoping it's a company I can work with easily, although with the parade so close it doesn't matter.

'This is a party. I've already talked shop too much, and if Lee overhears they will not be pleased. Let's chat on Monday,' Maria Luisa says. I nod and try to keep my exterior calm. She goes to circulate and I walk back over to Beau who is still chatting with the morning show host and Housewife.

'Here he is,' Beau says as I arrive. 'Here's my *fiancé*.' He zings the word fiancé playfully at me.

Clink. Clink. Clink.

On the other side of the room Lee taps a butter knife against a glass. 'It's time to get started everyone. Find your partners.'

'I thought you'd be my partner,' Beau says in a panic. I look across the room. Delilah looks at me like an assassin.

'So did I but unfortunately you have Keegan. It was out of my control.' I turn my head to Beau. 'Just pretend you know him, okay? You *know* him.' I try to emphasize the word 'know', but it's too late to do much else since Keegan is fast approaching.

Chapter 26

Keegan sidles up to Beau. 'I'm afraid Chase belongs to me for the night,' he says. 'I'll make sure to return him without too many marks. I know you want to keep him spiffy for the live stream and show him off as the dutiful husband in front of all these execs. They don't need to know what we know, do they?'

'No, they don't Keegan. Just remember our deal,' I say.

'Your secret is safe with me.'

I laugh. Keegan laughs. Beau looks scared. Keegan has the audacity to grab Beau's hand and guide him away from me to one of the loveseats in the game room. As soon as I see their hands connect, I notice a pang of jealousy enters my chest. I shoo it away. It must just be nerves, not jealousy. I certainly never cared about Keegan and Chase before. But this is Keegan and Beau, though of course Keegan doesn't know that.

'Sit!' I hear a voice next to me say. Delilah is pointing to a hard-backed chair she has placed next to the comfy couch where she is sitting.

'Don't you want me to sit next to you? On the couch?'

'No,' she says. 'I want you where I can keep an eye on you. When I give clues, I expect you to pay attention.'

'Of course,' I say and swallow hard. America's Sweetheart is terrifying.

Lee makes sure everyone is ready and then announces that we're playing Celebrity. Beau looks at me from across the room. He has no idea what this game is. At least Lee is a stickler for rules and since there are a few new people around they explain it thoroughly, though Beau still looks totally confused. Everyone writes down the names of three famous people and puts them in the bowl. Each team then takes turns describing the person any way they can to get their teammate to guess. It's a game I usually like but tonight not so much.

I take my sheets of paper and write down the easiest names I can think of before popping them in a bowl and praying Beau picks some of them. Usually when we play Celebrity people like to show off how current they are so I decide to go in the opposite direction, hoping it will help Beau fake it. I have George Washington, John F Kennedy and Nixon. You can't go wrong with US presidents. There's no guarantee Beau will pick any of these names but at least it gives me a fighting chance. I look over at Delilah. She's writing down names, looking as serious as a heart attack. This is the same woman who hosts *Dunkin' Funkin'*, a game show that involves contestants dressed as cookies jumping into vats of milk to win prizes. Beau looks stumped.

'I'm totally focused tonight,' I say to Delilah even though I couldn't be more distracted.

Just before it's our turn Delilah says, 'If Drew Barrymore beats me again, I will find out where you live. Do you hear me, Ethan?' She's joking. I think.

Delilah gives the clues and we seem to speed through them.

'Famous ice skater. Male…'

Figure skating is out of my area of knowledge. I'm going through every Olympic opening ceremony I can remember. Then she says, 'First name is the same as my third husband.'

'Nathan,' I say. I know Nathan. 'Nathan Chen.'

'Yes,' Delilah says just as the buzzer goes off. She counts the number we got right and she seems pleased. But then it's Beau's turn and I can see that he's sweating it a bit.

Keegan is giving clues and the first ones are easy. Someone has written 'the Queen of England' and he even gets my George Washington. Then it takes a terrible turn. Keegan pulls out a piece of paper, reads the name and mutters, 'Too easy.' He turns to Beau. 'Your favorite designer.'

Beau's eyes are wide and he has no idea what to say. 'Someone...' is all he can manage to say. Everyone chuckles, probably thinking Chase must be making a joke since he worships Salvatore Ferragamo. Everyone knows this as Chase constantly makes such a big deal of it. He says their names in this affected accent that he thinks is Italian but is more of an Irish brogue.

'Can you be more specific...' Keegan says, thinking he is still pulling their leg.

The time is ticking. The giggles turn to nervous laughter. How could Chase not know who his favorite designer is? I don't see any way out of this. I could escort him out of the room quickly and claim he hit his head this morning and then pray Delilah doesn't have my body buried somewhere in New Jersey for making her forfeit. What are the laws surrounding screaming 'fire!' in a crowded room? It might be a risk I need to take. But then he says, 'Salvatore Fair-and-game-o.'

Now everyone laughs very hard at what they assume to be the mispronunciation of Ferragamo. Lee nods saying they will accept the answer and Keegan moves to the next one and we are out of the clear for the first round. Lee allows everyone a ten-minute break to refresh their drinks and so they and Maria Luisa can FaceTime with their kids.

I race over to Beau and pull him aside. He takes me by the waist and plants a kiss on my cheek. Totally normal for someone to do to their fiancé; not so normal for Chase, but at this point I don't care. I feel his soft lips against my stubble and I struggle to let the feeling stay in my head and not travel further down. I make sure no one is in earshot and ask, 'How did you do that? Do you even know who Salvatore Ferragamo is?'

'Do I look like I live in a cave?'

'Up until last week, yes, you did,' I answer.

'Fair enough. Actually, I've never heard of them, but I then I remembered that Chase has this picture of him outside their store and he has all these bottles of the most awful smelling perfume on his dresser with that name and I just put it all together.'

'That was amazing,' I say and I really mean it. He could have just flubbed or messed it up but he went out of his way to figure out a solution to the problem. Usually I'm the one who has to do that for everyone. Feeling Beau take some of the burden off my shoulders feels wonderful.

Beau's eyes dart to the corner. 'I think your boss is watching us,' he whispers.

'I'm not surprised,' I say without turning around to check. 'She wants to make sure we're in sync.'

'Well then…' He pauses and licks his lips. 'Let's make sure she sees what she wants. Isn't that why I'm here?'

Then he throws his head back with a laugh like I just said the funniest thing in the world. He circles his finger around my face and then gently touches the tip of my nose before kissing it sweetly and covering me with kisses over to my ear.

Suddenly everything falls away, the party, the people, the show, all of it is gone as my heart and mind try to sort out what I'm feeling.

'Beau...' I say his name softly and tentatively.

'Uh-uh. It's Chase,' he says, whispering so close in my ear that the hairs on my neck stand to attention.

Someone taps me on my shoulder and I turn around.

'Sorry you two, I hope I'm not disturbing an intimate moment,' Maria Luisa says. Beau smiles at me, clearly satisfied that his little PDA has gotten the attention we wanted. I snap back to reality although my hand goes to my cheek to feel the lingering sensation of his lips on my face. 'I have some interesting news.'

'What's that?' I ask and drop my hand to my side. Beau immediately grabs it and my heart starts racing. I notice Maria Luisa's eyes drop and she catches our intertwined fingers.

'You two are adorable, really. That's what I've been texting with Alexandra Petras. She's who you will report to if you get my job.'

'Is she?' I ask like I haven't studied the org chart.

'I was telling her about your engagement and she heard about our ideas for a show and...' She pauses for dramatic effect. 'She loves it. And I shouldn't tell you this but what the hell, it's a party, but she said something to the effect of, "Sounds like Ethan is ready to move up." Something like that and Alexandra *never* says stuff like that unless she means it. Never. But that's all I can say.' She mimes zipping her mouth shut.

'Maria Luisa!' Lee says from the other side of the room.

'If they find out I'm having a work conversation I'll be in hot water. You'll cover for me?' she asks, and I nod. She leaves and Beau and I are alone.

'That is amazing news for you, right?'

I'm in a state of shock but I don't know if my mind is still lingering on Beau's lips or Maria Luisa's news about the new sponsor and my new job. Maybe it's all of it. 'Yes,' I answer. 'Yes, yes. This is fantastic news. This is everything I've been wanting.' Again, I'm not sure what the 'this' I am referring to is exactly since it could be the promotion or the kisses, but either way I am giving him an honest answer.

'Congratulations,' he says and kisses me on the cheek. I assume it's for Maria Luisa's benefit but out of the corner of my eye I see that she's deeply engaged in a conversation with Lee, so it's clearly not. But then it hits me. All the stress I've been feeling releases just a bit and it feels great.

'Thank you. Let's celebrate after this,' I say, feeling spontaneous and open to the world. I'm able to push down the fact that Maria Luisa is potentially further complicating my life with Chase. But that's way in the future. Any number of larger disasters can take that one's place. 'I'm taking you to the best, most expensive restaurant in the city. Your choice.'

'You're going to let me pick?' he asks.

'Sure,' I say, knowing that it's not actually my usual way of operating. 'The best meal you can think of. On me. The sky's the limit. Le Bernadine. Bistro Po Po. Anything.' I'm riding an incredible high. No one suspected Beau is

Chase, we might have a new sponsor for the parade and I'm a step closer to getting the promotion I want. Tonight is an exhilarating win and I'm going to enjoy it.

Chapter 27

The first warm night of the summer is making the West Village feel like the center of the universe. We walk down Greenwich Street past bars and restaurants with groups of friends spilling out on to the sidewalk. I can hear different bits of conversations and live music as we stroll. I love when New York is like this; a big party where everyone is invited.

'Do you want me to get a car? I can call ahead and get a reservation. I know that...' I'm about to offer another helpful suggestion when Beau stops me.

'Ethan, I'm in charge for at least the next few hours and I know exactly what I'm doing. The best meal in the city. But first, since we're so close, a quick detour.'

I have no idea where we're going or what we're doing. Usually this would make me tense. Since meeting Beau I've been feeling like I've lost almost all control. I have no idea what's going to happen next or what bump we'll hit with this crazy plan. He's not the first person to allude to the fact that I like to be in control, but I honestly don't have a problem letting other people take the lead. As soon as the thought crosses my mind, I almost laugh out loud at the absurdity. *Of course I do*. He's right. Not knowing what restaurant we're going to walk into makes me uncomfortable.

'Can you at least tell me the neighborhood we're going to? Midtown? Some place further?'

'Ethan, I've got this. Don't worry.'

He puts his hand on my back. Beau's been physically attentive all night. At first it was a bit shocking, but I soon got used to it; in fact, I started to enjoy feeling his hand on my back or shoulder. But that was all part of the charade. We were playing the part of the happy couple and as long as there were people around, that made sense. But now we're alone. There's no one to put on a show for and the sensation of knowing that it's Beau touching me and not Beau playing Chase is quite different. It feels comfortable and exciting at the same time. A strange mix of feelings that I don't understand.

We walk across 8th Avenue near the border of Chelsea and into the winding streets and stunning brownstones of the far West Village. I'm enjoying the relief of not being in charge and he's definitely in a playful mood, so why not let him be the 'producer' of the evening? There are any number of excellent restaurants in this area that would be ideal for a celebration though I'm hoping he picks Marea because I've been dreaming about their sticky huckleberry *mostarda di frutta* drizzling over a scoop of tart prickly pear sorbet lately.

We make a turn on to Perry and he stops. 'Do you need directions? I can check my phone,' I suggest.

'No, it's not that,' he says, looking down the block. 'It's just that… I haven't been back since… I think I'm ready.'

His tone is more serious than it has been since we left the party. We walk down Perry Street and he stops in front of a somewhat new women's jewelry store featuring gold necklaces in organic forms with large stones in the center. The store is closed for the night but there are enough lights on to see that it's super tiny. It might be smaller than my apartment.

'This was it,' he says, standing in front of the window and peering in.

'Was what? Did you sell jewelry?' He probably studied silversmithing at some point.

'This was my restaurant.'

'Oh,' I say, because I really don't know what to say. This is a big deal but I don't want to over-determine his reaction, so I let him take the lead.

'Actually it was an underground ghost kitchen.'

'So no dining room, just deliveries and takeaway,' I say. It's a great location for a ghost kitchen since it's close to so many downtown neighborhoods. Still, I can imagine wealthy hipsters from this part of town could be brutal on social media. 'What kind of food?' I ask, hoping it's an easy enough question.

'Promise you won't laugh?' I nod and then he squints his eyes and says, 'Regional varieties of... pork barbecue.'

I laugh. I can't help it after everything he has put me through with his vegan recipes.

'You promised,' he says, but he's laughing as well. 'I know. I know. Look, I have to confess I still eat meat but I've come to learn the importance of not depending on it. Back when I had this place, it was meat, all day, every day. But it was all mine. Until it wasn't.'

His eyes dart around the place and I can see he's imagining the space as how it once was. It must be so hard to see something you built just disappear. He's such a talented chef.

'Things got screwed up. I screwed it up. I wasn't able to handle it and I lost it. I was too focused on pleasing everyone around me and the foodies and social media instead of cooking the food I wanted. I was trying to impress everybody so I kept taking on more and expanding what we could do and it was too much. I couldn't keep up with all the suppliers and orders and billings and making everyone happy. Then, well...'

He stops. It seems like he was just about to get to the heart of what happened but he wasn't able to make it. I'm quiet. I don't say anything and wait to see where he needs to go with it.

'There was some family stuff that was... not good. It was very not good and I got into some debt I couldn't get out of. I had to downsize my life so I could pay things off and I had to get my head on straight.'

I think about the payment that I had Tina send once he agreed to help me. I didn't really think about how or why he had so much debt but now it all makes sense.

'I'm sorry. Is it hard to see it again?'

'I thought it would be.' He looks through the window of the shop and then takes a step back to see the whole building and the block around it. 'But it's the opposite. It's inspiring. I did it once; I can do it again. This time I know what not to do. Also, with what you're paying me I'll have a clean slate soon enough and that feels amazing. Maybe I can get back in the game, but now I know it has to be about feeding people's bodies and spirits. No more reading reviews and letting strangers decide how I feel about what I make. Tonight is a celebration on multiple levels and we have some very fine dining ahead of us,' he says and we keep walking.

We walk away from the place that must have caused Beau so much stress and heartache and I feel his step is a bit lighter than when we approached. Maybe this is exactly what he needed. It's been a great night but seeing Beau so at peace and thinking about making a new start makes me feel an even higher level of joy.

Chapter 28

After a few more blocks we reach the end of the sidewalk, or at least the Westside highway. We are officially past any type of a neighborhood or even a building. Beyond the throughfare is a small strip of parking lots and abandoned piers. Just beyond that, the Hudson River flows.

'We're almost there,' Beau says.

'That can't be it unless we're eating in the water. The other option is the parking lot on the pier.'

'Exactly,' he says. He points across the highway and I see a small collection of food trucks with some lights strung up between them. 'Did you expect me to want to go to some stuffy dining room and eat some over-priced chicken breast? No thanks. Come on,' he says, and he holds out his hand.

I stare at it.

What am I supposed to do with that? I want to say, 'Put that thing away.' His hand behind my back over my clothes is one thing. I don't know what will happen if we touch, but instead of trying to predict the outcome I just grab it. Immediately the warmth of his hand connects with mine and their synergy generates heat throughout my body. He heads right for a yellow and red truck with a hot dog on it painted to look like a person wearing a hot dog suit. He pauses in front of the truck and says, 'Ethan, I want you to taste a big fat greasy wiener.'

I trip on the pavement. I know he's referring to the food truck in front of us with name 'The Greasy Weiner' painted on it but still to hear him say those words to me makes that part of my anatomy reserved for my filthiest thoughts stand up and take notice.

'What the hell are you doing here? I thought you were living in Maine or some tent.' A woman about our age rolls down a ramp at the back of the truck. She wheels her chair over to us and Beau bends down to give her a tender but fierce hug.

'It's a long story. A long, long story.' Beau looks at me with a smirk instead of a scowl and that makes me feel relieved. 'I wanted to have this guy try the best vegan hot dogs in the country. Ethan, this is Lisa. Lisa and I studied together.'

'Studied together? More like Beau was my private tutor. I didn't come anywhere close to his expertise in food ecology or finance. I barely passed,' she says with a big robust laugh. She has chubby cheeks and a vintage apron with red polka dots tied around her full figure. I like her immediately. She's warm and easy-going and I can see why she and Beau would be friends.

'Beau, before I fix you something, let me show you all the mods I did to the truck to make it accessible.' She rolls up the ramp and Beau follows her as she guides him around the changes she's made to the cooking surfaces and storage areas. I watch from the back entrance.

'I can cook hot dogs for over a hundred or a gourmet meal for two from this thing. And I can do it anywhere in the world,' she says.

'It's amazing,' I say, peering into the truck. I'm truly in awe of the freedom and independence something so portable and so complete can give a person.

'Thanks. I got tired of working at places with kitchens that weren't accessible so I made one myself and then I put it on wheels,' she says, laughing. She has a big personality and it immediately makes me think of Uncle Clams. Now that his ankle is healed he'd love to walk over here with his friends and meet her. She creates what she wants on her terms. I'm not sure a parking lot is my natural habitat but I certainly admire the fact that she doesn't have to worry about making sponsors happy.

Beau hops out of the truck and we both stare up at the menu.

'I've got something special,' Lisa says and heads back into the truck. It's a clear night with the moon as bright as a streetlight. A few couples are walking hand in hand on the edge of the parking lot near the shoreline. Behind us the Manhattan skyline twinkles, making it feel like the Emerald City.

'I love her truck,' I say.

'It's amazing, right? I shouldn't have gone this long without seeing her. I'm beginning to realize what I've been missing.'

'Here you go,' Lisa says and reaches down from the truck to hand us a small shallow box of hot dogs. One has a dark golden mustard and relish. Another is simply served with a chunky artisanal ketchup and one has what looks like a type of slaw made from Japanese daikon.

'Thanks,' Beau says, taking the box.

'Are you here for a while?' Lisa asks.

'At least through Pride,' he says, looking at me and then adds, 'Maybe longer.'

Maybe longer? What does that mean? He's thinking of staying around. Is there something here that makes him want to stay, or is it just the fact that his brother isn't here that makes him more comfortable with the idea?

'Come on,' he says, and we find our way to the bench overlooking the water. A gentle wind rises from the river and should make me shiver but I don't feel cold at all. We sit down and face the river. The aqua patina of the Statue of Liberty glows in the distance and a few blocks up the concrete pedestals that make up Little Island anchor our view. He hands me a wiener. The savory smell of sautéed root vegetables and some kind of earth spice wafts up from the hot dog.

'There's no meat in this?' I ask before putting it in my mouth.

'Nope. Lisa grew up in a family that ran a kosher butcher shop and she stopped eating meat the minute she left home. She can cook anything. I'd drink her leftover poaching water.' I laugh. It's gross but funny, just like him. 'Are you ready?' he asks and he grabs a wiener and holds it up to his mouth. I nod and we both take bites at the same time.

The crunch of the Japanese radish and the tenderness of whatever is in the dog mixes together to make an incredible sensation of textures accompanied by a mix of sweet and savory. 'It's so good,' I say.

Beau is clearly in heaven. His face displays utter joy as he eats. I've spent so much time manufacturing a look of joy on Chase for the cameras that when I see the real thing the difference is palpable.

'I know, right?' he asks, raising his voice just a bit so he can be heard over an eruption of honking horns behind us. He smiles and stuffs another bite of the deliciousness into his mouth but this time he gets a bit of ketchup above his lip. I don't think. I just go to wipe it away. I'm so used to erasing any smudge of imperfection on Chase that I automatically do it. I can't help myself.

Beau gently grabs my hand as I reach for his mouth. 'What are you doing?' His voice is playful and inviting.

'Sorry,' I say. 'It's an immediate reaction. You have a smudge of ketchup on your mouth.' I'm very aware of the fact that he has my hand in his and that technically we are holding hands.

'Ethan, not everything needs to be perfect,' he says, putting his hot dog on the bench next to him but not letting go of my hand.

Not everything needs to be perfect. Before meeting Beau I might have had a tantrum being told this but hearing it from Beau after this incredible evening makes me really listen and hear it. *Not everything needs to be perfect.*

'What would happen if we lived with the mess?' he says, and his other hand reaches for his snack. I can't exactly see what he's doing but I then see his finger rise in front of my face with a glob of ketchup on it.

'What are you doing?' I ask. There might as well be blood on his finger.

'An experiment. I want to see if you can live with thirty seconds of a mess.' He takes his fingers and places a dab of ketchup on my lower lip.

'This is silly,' I say and go to wipe it off. He squeezes my hand gently.

'Just thirty seconds and I promise you'll get a reward.' He starts counting and I wonder if we are both thinking of the same reward. It turns out that not wiping away the mess is harder for me than I thought it would be.

'Fifteen. Fourteen.' Beau keeps counting down and he's still holding my hand. I feel the ketchup drip from my lip to my shirt as our eyes are locked on each other and

I don't care. He squeezes my hand to help me through. I'm wearing a Helmut Lang shirt that will never survive the stain and I don't care. I'm just looking at Beau and he's returning the gaze, really seeing me and I think I'm seeing him for the incredible, unique and intelligent person he is.

'Two, one,' he says and then uses his finger to wipe what's left off my lip. The touch of his finger feels electric. 'Are you ready for your reward?' he asks. By this point we both know what's coming. Delaying it is only making the anticipation greater.

'Uh, huh,' I say, nodding my head and gently moving it to the side indicating that I'm ready for what I hope he is about to do. He angles his head and closes his eyes. This is it. I can't wait a second longer and I go to kiss him. He's surprised. I guess he thought he was going to make the first move but I couldn't wait a second longer. I had to feel his lips against mine in that moment. His mouth moves slowly and gently in sync with me but then he puts his arm around my waist and pulls me tighter, preventing the air from moving between us as our two bodies press up against each other. His mouth begins to open and invite mine in. His kissing is as confident and bold as his personality. I can feel him wanting me and not being shy about it in any way. His lips start traveling around my mouth and kissing the side of my face. Then mine do the same and I feel his rough stubble against them.

'Ethan, Ethan,' he says, and the sound of my name whispered in my ear makes me tremble. My mouth finds its way back to his and we stay this way, pushing closer and deeper toward each other. I let my hand move between our bodies toward his chest and he does the same. His muscular torso is as spectacular as I thought it would be.

I feel his hand wander over my shirt until it finds a hole between the buttons just large enough for his hand. He pushes his hand through the opening, popping one of the buttons. I don't care. I want his hand on me. I want to feel him on my chest. I hold his wrist for a second and then guide it around my body. I let out a moan with the words, 'Yes, yes.'

I pull myself away from him just enough to see him smiling. 'You like that?' he asks. I beam from ear to ear and then nuzzle my head into his chest as I enjoy the sensation for a few seconds before bringing my mouth back to his. We move from kissing to full-on making out. I'm not thinking about the rights and wrongs of what I'm doing and how it will have larger implications tomorrow morning. I'm just thinking about this handsome and incredible guy in front of me.

'Would this be better back at the apartment?' he says in a low growl, moving his mouth down my neck with kisses.

It doesn't take much for my mind to go to a naked sex romp with him back at the apartment. Running toward the front door and ripping each other's clothes off, barely making it to the bed and then exploring each other's tastes and inclinations until we settle on something that makes us both wild with sexual passion. His hand starts to explore below my waist and then he stops. He removes his hand and his body shifts away from me. A sudden wind blows between us.

'Wait,' he says.

'What?' I ask softly. The moment has been so tender and precious but those are also the most fragile.

'You're with my brother. I can't do this. It's wrong. Totally wrong. I wasn't thinking.' He pulls completely away and then sits back. I guess he realized the apartment we would be going back to is his brother's. Beau runs his hands through his hair, shaking his bangs.

'But...' I say, so overcome with desire for the man in front of me I can barely put together the words he is saying.

'You and Chase are a couple. You're engaged. I wasn't thinking,' he repeats.

I could tell him right now that Chase and I aren't really a thing; that it was just a mutually agreeable situation. That we pretended to be together for the cameras, but that there wasn't anything real between us.

'Uhm... no,' I say, at a loss for how to begin.

'Or is that another lie for the camera?' he asks.

Now I'm the one to pull back. Ouch. 'Lie for the camera? Is that how you see me? As a liar?' I shift away from him. I thought he was down with everything. Why would he kiss me and then call me a liar?

'That's not what I meant, Ethan. I just don't know what's real and what's for the camera with you. Half the time I don't think you even know yourself.'

It's so self-righteous of him to say that. He doesn't know me well enough to make these big leaps. A siren from the West Side Highway blares and the bubble around whatever magic we were experiencing bursts. The warmth of his physical affection no longer distracts me from reality. This was a mistake. I wanted it to happen, but I shouldn't have let it. Kissing the brother of the star I created, who I have paid to pose as his twin, is more complicated than I can handle. I'm not ready for this. I get up from the bench.

'Where are you going?' he asks.

'It's been a long night and we should get you back to the apartment before it gets too late.' Our relationship is a professional one and I should not have allowed it to even hint at being anything else.

'All I did was ask you a question about my brother. It's a fair question.'

I guess it is but why bring it up now in the middle of a make out session after feeling so close to each other? 'You didn't just ask me a question. You also called me a liar and I don't like that. Yes, I'm not being completely honest about some things on the show and things related to the show.' I take out my phone and start searching for a ride back. What was I thinking? That I was going to hop in a food truck with this guy and give up everything I've worked so hard for? The parade is less than two weeks away. As soon as the last float finishes he's going to be out of here and back to Stark or someplace else. He'll finish his obligation and walk out. That's fine. That's the deal. I've handled people walking out before. Better not to make it messier than it needs to be. There is some truth in what he's saying but that only makes me want to run away faster.

'Let's go,' I say, walking away from Beau. I don't even check to see if he's behind me.

Beau catches up to me. 'Ethan, I'm sorry.'

'For what? You didn't do anything wrong. Beau, you're a nice guy. I get that. You're a nice, honest guy who would never do anything to hurt someone else and even though your brother is, well, your brother, you don't want to mess things up for him, and the truth is Chase and I are so tangled up I don't know if we will ever be free of one another.'

He thinks I'm engaged to his brother. Instead of telling him the truth I decide to do the opposite, prophylactically.

As long as he *believes* I'm engaged to Chase I don't have to worry about getting too close. I don't have to repeat the fib, but I don't have to correct him. I stare down at my phone as I enter the details to get us out of here. I make sure I don't look at him since I know that if I see his eyes I might change my mind.

'Ethan, I have to tell you something,' he says, and I finally surrender and look up from my phone. His face looks serious. His usual confidence and joy are definitely missing at the moment. I walk away toward the edge of a parking lot when I see a car enter that fits the description from the app.

'This is our ride,' I say as I open the door. I'm not thinking, I'm not feeling. I'm just moving forward. It's the thing I'm best at and I need all my talents right now. I take out my phone and pretend I'm going through some tasks to avoid talking to Beau. All I'm thinking about is what he wants to tell me. I'm too angry, hurt and confused to even ask him what he thinks I need to know. We pull up to the apartment and Beau begins to get out of the car but instead of going inside he comes around to my side and knocks on the window. I roll it down.

'What you said before about me being a nice guy. It's not true. It's not true at all,' he says and then moves away from the car. As we move down the block I look out the back window and I see Beau. He's watching me drive away and even though he gets further away with each second, I can feel his eyes on me.

Chapter 29

No one misses Maria Luisa's mid-month programming one-on-ones. Every producer of every show on her team makes it no matter what. Patrice, who produces a popular dating show, was in a car accident once the weekend before and she showed up to her one-on-one in a partial body cast. Missing the meeting is not an option.

My body is waiting outside Maria Luisa's office but my mind is not. I'm thinking about Beau and that kiss at the pier. What if we hadn't stopped? What if I was able to explain that Chase isn't my boyfriend or even worse, my fiancé? What if I told Beau that everything with Chase is fake but everything with him pretending to be fake is starting to feel real? My brain might explode. I need a pad and pencil to keep straight who is what and what is real. Less than a week and a half until Pride and then the show will be on hiatus and my life can go back to normal. Good lord, I'm getting good at lying to myself.

My phone vibrates and I look down and see it's Chase. What does he want? I react mindlessly and then I realize it's actually Chase. It's not Beau as Chase. It's Chase as Chase. It's not an Abu Dhabi exchange but Chase's actual number. I checked his location this morning, so I know he isn't back in New York. My heart sinks to my stomach. I leap up and Beverly scolds me with her eyes.

'Doctor's office. Test results. Be right back,' I say, holding my finger up to her. I cough quickly to add texture to my fib, then run out to the stairwell and answer.

'Hello, Ethan, this is Beau,' a falsely deep voice says. This idiot thinks he can make me think he's Beau.

'Chase, I know it's you. I see your number.'

'Well, good for you,' he says, his normal whine returning. 'You think you're so smart getting my brother to be me. You think you're fooling everyone. You're the one being fooled.'

'What are you talking about?' I whisper into the phone.

'Everyone thinks my brother is such a nice guy. Ha! What a joke,' Chase says bitterly. What does he mean by that? Is this what Beau was talking about at the car window? I haven't had the courage to ask. Every layer I peel back on Beau only reveals more integrity. I find it hard to believe my gut is wrong about him and considering who I'm talking to right now, I'll go with my instincts.

'Chase, why are you calling me?' I ask. I don't want him causing any more problems. 'I thought you were embarking on a new career in the cinema.'

'Wrong again. I'm going to be in a movie. One more callback at the producer's hotel suite and the part is mine.' I don't want to know any of the details although there is no telling how much trouble he could get into.

'Chase, seriously, are you okay? Are you safe?' I ask. I hate him the way I hate white after Labor Day, but I don't want him hurt in anyway. He's not in a place known for their pioneering efforts in LGBTQ rights and a callback at a hotel is a red flag. Not to mention I've been feeling guilty about not treating him better before he left. 'Be careful,' I say.

'Oh, the irony! You, worrying about me!' I'm about to correct him on his use of irony but I think he's pretty close. 'If I didn't have to get my anus bleached tomorrow' – I wince – 'I'd fly back to New York and show you who's really fooling who.'

'Chase. No. Don't you dare. Stay where you are. For now, at least.' What am I saying? I could have Chase back here in a day and everything could go back to the way it was. I'd have my star and my promotion wouldn't be hanging by a thread.

'You think you've got it made with golden boy standing in for me. I'm the real deal. He's the real fake. Don't think you're going to get away with this.'

'Chase. Chase,' I yell into the phone but it's too late. He's hung up. I put my hand on the wall to steady myself and then take a seat on a step in the stairwell. Without thinking my hand grabs the antique case where I keep my antacids. I open it, but it's empty.

I want to scream but the sound would echo down to the ground. How dare he? I'm appalled by Chase's behavior but I'm more disturbed by his comments about Beau. What did he mean? What am I missing?

I run my hands over my hair and then shake them out. I'm sure Maria Luisa is waiting for me. I head back to Beverly's desk. She doesn't speak. She points to the open door. In my head I delete my conversation with Chase and shift gears. I don't have any other choice.

Beverly shuttles me into the meeting. Maria Luisa's suit is deepest black with a high-waisted skirt. Very Prada-esque. It's new so I haven't given it a name yet. She's with a man in a non-ironic cowboy hat who takes it off to nod his head and reveal a non-ironic mullet.

'Ethan, please meet Buck Kerr.' I think I almost recognize the guy. He has narrow shoulders, a pinched face and a bulbous midsection with a belt buckle so big you could eat lunch off it.

'How do you do?' he says and we all take a seat at the table.

'The word for the day is synergies,' Maria Luisa says. As soon as she says the word I think about my lips on Beau's. That's exactly what that felt like: a synergy. I rub my eyes quickly, hoping to shake the thought of him.

'We hope we can find some great synergies here with someone we're welcoming to our constantly growing, streaming family.' Now that is a word I truly hate hearing in this context. Family. Mutual exploitation of sponsors and programs is not a family.

'Happy to meet so many of you interesting creative types here at this network.' His voice has a drawl to it that makes him sound like Yosemite Sam on a Bugs Bunny cartoon. 'Oh, and happy to meet and sit down with gays. Happy to. Very happy.' He has rehearsed this and rehearsed it poorly. Where do I recognize this guy from? Then it hits me. No. It can't be. 'Beefy Boy has been getting some bad press. Some very bad press,' he says.

I don't say anything. I don't know how I can be in the same room as this human. He is vile. His fast-food empire is notorious for spending millions of dollars opposing gay marriage and holding back equality. He uses the term 'family values' as a dog whistle to mean gays, and anyone who doesn't fit his narrow definition of family isn't allowed. It's hard to avoid their commercials or seeing their slogan 'Tradition tastes better.' I make eye contact with Maria Luisa who must sense that I am about to walk out.

'Ethan, I know this has many complications.' Maria Luisa does not know the meaning of the word complications. I just had a conversation in the stairwell with the man she thinks is going to be on a float while I'm trying not to kiss the brother pretending to be him. That's a complication. 'But Buck has come here to make changes and I think we can listen to him. There is a backside gain and I want you to hear it through. It's important to think about the network as a whole.'

If she thinks there's a reason to listen to this person then there must be something. I trust Maria Luisa. She's worked hard to create inclusive programming and I have to believe that she knows what she's doing. *Maria Luisa is a definitely a good witch.* Buck explains that he's looking to become a major sponsor for *Myles of Style*. In theory this is great. In reality it's like Lucifer is sitting across from me with a fiddle.

'I can't imagine our viewers are going to put up with a sponsor that doesn't align with our values,' I say as politely as possible, which is like spitting on someone politely.

'But we do. I'm trying to explain that we're changing. Maria Luisa knows that we are. I made it clear before she even opened the door.' I'm glad to know this since I respect her so much. 'We're even launching an LGBTQ Onion Ring this summer. Did you mention that gay onion thing?'

'Oh right,' Maria Luisa says. 'They're planning on adding a gay onion ring to the menu. Super excited about that. Can't wait to try it.' I know for a fact Maria Luisa hasn't eaten a piece of fried food in almost a decade, but the words flow out of her mouth with a tone of authenticity. Of course, once I'm in her position I'll be the one with the words flowing out of my mouth. She allows me to have more snark than most bosses would but once I'm in charge I won't have that latitude.

And what the hell is a gay onion? All I can picture is some hideous stack of fried heart attack with a small rainbow flag stuck in it. I don't pretend that our show is about activism but I'm not going to promote a sponsor that doesn't align with our values just because they've created a gay side dish.

'I'm afraid I don't see how we could make this work,' I say. I am about to give a speech that would make Julia Sugarbaker proud when Maria Luisa stops me.

'Ethan, Beefy Boy wants to replace Hairlucinations.'

'That's correct,' Buck says. 'We want to see Chase represent Beefy Boy at your Pride party stuff.'

'It's not a party. It's a celebration of...' I'm about to repeat the words Beau said to me when he first arrived.

Maria Luisa steps in. 'They've agreed to sponsor our float for the *Myles of Style* live stream. Isn't that great?'

The two of them keep pitching me the idea and each new detail is worse than the one before. A Beefy Boy branded Speedo? An onion ring toss-off? No; just no.

'I believe in getting right to the point. Ethan,' Bucks says. 'I know Beefy Boy has made some controversial statements, but we underestimated the potential buying power of people like you. There's a lot of disposable income there.' He makes some other empty promises, tells us he has to get on a jet to his next meeting and leaves. I'm alone with Maria Luisa and we wait for the code from Beverly that Buck is gone.

'I know. It's ridiculous. I know,' Maria Luisa starts. She disparages the sponsor but in the end we do what they say. 'I really struggled with even entertaining the idea but they bring a lot of money to the table and we can't ignore that. We need to make up for the Hairlucination loss.'

'I see,' is all I say.

'Our hands are tied, really. I have to answer to the people above me and they have a board and they have shareholders. If I had a choice I would tell him to go back to Arizona and screw off.'

'Beefy Boy is from Nevada,' I remind her.

'Then Nevada or wherever but the fact is he's bringing in a tremendous amount of money across the network. If we want to have a seat at the table for diversity programming, we have to bring in the revenue the way every other division does. I hate making decisions like this. But with this money we could reach more people in the community and have even more diverse programming.'

'What about our viewers? Our followers? They won't be happy.'

'I know, they'll make a fuss online but you're in a unique position to "weather the storm", shall we say.'

'I don't follow,' I say, my arms folded in front of my chest.

'Let me speak frankly. You are a gay man...' she starts.

'So I've been told.'

'You are an out gay man about to marry another man. I'm just an executive. Chase is out front with you next to him. If viewers see that your show and someone like you can support Beefy Boy then...' She sways her head from side to side.

Someone like me? The phrase rings in my ears. I'm beginning to feel less like I am *me* and more that I am *someone like me* and those two things are totally different. Is Maria Luisa more concerned about who I appear to be than who I am? As soon as the question forms in my mind

I realize that it's not really a question for her. It's a question for me. I've been so driven by ambition and moving up that I've become a stereotype of myself and I'm beginning not to like it. I know I'm gay. I'm gay all day, every day, but I don't like being forced to have my identity take center stage over my personhood.

'Look, Ethan…' Maria Luisa gets up from the table and walks to the window and stares out of it for a few seconds. She turns back to me. 'I don't know how to say this but if we don't play with Beefy Boy, it will look bad. I'd hate to see people, shall we say, undo decisions that may have already been made based on your perceived commitment.'

I remain silent.

'This is not a partner I would have chosen in a million years. I get that it's not a perfect match but they're trying to change and we need a new sponsor to replace the one who left. So we have to find a way to live with this.'

I can't even imagine how I'll be able to ride on a float sponsored by Beefy Boy. I think about all the times I've been in the parade over the years. Usually I've got the Giblet Mobile in low gear as my uncle and his friends wave to their adoring fans. Am I really trading giblets for a gravy train? Maybe I'm having my own Hairlucination.

Chapter 30

'Is there enough ice in the cooler? Do you have the ferry tickets? Does Amnesia know the arrival time for the ferry we'll be on?'

'Yes, yes and yes,' I say. I have answered almost a thousand questions since we picked up Uncle Clams this morning. When I figured out I could combine our annual trip to Fire Island with some on location shoots for the show I thought it was a great idea. Of course that was before Chase ran off, before Beau took his place and before my fake relationship with Chase became an almost real relationship with Beau. Before I agreed to have a notorious anti-equality corporation sponsor our Pride float.

Clams will stay with Amnesia in the owner's suite of the Starlight and I have one room booked for Beau and a separate room on the other side of the hotel booked for me. The past week I've managed to keep my distance from Beau but it hasn't been easy. On the outside I've been able to explain that we need to keep things professional and cordial. On the inside I'm a knot of stress and confusion.

What did Beau mean when he said he wasn't as good a person as I have been led to believe? All week I've thought about finally asking him what he meant but it's so hard for me to come right out with the question. I'm always worried about the consequences of tearing down the walls between myself and other people. That's why I work so hard to make sure those walls are spectacularly decorated. Something about Beau makes me think it's time for a demolition renovation. And I think that something has to do with how it felt to have his lips on mine and his body pressed against me that night near the Hudson.

Beau, of course, has been unflappable, continuing on like our lip lock didn't even happen – friendly but professional. I've tried to do the same. Maybe he regrets revealing too much and that final comment in the car. Still, when we went over details for the parade I conveniently forgot to mention that we now have Beefy Boy as a sponsor. I also never cleared up the fact that his brother and I are not actually engaged in any real way. As long as I have that wall up, I think I can make it to the literal finish line of the parade.

I take out my phone and discreetly check the SecretSlam app. Chase is still somewhere in the Middle East. At this point I hope he stays in the desert.

I close my eyes and let the salt air fill my lungs. The wind is always strong crossing the water like it's blowing away all your cares and stress. For decades Fire Island has been a sanctuary for queer people where they can forget about the real world among like-minded people. There's nothing I can do about any of my problems this weekend so I decide to focus on work and leave my concerns back on the mainland. I try to let the wind push everything away although we'd need to be crossing in a category-five hurricane to have it truly erase all my worries.

I wanted to shoot a few segments here to explain to our crossover audience the importance of this place in our community. My cousin Sheila refuses to step foot out here since she thinks it's just one big orgy. The Meat Rack certainly can be one but the communities on either side of that preserved grove are just regular beach towns that have the fabulousness turned up to an eleven. People are shocked to find out I prefer the coziness of Cherry Grove to the glossiness of The Pines. It shocks me too but I first came to Fire Island with Uncle Clams and he took me to Cherry Grove so that's what I prefer. It's hard to get away from your roots.

As the ferry approaches the dock, The Starlight Inn appears on the horizon with its rainbow flags flapping wildly in the breeze and all the bizarre jigsaw puzzle pieces of the eclectic architecture blending together under the bright sunlight. The inn looks like a gay man's idea of what a gothic mansion might look like if it were put together between disco naps.

'How is it that you've never been to Fire Island before?' Clams asks Beau over the whirl of the ferry's engine.

'I was working pretty hard when I was in New York. Restaurants don't give you a lot of time off and when they do you pretty much need to recover.'

I think about the hole in the wall where he had his ghost restaurant and how hard he worked to keep it open as long as he did. It must have been challenging to see it again. I wish I could tell him how much it meant to me that he shared all that.

'Oh, restaurants are hard,' Clams says. 'Amnesia had a whole cafe built overlooking the bay on the south side of the hotel and she could only keep it open one summer, maybe two. Too much work. She converted it into a gym more or less.'

'Please,' I chime in. 'Converted? There's a weight bench next to an industrial stove.'

Clams takes off his sunglasses just to roll his eyes at me. 'Beau, you make sure you get as much time as you need on the beach and in the waves. Just soak it all in since it's your first time,' Uncle Clams says. 'Did I mention the beaches are clothing-optional?'

'Yes, Uncle Clams. Like a hundred times. We're only here through the weekend. That's it. We have to get back to the city on Monday to prepare for the parade. This isn't a vacation for him. Or for me,' I say, taking a second to look up from my phone.

'You can't work every hour of every day,' Clams says.

'You can if you want a big promotion,' I say.

Clams sighs. 'He wasn't always like this, Beau.'

'Oh, really, what was he like?' Beau asks.

'Land ho!' I say in an attempt to detour any trip down memory lane. I can see the dock and The Ice Palace nightclub where they say Disco was born or at least spread its wings. Amnesia is waving her arms wildly as we approach. She's wearing a bright daffodil yellow kaftan trimmed with matching feathers.

'My darlins, my darlins. How y'all doing?' she coos as we disembark. Amnesia has one of the thickest Southern accents I've ever heard despite the fact that she was born in Istanbul and spent most of her adult life in Secaucus, New Jersey. She hugs Uncle Clams and the embrace makes them both tear up a bit. 'I'm so glad you're here. Ethan, did you know your uncle arrived in this country by boat as well?' She pauses for dramatic effect and then says, '*The Mayflower*.'

'Oh, Milk of Amnesia, sweetheart, I'm so glad you could take a break from the reception desk at the Starlight to meet us. Do you have someone else giving the blowjobs or are they just giving out rainchecks until you get back?'

'Let's save some of the shade for later,' I say, interrupting them. They could read each other for days on end. It's how they show they love each other.

'Give your Auntie Amnesia a hug,' Amnesia says, and I embrace her. I've known Amnesia since I was a kid. She bought me my first Easy-Bake Oven and taught me how to zest a lemon properly. Amnesia turns to Beau and looks him up and down and then says, 'Come here, young man. I want you to hear this.'

Beau bends down so his face is right next to hers. 'Have you ever considered running away with a sixty-eight-year-old non-binary drag queen?'

Beau doesn't miss a beat. 'Not until this very moment.'

Amnesia lets out a cackle.

'I told you this one is a *vast* improvement,' Clams says to Amnesia.

'Clams, did you tell…' I start.

'Oh please, Amnesia is family and you know it. She burped you when you were a baby and you threw up on her aqua hostess gown.'

'I hated that dress. Good choice. Even as an infant you had exquisite taste,' Amnesia says. The compliment, although absurd, makes me smile.

Amnesia pats the passenger seat of the golf cart she drove here from the hotel. 'Put that amazing ass right there. You're sitting next to me,' she says to Beau. 'Clams and Ethan, sit wherever you want.'

Beau does as he's told and we take the golf cart over the bumpy wooden boardwalk to The Starlight Inn. Fire Island is barely more than a sandbar between the Atlantic Ocean and the Great South Bay of Long Island. Decades ago Amnesia built the Starlight with her lover – that was the preferred language of the time – a wealthy but closeted banker who only stayed with her one month every year, each summer. The other eleven months of the year he was with his wife and kids somewhere outside of Boston. The banker guy passed away more than a decade ago so Amnesia runs the Starlight on her own. The entrance is through a small ornate passageway adorned with hanging baskets overflowing with yellow flowers. There are so many miniature fountains that it sounds like it's raining.

'Hey, Marco,' I say to the shirtless man behind the desk. I don't think I've ever seen him in anything other than a pair of cut-off jeans. He's been helping Amnesia with the place the past few seasons. Amnesia couldn't really operate it on her own.

'Hi Ethan,' Marco says with a big smile and then his lips even out quickly as he says, 'Chase.' Chase and Marco had a fling that ended badly. I tried to warn Marco but he wouldn't listen. Amnesia and Uncle Clams look at each other like they are water balloons about to burst hearing Beau being called Chase. I give them each a sharp look.

'Having a good summer, Marco?' I ask quickly so they won't blow Beau's cover.

'It's been great. Perfect weather. I'm going to really miss it here,' he says.

'Can you believe it? Leaving the glory and beauty of the Starlight for that dump in England,' Amnesia says.

'I'm sure I'll regret it,' Marco says.

'Where are you going?' I ask. I know Marco was only working at the hotel until he figured out what he wanted to do next.

'Oxford. I got a scholarship. I leave at the end of the summer.'

'A waste of time if you ask me. What can they teach him you can't learn here? I don't know,' Amnesia says and I'm sure she believes what's she's saying.

'Are our rooms ready?' I ask, hoping it will be enough to distract Amnesia from putting Marco on the spot.

'Yes, you're in the Sunflower room and Chase is in Purple Passion,' Marco says.

'I thought you said the Sunflower room had a leak, Amnesia,' Clams says, pointing his words at her.

'I did? Oh right. I did. Terrible leak. Pipe burst just the other day.' Amnesia waves her hands around wildly as she talks.

'That's horrible. Such a shame,' Uncle Clams says, hamming up his performance.

'You two are both in the Purple Passion room.' Amnesia holds up a key with a purple tassel on it. I know that room only has one queen bed.

'What about the Blue Dahlia or the Green Mountain rooms?' I ask, scrambling. 'Are either of those available? I thought I made it clear we wanted two rooms.'

'I'm afraid we're all booked,' Marco says with a grimace. At least hearing it from Marco I believe it. 'Let me go get some extra towels for you, Ethan.' He makes it clear the towels are for me and not for the man he thinks is Chase.

'The Purple Passion is around the other side of the pool, just up the short staircase. Wonderful view from the terrace. Very private. You can't hear any sounds coming out of it,' Uncle Clams says.

'Especially sounds that accompany an unbridled night of lovemaking,' Amnesia says. She snaps open her yellow bedazzled fan and moves it around her face dramatically.

'Thanks for the tip. I know where it is,' I say dryly. 'We are here to work. I have a crew arriving on the first ferry tomorrow morning. We'll be getting footage all weekend.'

'Well, not all weekend. Don't forget The Giblet Triplets are performing tomorrow night at Tea,' Amnesia says.

'Who are The Giblet Triplets?' Beau asks and as soon as he does I know he's in for it. Uncle Clams pretends to hyperventilate and Amnesia stumbles around like she's going to faint.

'Dear boy, have you been living under a rock?' Amnesia asks.

'As a matter of fact I have more or less.'

'Well, that was one lucky rock,' Amnesia says in her best Mae West. This makes Beau laugh.

'The Giblet Triplets is the name held by three of the most internationally ignored drag queens in the world. Milk of Amnesia, Joan of Arse and I, Clams Casino. Joan is coming in tomorrow so we can rehearse before the show.'

'Not that we need it,' Amnesia says.

'Be warned,' I say. 'If you think these two are a handful wait until all three of them are together. It's like a small storm of sequins and rude jokes.'

'Is that why you have forsaken us?' Amnesia asks. I assume she is referring to the fact that I'm unable to drive them in the parade this year.

'I have not forsaken you. You know I'd love to drive the convertible with the Giblets but I have to work. We have to work. Anyway, you only need me because you don't know anyone else who can drive a stick shift.'

'We've driven that car all over this country. I'll have you know Amnesia can drive a stick shift.'

'Let me clarify. You don't know anyone who can drive a stick shift and doesn't have cataracts. Kiara is learning to drive stick as we speak. I think she had another lesson.'

'How's it going?' Amnesia asks.

'Fine,' I say. I don't tell them that her last lesson went so poorly the teacher cried.

'But you know how temperamental that car is,' Clams says.

'You'll be fine,' I say.

'What about you?' Amnesia asks. 'I bet you know your way around a crank shaft.'

Before Beau can answer I jump in. 'He's working with me that day.'

'Honestly, your generation has a terrible work ethic. You do too much of it. No excuses. I expect you both at the annual performance of The Giblet Triplets,' Uncle Clams says.

'I wouldn't miss it for the world,' Beau says. They both squeal with joy and we head up to our room.

Chapter 31

We walk across the pool area and a number of people recognize Beau and think he's Chase. When this first started, I thought this was a sign that everything was working to plan but now I can't help thinking about the impact this has on Beau. I want to stop people and tell them that he isn't his brother at all. He's so much more than Chase ever could be. Still, Beau doesn't seem to mind. He smiles and lets people take pictures. With Chase it's the attention that gets him off. Beau likes making a connection and the difference is palpable.

I open the door to the room and, as I remember, it's a purple paisley fantasy of clashing prints and mismatched fabrics with one queen bed smack dab in the middle. And a mirror over that. *Oh boy.*

'I'm sorry about the sleeping arrangements,' I say.

'I'm not. This place is fantastic and this room is something else,' Beau says and he starts peeking around, taking in the details. He's avoiding the bed issue and I can get on board with that.

'When I first came here during college I thought the entire place was so tacky. Uncle Clams was doing his show and I'd spend a week or so helping Amnesia. I'd beg her to let me re-do the rooms, but after coming here year after year I've grown to love the charm, though it could certainly use a refresh.' I open the window facing the bay and a cool breeze makes the sheer lavender curtains billow.

'It's very different from your aesthetic on the show,' he says, gesturing to a ceramic lamp in the shape of a Grecian statue.

'I know but it all fits here. I mean if I was in charge I'd make it all more modern. I'd keep the kitsch sensibility but I'd integrate it with something cleaner and sleeker. Mid-century, of course, but nothing too nautical. I'd get Belgian linen spa towels for every room and have plenty of extras rolled and stuffed into hand-woven baskets by the pool. I'd change the plantings so that they bloomed in sequence throughout the summer and I'd reopen the cafe that overlooks the bay with a great menu that was indulgent but simple.'

'Sounds like you've given this a lot of thought,' he says.

I used to think about it all the time. How much fun it would be to own a hotel. I still think about it when I'm stressed. I like to imagine the things I would keep exactly the same and how I would update other things. Guests coming from the ferry and making them feel welcome and cared for during their stay. Making them feel safe.

'I have,' I say. 'When I was a kid I wanted a dollhouse to play with and my mother, bless her heart, bought me a used handmade one that I immediately began construction on. I turned it into the Sparkle Plenty Inn, a lavish hotel where everyone is welcome including a few horse couples since I had a ton of My Pretty Ponies. I was obsessed with renovation shows and I knocked down walls and painted the ceilings in the little building. Eventually the entire thing came crashing down. As my mother suspected. Nothing was done to code.'

'You were really a creative kid,' he says.

'I guess so,' I say.

'Do you miss it?' he asks, and my immediate impulse is to lash out and tell him that I'm still creative. I am in some ways but not in the way I was as a child. He sees that most of my life is dealing with business and I think I'm beginning to see that too. What I do now is more about managing things and less about creativity. There is a satisfaction in that but it's not the same thing.

I'm about to answer Beau when my phone buzzes. I look at it and see a bunch of notifications I've missed. The most recent from Maria Luisa and the subject is Beefy Boy. I need to tell Beau that they'll be sponsoring the float he'll be riding on at Pride, but this weekend is not the moment.

'I better answer these,' I say to Beau instead of answering his question.

'I've got a better idea,' he says, and he pulls back the sheer curtains to open the sliding door for the terrace. The sun is sinking lower into the horizon with just enough peachy light to bathe everything in a gentle glow.

'Join me out here. This is the absolute best time to do yoga.' He grabs two towels from the shelf next to bathroom and lays them out.

'I can't. I haven't done yoga in years. And I have all these texts. And...' I stop because I've run out of excuses and the desire to make them. Beau and I haven't been alone since that fateful night and the fact is I miss it. I miss sharing space with him and feeling close. What's wrong with a few yoga poses? I look out toward the terrace and the atmosphere is heavenly. Without saying anything, I silence my phone and throw it on the bed. I walk outside, take off my shirt and stand on the edge of the towel just as Beau is positioned.

The sun eases into the water making the sky a melted popsicle of orange and purple. I can hear the waves gently lapping against the shore. Each minute moves me further away from my stress. Soon the rest of the world fades as we move through the poses together. I'm able to forget everything and follow Beau and just focus on the light, the air and the feeling of the moment.

'Knock, knock,' I hear Amnesia shout from the other side of the door.

'We don't want to catch the two of you indisposed,' Clams says.

I've lost track of time. I'm not sure how long we've been on the terrace. I throw Beau his shirt and grab mine and pull it on. I don't want to give them any ideas. I open the door and the two of them have their hands over their eyes.

'You can open your eyes. Nothing indecent going on here,' I say.

'Well, not yet,' Beau says, coming in from the terrace. He has not put on his shirt.

'Please don't encourage them.'

'You two are certainly sweaty for being so innocent,' Clams says, walking into the room.

'We were doing yoga on the terrace,' Beau says as he finally puts his shirt on.

'Don't let us stop you,' Amnesia says. 'No really. I mean don't put your shirt back on. You're right, Clams. This one is so much hotter than the other one. You can feel it.' Her shoulders shake like she's gotten a chill.

'The two of you remember that this little switcheroo is a secret. Family only,' I admonish them.

'Speaking of family. We're having our family dinner tonight at our place.' Amnesia turns to Beau. 'It's a

253

tradition. I make dinner the first night. I use a secret recipe but I'm known for my loose lips so you might get lucky.' She runs her tongue over her teeth and I want to die from embarrassment. 'Just get undressed and come on down.'

'She means dressed,' I correct.

'Do I?' Amnesia says and she and Clams head down.

I make sure they're in earshot and say loudly. 'I'm sorry about those two.' I can hear them laughing and making a fuss as they walk away.

'They're like a car radio, you know. It's easy to turn their volume up or down. I'm used to it so it barely registers with me but if they're offending you or making you uncomfortable in any way...'

'Quite the opposite,' he says 'I like it. They're a riot. I can see where you get your wicked sense of humor from.' He heads to the bathroom and turns on the shower. I think about getting my phone and replying to some emails but instead I grab a chair and sit on the terrace watching the lights twinkle across the sky. I can't help smiling over Beau's comment. He really pays attention to the people around him and I'm feeling lucky to be in his orbit.

–

Dinner is fabulous. All four of us love food and love to cook. Amnesia prepares so many dishes I can't imagine there's a plate left in her entire kitchen. She always makes a table full of *mezes*. Her background is Armenian but she grew up in Turkey. Beau is fascinated by each dish. He wants to know how the grape leaves are prepared for the *dolma* and if the pine nut and rice stuffing ever uses preserved lemons. He enthusiastically dips the lavash in the eggplant ragout and can't get enough of the expertly prepared chickpea pate called *topik*. I've eaten these foods hundreds of times so for me this is as close to a home-cooked meal as I get. Amnesia loves the attention from Beau. He is sweet and thoughtful. He asks a ton of questions but is never pushy or overbearing. He's genuinely curious about the culture and the food. He follows Amnesia into the kitchen so she can show him how a Turkish coffee should be made.

As soon as I'm alone with Clams I grab my phone. Not that I have any intention of responding to work emails. I don't. I just want to ignore the line of questioning that he's about to throw at me.

'Ethan, what are you waiting for? Do you want an engraved invitation to jump that man's body? He's charming, intelligent and he laughs at Amnesia's awful jokes. What more could you want?'

'Uncle Clams, please. He's technically an employee of mine.'

'I bet you have a list of reasons from here to the ferry terminal why you shouldn't do it. But there's only one reason you should do it.'

'What reason would that be?' I ask.

'That you might like him. Why not give it a try? It's been ages since you've had a real boyfriend and please, we all know the only reason you pretend to be with Chase is for that dumb show. You've never had a romantic thought about that department store mannequin in your entire life.'

'Why are you suddenly so down on the show? You were the one who encouraged me to pursue the first season.' I was nervous about doing it and Uncle Clams was my biggest cheerleader. He helped me design the entire show bible when I started.

'I thought it would be great for you and it has been. You think the problem is Chase. But it's not Chase who has taken over your life. It's that show.'

'What's that supposed to mean?'

'Ethan, stand up and look out there.' He walks out the sliding glass door and turns back to me. 'Look out across the water.' I do as he says and join him. 'Do you see that bright shining light across the way?' he asks, pointing his finger. 'That's your North Star and you need to follow it.'

I look, closely inspecting the glimmer he's referring to and say, 'Uncle Clams, that's a broken light from the Target parking lot in Sayville on the mainland.'

He turns away quickly. 'Oh piddle-paddle, that's not the point. But it does remind me I want to stop at that Target on the way home. They have paper towels on sale.'

I sigh loudly but also make a mental note to get paper towels.

'You think this show is pushing you toward your destiny but it's taking you away from it. You're so worried about pleasing the network and the sponsors.'

I immediately think about my meeting with that sleazy Buck. What an awful creature, and having to go along with his pretend support of the LGBTQ community is nauseating. Uncle Clams would rather starve than eat at a Beefy Boy and I'm about to have them sponsor our Pride float.

'What am I supposed to do? That's how you get ahead.'

'You keep thinking there's something at the end of the rainbow. But you're asleep in the field of poppies. It's time to wake up. Amnesia and I were talking, and this was her idea not mine, although I agree with it. She was thinking you could take over the Starlight.'

'Me?'

'Why not? You're on hiatus most of the summer anyway. That's the busy season out here. It's *your* hotel. I mean it will be. Amnesia is leaving the hotel to you; you must have figured that out.'

'That's a long way away,' I say. She's mentioned leaving me the place before. She doesn't have any heirs and we've all been a family for so long but she's a force of nature. It's hard to imagine her not being here.

'Marco isn't coming back next season to help. Why don't you do it instead? You adore being out here and you'd get to do what you love.'

The swinging door on the kitchen opens and Amnesia comes out wearing a new outfit. This kaftan is goldenrod yellow and has a daisy applique on the sleeves. Her hair is now strawberry blonde.

'You had time to make coffee and change wigs?' Clams asks.

'And flirt. Don't forget flirt. I tell you if I was ten years younger, I'd...' Amnesia starts.

'If you were ten years younger, you'd be fifty-eight and still twenty years too old for him.'

We all laugh and then Beau says, 'Amnesia showed me the gym that used to be the old cafe space. It's amazing. She has everything you need to make it operational. The stoves are top of the line.'

'Wouldn't it be great if you could get that cafe going next summer and maybe we could find someone young and just as handsome as you who doesn't know a good thing when it's in front of his face to...' Calms says.

'Enough. Enough,' I say before Beau can put it altogether, although I'm sure he already has. 'Let's enjoy our coffee on the deck.' I grab the tray and Beau opens the door. The moon is now dominating the sky and I can see it reflected clearly in the water. The air is humid but the breeze off the bay creates a pleasant balance in temperature. Luckily we spend the rest of the evening talking about the Giblets and their upcoming performance.

We thank them both for dinner and head back up to our room on the other side of the inn.

'I'll just sleep on the floor or out on the chaise lounge on the terrace. It's not an issue,' I say.

'I can take the terrace. My cot in the yurt is harder.'

'No way. I want you fresher than the daisies on Amnesia's kaftan tomorrow. We have a whole day of shooting and a remote crew arriving on the first ferry.' He nods and as much as I've been able to ignore work there are a few last-minute details I need to attend to so tomorrow runs smoothly. 'I'll let you get to sleep. I have to follow up on some of the lighting rentals and locations for tomorrow.'

'You're really lucky, Ethan,' Beau says as he climbs into bed.

'I'm calling equipment rental facilities in Queens. How am I lucky again?'

'You really don't see it, do you?'

'Enlighten me Beau, please.' I'm trying not to be snarky but I truly miss the point.

'You're surrounded by people who love you. Clams, Amnesia, Kiara. They're wonderful. Tina would do anything for you. Actually, everyone on set adores you. I know you gave Tina the whole month off when her dad was sick and you even found them a great oncologist in Seattle.'

'Oh, that doctor was a friend from college. I was his RA and didn't write him up when I found him drunk in a stairwell so he owed me. But that reminds me.' I grab my phone and make a voice memo. 'Find present for Jackie,' I say into my phone and then turn to Beau. 'His kid turns ten next week and I don't want to forget.'

'You really take care of people, Ethan. Sometimes it's big things but sometimes it's small things like a present for this guy's kid. You've built a life around love and I think it's pretty incredible.' He pulls the covers over him and says good night.

I walk out to the terrace. I am surrounded by people I love and who I know love me but it's beginning to feel like there's something missing at the center of it all. A beautifully set table with nothing to eat? Not exactly. It's more like a sumptuous banquet but no one to share it with. For the first time in my life I feel like I need someone at the center of it all with me. Someone who makes each morsel more delicious. When I think about my life right now I see all the stress and obligations. Everything seems challenging and gray. Beau sees my life in color and it makes my heart feel full.

Chapter 32

We finish the sun-safety segment on a patch of boardwalk close to the preserved area. A deer walks by and tries to peck at the display of lotions we have set up but other than that shooting has gone incredibly well. Tina is in charge of everything and she's doing a great job. One bonus of working with a temporary weekend crew is that they don't know Chase or the show at all. They're freelancers who get what we need and don't ask a lot of questions.

On the dock we shoot a segment on survival gear for the beach between ferry departures. It includes a tacky rainbow water bottle with a fan that's supposed to cool you down. Despite the silliness of the product, Beau is easy-going and, dare I say, even fun to work with. He takes Tina's notes and doesn't complain about last-minute changes. He even makes contributions that are on point. While we're filming the segment called 'How to Pack the Perfect Beach Bag' he suggests we change the title to 'How to Pack a Great Beach Bag.'

Tina pipes in. 'I mean perfect suggests there is one way of doing it.'

'Exactly,' Beau says. 'Going to the beach is supposed to be relaxing. Why add a layer of anxiety?'

I tell Tina this is her shoot and I'm glad when she decides to revise my original title to Beau's suggestion.

A small change but I'm beginning to understand it's important.

As we prepare to travel to the next location the crowds of day-trippers begin to arrive. Beau takes selfies when people ask and makes small talk. It's very vague and general so it's easy to get through it. Everyone knows about the big live stream coming up and the ribbon cutting at the parade. Most of the people here will be at the parade in the city but more than a few people tell us that they have friends or family in other places who are excited to see how big the celebration is. I wonder what they'll think when they see the Beefy Boy logo on the float.

We head to the dunes on the beach to film a segment on making the signature *Myles of Style* summer cocktail – gin-spiked lemonade with blackberry liqueur, a splash of club soda and a basil garnish. Tina has found a crafty way to make a beachside bar complete with ice bucket, cocktail shaker and mixers. When Beau holds the shaker over his head to mix the cocktail and his muscles flex, a small crowd of fans gather. It doesn't faze him at all. In fact, he digs out some cups from the lunch we had and offers samples.

After we wrap and the crew leaves, Beau and I are walking back on the beach and a person comes up to us wearing a lavender halter top and cut-off shorts with strawberries embroidered across. They have a slight beard and a floppy sun hat.

'Hi Chase. I can't believe you're here. I'm Andy.'

'Nice to meet you, Andy,' Beau says. This is the one area where he has needed no training at all. With Chase I constantly had to remind him that when fans approach him he needs to be gracious and kind. He always saw it as an irritant unless they were hot enough to turn his head.

'I've always wanted to DM you or something to thank you.'

'For what?' Beau asks.

'In that first season of *Myles of Style*, you had that series on coming out at home and office. You had that social worker, and you gave all these great suggestions about how to come out as gay or non-binary or a with disability and it was so helpful.'

'I'm glad to hear that. It's hard to come out, and everyone does it in their own way. In their own time.'

'Totally,' Andy says and then, 'Also, thank you for this.' Andy pulls up their halter top a bit to reveal a tattoo of a frying pan with arms and legs. 'That segment on getting the tattoo of your dreams convinced me to get this. Thanks Chase. See you at Tea,' they say and head up the steps that lead over the dunes to town.

'You did segments on coming out?' Beau asks.

'Of course,' I say. 'We used to do stuff like that all the time. Wellness. Mental health...' Our first season I wanted to make sure that all the lifestyle stuff was balanced with stories about coping. It's been a while since we've had that balance. Now we're sponsor driven.

'But not so much anymore?' Beau asks.

'No,' I say. He doesn't say anything. I'm expecting him to chastise me, but he doesn't. Maybe he knows he doesn't need to. I feel crappy about it all on my own. I run that first season through my head and it bears little resemblance to the show I'm currently producing.

We start walking up the beach back toward Cherry Grove and the boardwalk that leads to the Starlight. The sun is already low enough in the sky to create long shadows that stretch in front of us on the sand. I'm studying his shadow and noticing the way his arms swing and a tiny bit of his swagger seems to be missing.

'It took me a while to come out,' he says, and he stops walking.

I was the kind of kid who really didn't get much of a choice but I don't think that was true for Beau. I used to think having the option to come out made things easier for other people but as I've gotten older, I've realized it's all hard.

'Like you said, "everyone does it in their own time",' I say. A seagull squawks above us and swoops into the water.

'But there were consequences,' he says. His tone is serious.

I'm very aware that my heart is in my throat. At first I thought that everything must come easy to him but I'm beginning to understand that his good nature is hard won and the thought of him struggling makes me upset. He sits down on the sand. I join him.

'What do you mean?' I ask, but the question feels empty and I want to convey something more so I add, 'I want to understand.' He looks at me tenderly and I think I must have found the right words.

'Thank you. It's complicated,' he says and takes a breath in and then releases it slowly. He repeats that process again before he starts speaking.

'Chase has always been out. It's who he is. He told the whole family he was gay after college. My parents were furious. I mean they really lost it. Kicked him out. Chase got all their anger and their ugliness and instead of coming out at the same time, I just avoided everything. I couldn't bear to have them treat me the way they treated him. So I said nothing. I didn't help them understand Chase. I didn't help him. I didn't tell them that I'm bi. Instead I was silent and then I left. Chase stayed in Wisconsin and had to deal with their anger alone. That was very shitty of me.'

I feel bad for Chase. No one deserves that treatment for coming out. Maybe it even helps me understand why Chase can be so difficult. It doesn't excuse him for breaking his commitment to the show, but it helps me understand. I'm grateful that Beau is telling me.

'I had this girlfriend in high school and I knew I had these other feelings but I thought maybe they'd go away or something. I don't know. They didn't go away and I never told my parents because I was scared of their reaction. Then they were gone.'

'I'm sorry. I know your parents died in a car accident.'

'They died not knowing who I am. Not knowing who I really am and that's my fault.'

'That's hard. Very hard to live with. But if you saw their reaction to your brother, you were just protecting yourself.'

'But when your brother, your twin, comes out and gets treated like that… I should have stood up for him. I should have stood up *with* him. I thought I would one day but I kept putting it off and then they died and things got even more complicated.' A wave comes toward us and almost reaches our toes but then recedes. 'They cut Chase out of their lives. We weren't rich by any stretch of the imagination but they made it clear that *I* was their only son. And their will made it even clearer. I was the only heir.' Beau puts his hand in the sand. He squeezes a clump tightly and then lets it go.

'That is majorly messed up,' I say.

'I know,' Beau says. 'Once Chase came out and I didn't, things weren't the same between us but I tried to make it right. So, I took the money from the inheritance and gave it to Chase. All of it. I told you how things spiraled at the restaurant. I was struggling to meet payroll and pay vendors but I couldn't keep the money. Not like that. If I had come out when I should have, they would have disinherited us both or maybe they would have found a way to accept us both. I don't know. But I didn't feel right keeping the money.'

'Beau, you couldn't have known they would die or that they would do that,' I say, hoping it comforts him. I wonder what I would have done. I wonder if I would have had the grace to do what he did to try to make peace.

'Giving him the money was the only way I thought I could make it right. He came out and I hid, which is what I guess I've been doing upstate also.' A seagull digs his beak into the sand searching for something to eat and then flies away, spreading his wings. 'We were both in the city by then but things got so bad we had stopped speaking. I found him and told him the money was his. Every dime. He was really touched. For a few moments we found our way back and it was nice… for a while.'

This story is about to take another turn and I brace myself.

'I told him about the kitchen and the problems I was having and he offered to help me out and split the money. I told him no but he said it was the only thing to do. He wanted to use all the money to invest in the restaurant. I needed the cash so I agreed and started getting some more resources to help me get out of my hole. I knew I was overextending my debt beyond my means but I also knew I had this extra cash coming in. We decided to become partners. It felt great. We were brothers again. But then I start calling Chase and he's ghosting me and I can't find him. I'm calling and texting him. No response.'

Boy, do I know that feeling.

'Finally he answers his phone. He tells me he cashed the check, flew to Vegas and gambled, drank it away or who knows what and it was gone. Poof. Just like that. It was his money. I gave it to him. No strings. But he was the one who wanted to have a new start together. We'd both decided to become partners in the business. He knew I was struggling with the debt. We had a huge blowout fight. I'm not proud of some of the things I said to him. Maybe they were unforgiveable.' I don't ask. Family can hurt you in ways no one else can. 'At that point I owed a lot of money and not all of it to a bank.'

I suddenly remember the scary guy back at the diner in Stark.

'I'm sorry Beau. I'm really sorry.' I know Beau loved his restaurant and his brother and his parents, though I'm not sure the latter two deserved it. Still, he lost everything all at once and in such a devastating way. I put my hand over his and gently brush his knuckles with my fingers.

'Thanks. It's in the past now but after we saw where the restaurant used to be the other day, I didn't tell you any of this and I wanted you to know. Chase can be an jackass, but my hands aren't clean either. I was under a lot of stress, but I shouldn't have let it get out of hand.'

His words remind me that my hands aren't clean with Chase either. In some ways I pushed him away from the show. I see that more now.

'I should have been more honest about who I am and all of this would have been avoided.' There is a shadow of anger in his voice but the feeling of loss seems to flood everything else out.

'Things at the restaurant became impossible and the panic attacks returned. I ran away upstate. I needed to be far from everything. I figured a lot out by being up there. I learned to meditate and get quiet. I learned to live in the moment. I learned that my connection to food was really through wellness and that made the biggest change.' Beau looks down at the sand and grabs a stick. Then he throws it in the ocean as the waves approach us.

'I really appreciate you telling me all this. It means a lot to me,' I say. It's been a while since I've met a guy who I can connect to like this. I usually jump away at the first signs of intimacy and retreat to my work world or, worse, I manipulate the conversation to keep it focused on surface details and the way things look. With Beau, I don't need to do that, not to mention he wouldn't let me. Connecting with a man in this way feels powerful.

'It means a lot to me that I can tell you,' he says. 'There aren't a lot of people I really talk to like this upstate. None really. I thought once I got my debt under control I'd just stay up there because I almost forgot the part I loved the most about being a chef.'

'What's that?'

'We just had it. With that fan, Andy. "The tug at the end of the line." Like when you go fishing. When you're in a kitchen and you know the plate you're focused on has a destination. A hungry and eager person waiting for it. Feeling that tug is everything. Like with that fan.'

'I can understand that. Knowing something I do connects with someone feels great,' I say.

'Right. But before I was too focused on the people I couldn't connect with. The bad reviews or the complaints. But now I've figured out it's more about where I place my energy. Appreciating the places where I do connect. Not letting anyone else get in my head so I can actually take in the good stuff.'

'That's the tug you mean?' I ask.

'Exactly but it doesn't have to be a stranger at your restaurant or a fan. You can also feel it with people you feel close to...' His words fade out a bit but then he starts again. 'Or people you know but want to feel even closer to.'

He gets up and extends his hand to help me. I grab it and stand. I brush some sand off him and then he returns the favor and brushes some off me. When I hold his hand I'm not even thinking. I'm just reaching out to be close to him because I know it's the right thing to do in that moment. We begin to walk back to the hotel.

I'm so moved by his honesty with me that I feel compelled to tell him the truth about me and his brother. I want to. He deserves it but that was a lot. I can't pile on more. Not right now and I don't want to disrupt the mellow warmth of closeness that envelopes us. We keep walking side by side in silence.

Our peace however is broken a few yards before we approach the hotel. We can hear shrieking and moans of anguish. When we get to the front desk of the Starlight we find Uncle Clams and Amnesia freaking out. The quiet confessions of the beach quickly fade as we enter the madhouse.

'What's wrong?' I ask. They are often hysterical so I don't know if I should expect a death in the family or a chipped nail.

'A disaster. Calamity!' Clams says.

'I don't know what we're going to do,' Amnesia says. 'Joan of Arse can't make it.'

'Who?' Beau asks.

'Joan of Arse is the third member of The Giblet Triplets. She performs with Clams and Amnesia,' I explain to Beau. 'What happened?' I ask. Apparently Justin, Joan's alter ego, had to have a double root canal and can't make the show.

'The two of you will be great,' I say, trying to reassure them. This isn't quite the emergency they think it is, but I guess emergencies are relative.

Clams shrieks and Amnesia bows her head. 'Ethan, this is a trio. It will not be great. You've seen the show before. It's choreographed for three people, not two,' Amnesia says.

'What's the song?' Beau asks.

'We do a dramatic lip-sync to Wilson Phillips' "Hold On". I play Carnie, Amnesia plays Chynna and Joan plays the other one. We've done it for years.'

'I wish I could do something to help,' I say and I mean it. I'd take a ferry back and drive Justin aka Joan in but that would take too long and I'm not sure it would help in the end since Justin is having teeth problems. Justin is a great guy but not exactly a Navy Seal when it comes to pain. One summer he got a splinter in his toe and I thought they were going to have to Medivac him off the island.

'Now that you mention it we thought you could do something,' Amnesia says, giving my uncle a sly look.

'What?' I ask.

'Fill in,' Clams says with a big smile. 'You know the song and it hardly involves any dancing.'

'No. No way. Absolutely not,' I say. This is not up for discussion. My stomach roils just thinking about being in front of an audience of more than two.

'You are not an attractive woman. I've seen you in my wigs and it's bad but we can work with it,' Clams says.

'Is this you trying to soften me up?' I ask.

'But you're our only hope. No one else is available,' Amnesia says.

I'm about to give an even firmer no and maybe slam my fist on the counter when Beau says, 'I'll do it. I know that song. They go crazy for it in Paris.'

'What?' Clams asks.

'Really?' Amnesia asks. They are both smiling and push past me like I'm an annoying speed bump on the way to heaven.

'Beau, you don't have to do this. It's not part of the deal. It involves dancing,' I say.

'No one asked you. If this handsome young man wants to make his drag debut tonight at The Ice Palace with me and Amnesia, it's his choice,' Clams says.

'Who says it's my debut?' Beau asks, oozing charm. This makes them both squeal.

'Oh, calm down you two,' I say to them. They love any opportunity to get anyone on stage. I turn to Beau. 'Fine. If you're sure you want to.'

'Why not? They need someone. I'm here.'

'The fire engine red gown with all the silver,' Clams says.

'Fire engine red? With his skin tone? Have you lost your mind you addled queen? He needs something green,' Amnesia chides.

'Green? He isn't the Creature from the Black Lagoon. You're the one who has lost her mind. Let me show you what I'm thinking...' They leave and head to the room where they keep all the costumes and materials.

Beau is smiling from ear to ear. 'Do you have any idea what you're getting yourself into?' I ask. 'Being directed by those two divas is like...'

'Being directed by you,' he says, still smiling. 'I think it'll be fun. Fire Island is different than I thought it would be. I'm having a great time. The people we met today were super nice and Clams and Amnesia are wonderful.'

'What were you expecting?' I ask.

'I guess a lot of attitude and pretension. I lied when I said I was too busy to come to Fire Island when I lived in New York. I was invited but it always seemed way too intimidating. Chase was always able to fit in with that group and I never thought there was a place for me.'

Beau is serious and I can tell it's hard for him to say these words out loud. I wonder if it's the first time he has admitted it to himself.

'Bella! Bella!' I hear Clams yell from the other room.

'Ms D'ball. Ms Bella D Ball, you are needed for a fitting and rehearsal,' Amnesia says. He looks at me and smiles before Clams and Amnesia come out and grab his arms.

'He's ours now. We'll see you tonight at the show, Ethan. Come on, Bella,' Clams says and then he lassos him with a bright purple feather boa and they take Beau away.

Chapter 33

Clams and Amnesia have forbidden me from interrupting their rehearsal. When they ask why I can't buy a ticket like everyone else I yell back in my best Christina Crawford, 'Because I am not one of your fans.' They, of course, love my *Mommie Dearest* reference but I follow their orders.

The early evening is peaceful on the island. The day-trippers head back home on the late afternoon ferries and the people staying overnight take their disco naps to prepare for hours of partying. I start strolling down Bayview Walk by myself. There are no cars on the island. No roads. No traffic jams. A series of narrow-planked boardwalks serve as streets. The dollhouse-like homes are just feet away from the paths and nestled between the bamboo reeds and pitch pine trees that make the little island so green. New York City is massive overwhelming chaos. Fire Island is quaint and completely comprehensible but filled with all the same people.

I think about the rift between Beau and Chase as I walk. I really do feel bad for Chase being treated so poorly by his family. It sounds like Beau tried to make things right but in the end they both got screwed. I've never met anyone like Beau who would make such a sacrifice to do what he believed needed to be done.

I walk down Kingwood Lane and turn at the end to admire my favorite house on Summer Walk. It's a quaint salt box with cedar siding and Essex green shutters. A small balcony from the second floor looks over the deck in the front. The houses in this part aren't grand like the ones in the Pines with giant, sleek pools and multi-storied windows that capture every view. Everything in Cherry Grove is on a smaller scale and it makes it more inviting and charming.

The lights are coming on in the salt box. I linger a bit longer than I should and see someone setting up a meal on the deck with an April Cornell tablecloth, candles and a stunning porcelain bowl. I inch just a bit closer to make out some detail on the bowl and it looks like the Herend butterfly collection which makes me wonder if... but before I can finish that thought, I hear 'Ethan, is that you?' That answers my question. I wondered if the bowl came from The Silver Peacock on Madison Avenue, and it must have since I know it belongs to the shop's owner.

'Yonah, I'd recognize you or that bowl anywhere,' I say, wishing I hadn't lingered. This is awkward. 'How are things at The Peacock?' I ask politely.

Yonah was one of my few real boyfriends. He was a great guy with exquisite taste, but I couldn't handle my career and a romantic life. I never gave the relationship enough attention to find out if it could have become something.

'Great. How are things at the show? I've heard about the big live stream and Chase is the Grand Marshal or something like that. That's exciting.'

'Yes,' I say. 'It's something like that.'

Death by polite small talk.

'Hun, do you want me to dress the salad or...' An incredibly handsome man carrying a teak bowl filled with greens comes out.

273

'David, this is Ethan. Ethan, this is my husband, David.'
We nod to each other and smile since his hands are full.

'I don't want to interrupt your dinner. Nice seeing you again. I have to stop in your shop and see some of your marvelous things soon. Have a great night,' I say and continue my walk albeit at a slightly faster pace to get away from them and an invitation to stay for dinner. Yonah is a perfectly nice guy, and it looks like he's found an equally nice husband. That makes me happy. At one point Yonah and I talked about renting a house out here for the season. It wasn't something I think either of us ever thought would really happen. It's the kind of thing you do when you meet someone and start imaging what ifs. He's found a way to balance work and life and have a husband. I wonder if the trick is finding the right person with whom you can share the seesaw, someone to keep you anchored as you rise, someone to make sure you don't come crashing down.

I walk all the way to the ocean and then along the beach before heading to the dock to meet Kiara and Nisha. The lights on the ferry glow in the distance. The bay is calm tonight and the water looks almost black. I can hear the music beginning to pump from The Ice Palace where we'll go to watch tonight's surprise performance. I spot them immediately. Of course, a six-foot tall woman wearing a lime green wig and matching jumpsuit with cutaways running down both sides and a woman in a black sequined sleeveless tuxedo wearing a gorgeous gold arm cuff with dangling charms are hard to miss. Even on Fire Island.

'You both look fabulous,' I say as soon as they disembark. They do a twirl to show off. Kiara shakes the fringe on her jumpsuit. Nisha grabs the lapels on her jackets and runs her hand over her hair as she poses.

'Sorry we're late. The sitter got held up and the dog needed an extra walk and then we decided to rent a stick shift so I could practice,' Kiara says.

'How did that go?' I ask, unsure if I want the answer.

'I'm sure there are tiny bits of the transmission from here to Brooklyn,' Nisha says. 'But we wouldn't miss The Giblet Triplets for anything. How are the girls? Are they ready to perform?'

'I'm afraid Joan of Arse couldn't make it. Justin had a dental emergency but he's okay. Clams and Amnesia were crushed but luckily everybody's favorite understudy was able to step in.'

'Everybody's favorite understudy?' Kiara repeats my turn of phrase pushing some green bangs away from her eyes. 'You don't mean…?'

'Oh, I do.' We walk down the pier toward The Ice Palace and prepare for another Beau Myles stand-in performance.

The Giblet Triplets are the headliners of the night, so we enjoy some cocktails and sit through baby queens who weren't even born when Clams and his friends were impersonating Carol Channing or Donna Summer. By the time our queens are ready to perform it's way past midnight. The host for the evening, a gender-bending performer simply called The Limit, announces, 'The Giblet Triplets,' and the crowd erupts in cheers.

The familiar chords of the Wilson Phillips classic song chime through the speakers and the lights go dark and then gently rise as Clams Casino, Milk of Amnesia and, their long-lost sister, Bella D Ball take their opening poses and the music swells.

Beau is a hot guy. There is no doubt about that. It's always hard to know how someone will look in drag but I'm surprised to find out he is hideous. Clams and Amnesia did their best to beat his face but he definitely looks busted. However, Beau doesn't seem to care at all. The chorus of the song begins and he's flubbing lyrics, missing the steps, and looking like he's going to bust out of his strapless blue sequined gown, but throughout the number he looks like he's having the time of his life.

'I can't believe that's the same guy you brought me covered in hair and attitude,' Kiara says, sipping on her daiquiri. Like everyone her eyes are glued to the stage watching the crazy, spectacular performance. It's a train wreck but a sparkling one that's hard to turn away from. I can't believe this is the same guy either. The truth is I don't think he is the same guy but I'm also not the same person who drove up to find him. The difference is Beau has completely embraced the possibility of change and I'm still considering it from behind the scenes.

They do synchronous jazz hands and Beau, or rather Bella, looks right at me. No amount of makeup can diminish how piercing and warm his gaze feels. I sing along in my head. I'm connected to everyone else in the crowd as powerful vectors of joy bounce around the room like the reflections off the glitter ball.

They finish their number, and the audience goes crazy. A lot of people are filming and taking pictures. By the middle of the song people start to recognize Bella as Chase Myles, the host of *Myles of Style*. They're eating up seeing one of their favorite celebrities in drag. All publicity is good for the show, so I'm thrilled when I see people filming snippets and posting on their phones. I wonder if this might even trend. I should have thought of a clever hashtag to help it along but the fact is I'm just enjoying seeing Beau enjoying himself.

Kiara, Nisha and I run backstage as soon as the number is finished.

'You were all divine,' Kiara says.

'Redefining fabulous,' Nisha adds.

'Thank you, darlings,' Clams says. He and Amnesia are glowing.

'We could not have done it without this superstar,' Amnesia says putting her arm around Chase.

'How did it feel, Beau?' I ask.

'It was quite a rush I have to admit, and the two of them coached me through every step, but my feet! I admire anyone who wears things like that on their feet. The pain is incredible.' He's sitting in a chair in the dressing room almost completely de-dragged but rubbing his feet. 'It might be a while until you meet Bella again,' he says. 'My feet need to recover.'

'A round of drinks for everyone,' Amnesia says. She and Clams rush us out of the dressing room and back to the bar.

Eventually Beau comes out to the bar wearing an old T-shirt, his running shorts and a pair of flip-flops. There's nothing designer or fabulous about him but he looks so handsome dressed as himself.

I order a lite beer and when the bartender offers me a mug I make a big deal in front of Beau about not needing one. This makes him laugh and he orders a beer also. Clams and company have made it to the dance floor but Beau begs off insisting that his feet need more time to heal and I'd rather chop off my feet than dance, so we take our beers and head to a quiet spot on the deck overlooking the ocean. The moon reflects off the water and makes the foam on the crashing waves almost glow.

'It was really incredible seeing you up there,' I say.

'Thanks. Out of my comfort zone for sure but amazing,' he says.

'You realize that you now have two loyal and dedicated fans for the rest of your life. Clams and Amnesia will never forget you helping them like this.' His makeup is mostly off. There are a few smudges around his eyes and his hair is sweaty and pressed against his head in different places. He's kind of a mess almost like when I first saw him, but in a different way obviously. He's raw and without artifice and that is what's so incredibly sexy about him. I guess that's what's sexy about anyone – seeing them to their core. I'm remembering the kiss the other night on the pier and I want to experience it again.

'Beau,' I start, unsure of what I'm going to say. I can't announce that I'm going to kiss him and then kiss him. I look out over the ocean and see a ship in the distance. We're leaning on the railing of the deck side by side, and I move a bit closer to him, hoping he'll get the message. He does and he scooches closer. I put my beer down and look at him.

The music is pulsing behind us and the waves are crashing in front of us. The moon above and the sand below. Between us is nothing but salty air. I move through it and put my lips on his. His mouth responds, friendly at first as I find my footing kissing him, and then it quickly ramps up to something with more passion. My hands reach for him, and he puts his arm around me.

'Wait,' he says, stepping back, his breath heavy.

'You beat me to it. I wanted to say "wait" first but please let me say what I need to say.' I clear my throat to prepare for my confession.

'Okay,' he says.

I want to be close to him like this but I can't do that without coming clean first. 'Beau, my relationship with Chase doesn't exist. I should have told you. We aren't a couple. You were right. It's not real. It's a silly front for the dumb show.'

'Yes!' he says, pumping his fist in the air, going full out bro on me in this moment, and it's hotter than I thought it would be. I'm also relieved he isn't angry at me; or is that still to come?

'I'm sorry. I'm very sorry. I led you to believe we were together. I felt cornered. You had every right to corner me. I should have found a way to explain it all. I've never felt that way about him. Never.'

'I could not for the life of me figure out what someone as smart and caring as you could see in my brother. Except of course for his exceptional good looks.'

I laugh and he takes my face in his hands and kisses me softly. I can't tell if it's the beer or his lips but I'm definitely experiencing a buzz.

'There you are!' I hear someone say across the shadows. As they approach us I make out a muscular shirtless body with a tacky glo-in-the-dark necklace that provides just enough light for me to see that it's Keegan. Of course it's Keegan.

We separate like two school kids caught doing something they shouldn't be doing, although everything we were doing felt totally correct.

'Keegan, I hope you aren't here still trying to get an interview. I had Tina send you his answers to all the questions you sent for the *Mediapedia* piece on Pride.'

'Yes, I got them. I'll have it written this week but tonight I'm officially off the clock. I'm here to have a good time,' Keegan says. I think he might be drunk since he's slurring his words. 'Amazing to see you up there on stage Chase, with those old queens. They're a hoot.'

'Excuse me. Those old queens are my family,' I snap.

'Whoops. My bad. Apologies. Mean it. It was a great show. Seriously. So much respect for our queer elders. So much.'

Somehow, I find that hard to believe.

'I was just glad to finally see where the famous Chase Myles had been.' He stumbles a bit and puts his hand in his pocket, taking out his phone. He swipes around and then shows us a grid of bodies. 'Where is my magic ass?'

Beau looks at me totally confused.

'C'mon Chasey.' Keegan says. 'Say good night to your work colleague and let's head down to The Meat Rack.' He licks his lips like an animal preparing for a meal. It's disgusting.

'I think I'm good,' Beau says, which is exactly what the guy inside me who wants to kiss him more wants him to say. The producer inside me who needs to keep up this charade isn't so sure.

'Chase,' Keegan says. 'I've been seeing this new go-with-the-flow version of you and I don't believe it. The Chase I know could *never* spend a weekend on Fire Island without at least one pass through The Meat Rack for a romp in the sand. Unless the two of you are up to something.' He seems to sober up for a minute and looks at us with suspicion. I feel my heart sink. 'If you are, you better tell me right now so I can be first with the scoop.'

Keegan says all this playfully like it's a joke. It's no joke. Not at all and Keegan and I know that. Beau not so much. Keegan wants some action with Chase. Maybe I've kept them apart too long. Keegan is clever. He's been putting the pieces together since Maria Luisa's party. It feels like everything is about to blow up in this moment.

'Keegan, you know how Chase is. I couldn't keep him away from The Meat Rack on a Saturday if I chained him to the bed,' I say, but as soon as the words come out of my mouth I'm not sure I'm headed down the right path.

Keegan walks over to Chase and puts his hands on his chest. 'This big guy chained to a bed? Sounds like a win-win. See you later Chase. You know where I'll be and you already know what I like,' he says and lets his hands run over his own chest before walking away.

'No. No. What are we going to do about Keegan?' I'm not really asking him. I'm thinking out loud.

'Ah, nothing. Who cares what he does or thinks?' Beau reaches for me but I resist. 'I thought everyone thinks you and my brother are a couple.'

'Yes, the sponsors. The execs. But Keegan knows the truth. He's expecting some action. When you're queer, there's one way you present to the world and another way you behave in private. At least it's that way for Chase.'

'And for you it seems.' Beau pulls back. 'You're serious, aren't you?'

'Beau, this is serious. Keegan can ruin everything with one post or one mention in the article he's writing. He has the power to destroy everything. We are so close. Chase and Keegan have always hooked up. They have a long history of sexual escapades.'

'And you're okay with that?'

'Of course. Chase doesn't mean anything to me. You're going to have to at least take a stroll through The Meat Rack.'

'But I'll be the one doing it. Not Chase, me, Beau,' he says, thrusting his thumb toward himself. 'So I don't mean anything to you either?'

'I'm not suggesting you let Keegan have his way with you or anything like that at all. Just let him…' I don't know what I'm saying or what I even want to say. My mind is short–circuiting. 'I mean that's your business.' I don't have any right to be possessive over Beau. He isn't my boyfriend. We don't have any type of commitment. 'I'm just saying that you need to at least do a drive-by, maybe flex a bit,' I say but as soon as his face frowns I try to dial back. 'Or not…' Maybe I had one too many beers. My words are jumbled and confusing.

He looks at me with an expression I haven't seen before. He's not angry or confused or defiant. His eyes seem to have drooped a bit and the corners of his mouth have turned. 'Is that what you want?'

'It's not what I want, Beau. It's what I have to do. It's what *we* have to do. Just do a walk through, let Keegan see you and then we can pick up where we left off,' I say, putting my hand on his shoulder. His eyes dart to it and then his hand reaches for mine to remove it from his body.

'What's the big deal?' I ask. 'It's what you came here to do.'

'I did not come here to hook up with Keegan.'

'I know that. I didn't say you had to.' The truth is I don't know what I'm saying. I feel my buzz weaken and then strengthen. The threat of Keegan blowing everything up and figuring out this scam has me on autopilot. I'm a bear protecting a cub but my cub is this intangible beast I call The Show. I don't even know why I'm doing it except for the fact that I'm too scared to let my defenses down around it. If I let go, everything I've built will be taken away from me. I can't let that happen, can I?

'We can get back to where we were when you come back. I'll be waiting for you,' I say, and I mean it. I don't want what we have started to stop. Not at all.

'So you're into this now? Into me? You've come clean about the situation with my brother. I don't like that you misled me but I get why. But that's not the issue. The fact is the show comes first. It always comes first.'

'That's not true,' I say reactively but as the words come out of my mouth I wonder if they are true. I wonder if I should take them back, but I'm not thinking clearly and when I look down the boardwalk I see the entrance to The Meat Rack and wonder what it would mean if I asked Beau *not* to go, to stay with me tonight. But I don't know if I'm ready for that layer of complication at a time when things seem to be maxing out in terms of complications. I have to deal with what's in front of me, not what is possibly on the horizon with this guy I met a few weeks ago.

'It's not a matter of priorities,' I say. 'It's a matter of urgency. Can't you understand that?'

'So it's urgent that I hook up with some muscle head instead of stay here and make out with you and go back to our room at the Starlight.'

'I didn't say hook up with him.' I'm at that point in the argument where my mind and my heart are not speaking the same language.

'So let me get this straight. My instructions are to walk around The Meat Rack like a piece of meat.'

'I didn't give it that name,' I say but he keeps talking.

'Make sure Keegan sees me and come back and make love to you and show you everything I've been feeling since you drove me down here. Show you how great I thought you were. How much I appreciate what you've done for me.'

What I've done for *him*? He's the one helping me.

'There are so many rules for being in your world Ethan, or in the world you think you live in. You don't even see what's right in front of your face.'

'Beau, my hands are tied. You heard Keegan. If he figures out you aren't Chase, Maria Luisa will be furious and Beefy Boy will pull out.'

'Beefy Boy? That horrible homophobic sandwich place with the "tradition tastes better" BS? What does that have to do with anything?'

What have I done? Those words just slipped out. I didn't want to tell him this way. I didn't want to tell him about Beefy Boy at all but now I don't have a choice. 'This is not the way I wanted to tell you, but yes. They have decided to sponsor the float for Pride. It's awful, I know, but they are bringing a lot of money and…'

He looks disgusted with me and I can't blame him. 'The show always comes first. Doesn't it, Ethan? That is always your number one priority, your number one concern. I get it. It's important to you. But the part I can't watch is when you put it in front of yourself. I just can't understand that.' He turns and walks away. 'I'm off to the woods. Let me know if there's any special position you think Chase would use with Keegan or maybe I'll just experiment,' he says, and he's down the boardwalk on his way to The Meat Rack before I can even think of a response.

Chapter 34

A Monday meeting at seven a.m. in Maria Luisa's office is not exactly how I want to start the week. It's usually hard to leave the magic of Fire Island but this time I fled. After feeling so close to Beau and thinking we might have an incredible evening together, I spent the rest of the night waiting for him in our room only to fall asleep and wake up minutes before the sun came up. I found him sleeping on a bunch of towels on the terrace.

I packed and left notes for Clams who was staying with Amnesia until later in the week when they'll arrange to have the Giblet Mobile transferred by truck to Manhattan for the parade. I decided it would be better to wait by myself on the pier for the ferry. That was a mistake. I wasn't there very long until Keegan walked by looking like he hadn't been to sleep yet. Seeing him twice in twelve hours is more than I can take but when he told me that he ran into Chase in The Meat Rack right after our encounter on the boardwalk, I thought I was going to jump off the dock. Then he had the audacity to say to me, 'Ethan, your Chase Myles is magic, really magic.' I thought I was going to swim back to the mainland. Beau and I didn't speak the entire way back.

I guess he took my suggestion a bit too far and hooked up with Keegan. Keegan is an incredible specimen of everything people expect from a gay man. He's pumped and plucked. I can't imagine that's the kind of guy Beau would want to hook up with but I'm not oblivious to the fact that I pushed them together.

Up until the moments after the show at The Ice Palace, the weekend really had been magical but I've worked in media long enough to know that magic is just camera tricks and sleight of hand. Reality was coming home last night and finding a stream of texts and emails from Maria Luisa ordering me to be in her office first thing. The elevator beeps as I arrive on Maria Luisa's floor and I'm back on terra firma.

It's early enough that Beverly is not at her station so I knock directly on Maria Luisa's door. She's not alone. Buck is there. Now I'm confused.

'Ethan, thank you for coming,' Maria Luisa says like she's welcoming me to a wake. Buck's chubby face is red. He looks like he might have been crying. Did someone die?

'We have a problem,' Maria Luisa says.

'I'll say we have a problem,' Buck growls. The tone is clearly anger rather than sadness. But what is he angry about? I take a seat and remain silent. I still have no idea what's going on.

'As you know social media has been exploding this weekend,' Maria Luisa says. I nod. I haven't checked the social in hours, maybe days to be honest. A highly unusual circumstance due to the fact that I was actually living my life instead of staging one and photographing it.

'The *Myles of Style* account has almost tripled its followers,' Maria Luisa says. That should be a good thing, but I don't think I'd be invited to Thunderdome if that were the case.

'I thought you wanted more followers,' I say, knowing I'm missing something.

'Not like this,' Buck says. His anger is layered with more anger. Maybe he's eaten too much beef and I wonder if he has considered switching to a plant-based diet. I start to smile when I realize who I sound like but I quickly shut down any smirk that may result. This is not the time or place.

'Buck, we can fix this. It won't happen again,' Maria Luisa says. She's in power player mode. Her voice is firm and clear.

'It better not if Beefy Boy is involved,' Buck says, crossing his arms.

'This weekend it seems that Chase was on Fire Island,' Maria Luisa says.

Chase is in the Middle East according to my recent check of SecretSlam but she only need not know that for a few more days.

'Yes,' I say. 'We were shooting the beach segments for the live stream. That was our last location and now we have everything in the can for the parade this weekend.' I'm not saying anything Maria Luisa doesn't already know. I feel like she's reviewing the evidence in a case she's making but I have no idea what the charge is.

'I am aware,' Maria Luisa says. 'I'm also aware that Chase was quite busy at night,' she says, and my first thought is that the real Chase has made some kind of sex tape to bring the show down. Maybe there's footage of him dangling off some OnlyFans dude or dudes. My first thought is about Beau and how I hope Chase hasn't embarrassed him. Then I catch myself. I'm shocked by the fact that my first concern is a person and not The Show. And not just a person: Beau to be exact.

Then Maria Luisa holds up her phone and I cringe, fearful of what I'm about to see. But it isn't pornographic at all. She shows me some amateur footage of the drag number with Clams and Amnesia and Bella herself, dancing like an adorable fool.

'Oh, that's great,' I say immediately. 'I know the Giblets will be thrilled someone recorded it. I forgot to take my phone out. My uncle will be so relieved someone captured him on video.'

'One of *those people* is your uncle?' Buck asks. He's clearly horrified but I ignore it.

'Yeah, my Uncle Frank is Clams Casino but everyone calls him Clams in or out of drag.'

Buck is speechless. A deadly silence fills the room.

'Oh, isn't that fun,' Maria Luisa says, forcing a smile across her lips in an attempt to break the mood. 'But it's not exactly on brand for Chase, is it? *Myles of Style* is about class and elegance. A certain level of sophistication.'

Everything she's saying is directly from the media packets I wrote for the show. It's about all those things but maybe it's also about something more.

'It's actually a show about living your best life,' I say and that feels more accurate than anything else. That's what I want to produce. That's what I want people to do. That's what seems to happen on Fire Island. I want to bring that energy to the show. Lately it hasn't been part of it at all.

'I have a board meeting in an hour so I'm going to get to it,' Buck continues. 'I'm sorry I'm not part of the "everybody gets a trophy" crowd and making everyone feel good garbage. We did not bring a ton of money over to your show and this network to be represented by a drag queen. Chase is a handsome man according to popular opinion.' Buck is one of those straight people who can't even comment on the attractiveness of someone of the same sex. God forbid it might mean they're gay. 'He's a gay man in, what I have been told, is a solid committed relationship,' Buck says. 'My granddaddy would roll over in his grave at the very thought of a homosexual representing Beefy Boy.'

Really? He named the company like a subcategory on Gay Reddit but okay, Buck. If you say so. I'm about to interrupt but I look at Maria Luisa and there is a trapped look in her eyes. I can tell this is a conversation she has been having with Buck since before I walked in.

'We could have put our money into that other show with all the queens in it.' Buck rolls his eyes and shakes his head. 'That one with all the liberal guests talking to men dressed up as women. *Good Night Queen!*'

Now Buck is confusing *Queens of the Night* with one of my favorite childhood books, *Goodnight Moon*. Although *Good Night Queen is* an excellent title.

'I'm a progressive,' Buck says, and I want to throw up. 'Gay people are here now. We can't call them queer but they can call themselves queer. Fine. But we want normal gays. Not drag queens. That's why we are here. With you. You seem stable.'

'Wait a minute...' I say. I don't care if Maria Luisa stops me. The last thing someone should call me is stable and I don't like where this has been or where it is going.

'Listen, Ethan. I'm not a bad guy,' Buck says very sincerely. 'I'm the guy who wants to change Beefy Boy. I'm the guy who stopped our company from doubling down on its previous policy that was not very nice according to some pains in the asses with the online stuff. Okay, fine. But I'm also the guy pouring money into your show. I don't want to support every dang color of the rainbow. I don't think that should be a problem.'

With that Buck pushes himself away from the conference table, gets up and leaves the room. Usually I would at least wait for Maria Luisa to respond but I don't.

'Seriously?' I ask once he has left.

'I know,' Maria Luisa responds, rubbing her face with her hand. 'I hate this too but we have to be careful about how hard we push. The fact is corporations like Beefy Boy are fine with marginalized groups as long as they don't step outside the box they're put in. Mainstream personalities have more freedom, more flexibility but queer celebrities have to stay in their lane and the lane we have built for Chase is clean-cut, wholesome and sexy. He's your favorite uncle, the guy who never forgets a birthday, and the backup date you can bring to a family function without anyone turning a head. That's who Chase is.'

No. That's who I am and I'm not even sure I want to be that person anymore. I thought our show was breaking down stereotypes but maybe all we've done is create new ones. I want to tell Maria Luisa that we should tell Buck to screw off but I try to find a more professional way to say it. 'We can tell them that sponsors don't control content. They don't control me, and they don't control the host,' I say.

'That's not exactly true, is it, Ethan? The fact is we cater to what they want.' Maria Luisa gets up and moves from the conference table to her seat behind the desk. It's a power move but in this moment it seems empty. 'Ethan, you're so close to getting everything you wanted. You're almost across the finish line. I know this situation is not ideal but just stay on track and get through this week.

That's all you need to do. We can make adjustments on the other side of this. Stay on the path you're on.'

She picks up an envelope on her desk with the Beefy Boy logo emblazoned across it. She hands it to me. 'Buck took the privilege of writing the speech for Chase for the parade.'

'Buck? You let a straight man write the opening speech for the ribbon cutting of the Pride Parade?'

'I let the man who is funding your broadcast of the parade provide some input because that's how it works, Ethan. You pay, you play.' She slides the envelope across to me.

There is a version of me that picks up the envelope, rips it into tiny pieces and walks out the door, never to return. I can see that version of myself, but it still feels like a tart in the oven with a wobbly center. It's not ready to come out. So instead, I pick up the envelope, put it in my pocket and continuing playing my part.

Chapter 35

Of all the events leading up to Pride, the Pinnacle Music Awards was the one that I was most looking forward to but now I'm just counting the hours until all of this is over. After tonight I just have to get through the parade and I can put Beau on a bus back to where he came from. I can pick up my life and stay on track. Maybe then the nagging feeling I have that I should change direction will hop on a bus and get out of town too.

'If you fuss at me one more time when I am trying to do your eyebrows I will go back to the thread,' Kiara says.

Only one person could possibly complain about having to sit for glam more than Beau and that person is me.

'But it hurts,' I whine. 'It really hurts.'

Beau has already been made camera ready for the music awards tonight. He's been keeping his distance from me since our fiasco involving Keegan and The Meat Rack so I asked, or rather begged, Kiara to style Beau at the apartment and then come over and work on me at my place since there's a chance that I'll be on camera as 'Chase's fiancé'. The thought of marrying Chase makes me almost throw up and the thought of what I have lost with Beau makes me want to do the same thing, so finally the brothers are identical.

'I still don't understand. I thought you and Beau were getting closer but since we got back you won't be alone with the man. Baby, I'm your best friend and if you can't tell me...'

'I can't...' I say for the umpteenth time. Kiara has tried to get it out of me but I've been avoiding telling her exactly what happened. Now that we're alone in my apartment it's much harder. 'I just have to get through tonight and the weekend.' She knows not to push me too hard.

Tina texts me that she's put Beau in a car and that the next stop is my place. I should have prepped Beau for any unusual questions but I don't have the energy, or maybe I don't have the desire. I even forgot to check MagicAss on SecretSlam today – a ritual I've been doing with my espresso each morning.

Kiara and I walk out of the building and as we stand on the street waiting for the car to arrive she asks, 'Ethan, do you remember when I quit Kingsman, Kleinman and Kip?' She hated that law firm. She almost never mentions it directly by name.

'How could I not? We celebrated at every bar below 14th Street. I mean, it's still a blur but I remember it.'

'That was my last day. But I quit when I knew I couldn't work at a law firm one day longer. It was a long time coming. I always thought I had to be a professional. I thought I had to do something that was respectable and exemplary. Becoming a lawyer was never my dream. It was what I thought I should do, so that I could look anyone in the eye and show them what I had made of myself as a Black trans woman. But that doesn't come from having some powerful job that you think impresses people. That look comes from doing something you love and being who you are. What I really wanted to do and practicing law were so different. It was easier for me to see the gap. The Show is not making you happy. It's not too late to get back on track or at least change the direction a bit.' She kisses me on the cheek before hopping into the car taking her home. 'Ethan, I love you,' she says, and I watch her car drive down the block.

I'm waiting for Beau and thinking about what she said when the streetlight over me flickers, reminding me of the 'North Star' that Uncle Clams pointed out over the bay. Maybe it isn't too late to get back on track but I'm not even sure what direction I would go.

The black Escalade with Beau in it arrives and I get in. Beau looks incredible. He's wearing the blue suit he wore a few weeks ago when Kiara first worked her magic back in the apartment and seeing him in it again makes my heart flutter. He has more scruff than usual. Kiara has given just enough eyeliner and smoke around his eyes to make him look a bit more glam for the awards. The purple streak in his hair has had a touch up and almost looks violet. He's perfect.

I reach into my pocket and take out the envelope I need to give him. I could have asked Tina to do it but this is my decision and I need to handle it myself. 'These are the remarks for the ribbon cutting tomorrow at the parade,' I say, handing him the envelope marked 'Parade Speech' with the yellow and red Beefy Boy logo. 'When you get home put them on the shelf by the door so you don't forget them.'

I figure that kind of specific instruction will at least get him to spar with me but it doesn't. He says, 'On the shelf. Got it.' He looks down at the envelope. I can tell he's disappointed I didn't find a way to cut out Beefy Boy. I'm not exactly proud of myself either.

'Beefy Boy was very specific about what they want said and how they want it, so please just read these as written tomorrow and' – I stop. It's hard to say the last part – 'and then you can head back.'

I stare straight ahead. Seeing his eyes will hurt too much.

'You think after everything that's happened to me, I just go back to the wilderness and forget all the people I've connected with? You think I can just forget Kiara, Tina, Clams... you?' he says.

'And Keegan,' I say. 'Don't forget Keegan.' I shoot my voice like an arrow across the car.

'He's not as bad as you think,' Beau says.

I guess he had a better time with Keegan than I thought. His hands aren't clean either. Then I remember Keegan will of course be here tonight. As Beau walks the red carpet Keegan will be interviewing him, I'm sure. I can't imagine *Mediapedia* would have someone else covering this event. The thought of seeing the two of them together makes me sad and angry with myself. I stew thinking about them air kissing as lights flash and the crowd cheers.

Our car arrives at Radio City Music Hall, the doors open and it all begins.

Cameras surround us. 'Chase, over here! Over here!' The paparazzi are calling for his attention, but Beau turns back to me and lends me his hand as I get out of the Escalade. It's more than I deserve and I'm grateful he hasn't completely shunned me.

Ahead of us I see Jeremiah walking with one of the hosts of *Queens of the Night*. He sees us getting out of the car and we politely wave to each other.

We start walking down the red carpet and hit the entrance to the step and repeat banners. I've done this countless times before but tonight it feels like walking the gallows. On one side of us photographers are snapping away and behind us an endless display of sponsorship logos make up the backdrop. We're supposed to pose so they can capture pictures and, most importantly, get the sponsor logos in the shot. Beau and I are just the filling for this crap sandwich of celebrity and promotion.

We get halfway through and Beau grabs my hand. A rush of exhilaration gives way to sadness. I've destroyed everything that could have been between us but he's still willing to go along with my charade, although I think I should start calling it what it actually is: a lie. A big fat lie.

I feel my phone buzzing in my jacket pocket but I don't look at it until we're through with the red carpet photos. We'll have to do the press interviews before making our way into the auditorium. I finally look down at my phone to see a message from Maria Luisa. '*Is Chase wearing eye makeup?!!!!*'

I quickly count five exclamations points. What's the big deal? It's a music event; there's more makeup here than at the Sephora down the street and a lot of it's on the men. Still, Beefy Boy is not going to like this. I guess we're breaking their rules of what 'normal gays' should be.

We start the press circuit. Lots of celebrities are with their partners but the partners know to remain in the background and I'm happy to barely make it on camera. The first reporter is a thin young woman in a dress that can't be made of more than a yard of silver fabric.

'Everyone is talking about your show,' she says. Her enthusiasm is manufactured and over the top, as is the rule.

'I'm glad,' Beau says. 'We try to help people with queer lifestyle tips.'

'No, not that show,' the young woman says, pushing the microphone in his face. 'The one on Fire Island. Everyone is talking about the clips of Bella D Ball. When will we see her again?'

Beau laughs and starts to answer. I grab the microphone. 'That was a one night only performance. Chase was helping a friend. I don't think we'll see her again,' I say, hoping that will appease Maria Luisa and Buck.

'Well, never say never,' Beau says.

I laugh in that fake TV way. 'Well, this is one instance where never is a good word to use.'

We move on to the next reporter and while we're off camera I say, 'Do not mention the drag show again, and if they ask say it was a one-time thing,'

'Why?' he asks through a smile, although I can tell he's annoyed with this.

'It doesn't matter,' I say quickly as we wait for the next reporter. I look at his face. Damn, the eyeliner makes him look so sexy. Still, I wish we hadn't pushed the boundaries with his look. Everything is carefully orchestrated and when I start messing with the secret sauce it's an issue for the brand.

The next reporter doesn't ask about the drag show so we're in the clear but as soon as we arrive at the station for *Mediapedia* Beau is greeted with a big, 'Well if it isn't Bella D Ball,' by none other than Keegan Ellis.

'Hello,' Beau says. 'Nice to see you again.' Again. He had to add again. I watch him carefully. I wonder if they want to find a stall in the closest bathroom for a repeat performance of what happened at The Meat Rack.

'I loved your performance this weekend,' Keegan says. Oh, I'm sure you did Keegan. I can only image what level of sexual gymnastics the two of you performed together. 'Tell us when we can expect to see Bella return?' Keegan asks.

Say it was a one-time thing. Tell him that you are focused on the parade and next season. Anything.

'I'm not sure when you'll see Bella again. Soon, I hope. There really is a power in being able to express yourself freely. I think more people should feel that power, however they can.'

Keegan eats up this answer and I wonder if this is for the cameras or if there is some bizarre sexual chemistry between them. I can feel my phone buzzing in my pocket but I don't even need to look at it to know it's Maria Luisa.

He finishes the red carpet, and we move into the lobby outside the auditorium. Once we are away from the cameras I pull him aside.

'What is wrong with you?' I ask.

'What is wrong with you?' he counters.

'I told you not to mention the drag. I was very clear.'

'Who cares?' he shrugs.

'Our sponsors care,' I say without thinking.

'Ethan, you're so smart but you're being so stupid. You know they're just using you to try to rehabilitate their image and sell more beef.'

'No, you're wrong. It's the other way around. I'm using them to get more resources to have the show reach more people. I'm in control.'

'No, you've lost control. You aren't driving the bus, Ethan. You're under it. You loved watching me perform with Clams and Amnesia. I know it. I could see it.'

'So what? A drag show on Fire Island is not real life.'

'Oh, but some made-up music awards and a reality lifestyle show are? You've got everything backwards. You don't see what's real and what's made up anymore. You don't know the difference between what it means to be out and proud and what it means to be surrounded by the merchandise and products that supposedly *show* you are out and proud. You don't even know when someone is into you. Really into you.'

He looks at me intensely. Why did I let Kiara put that eyeliner on him? He looks so amazing with it on. I want to tell him that I'm really into him, but what does it matter? He'll be gone by the end of the weekend. Maria Luisa buzzes my phone again. I can almost feel her anger through the phone. I have to make the responsible choice. I can't throw years of hard work away to make this guy happy.

Buzz. Buzz.

I want to grab my phone and tell Maria Luisa to leave me alone for five minutes so I can tend to my personal life, but the truth is I don't have a personal life. My life *is* my work life and maybe that's the problem.

Buzz. Buzz.

I put my hand in my pocket and I suddenly remember what else is in there. It's the only choice I can make. I pull out the neatly folded towelette.

'Take off that eye makeup,' I say.

'Ethan…'

'Just do it before we go in there and get back on camera. We have a deal. This isn't your image of your show. It's mine.'

'Whose vision of style is this really? Is it still yours or is it your vision as ordered by sponsors and network executives?'

'You see how hard I work. I'm trying to represent queer people at a major network. Do you have any idea how difficult that is? It's a razor's edge. I have this opportunity and if I mess it up or don't follow orders, it's over.'

'Let it be over. You're so concerned about making sure everything is done right. That everything is perfect.' He's right. I think about how his first appearance on camera was such a mess, knocking over everything. 'But that's not how it is. Everything is messy,' he says.

'I do not like mess.'

Buzz. Buzz.

'Life is messy, Ethan. For example, I like you. I actually like you. When the cameras are off. And I'm not faking, like you do with Chase. You care about people and you want to do the right thing but you get so in your head that you can't function. But I've seen you. The real you. Why won't you let that person out?'

I know he's talking. He's saying words and I should be listening and responding but I can't. It's too much for me.

'Then why did you hook up with Keegan in The Meat Rack?' I ask, letting my hurt feelings show.

'Is that what you think happened? You think I would make out with you and then have sex with Keegan even if you told me to do it?'

'No, you don't get to treat me like I was pimping you out. I told you to just walk around. I didn't tell you to do anything like that. I made my instructions clear.' I was so buzzed that night that the details are foggy but I remember enough.

'Your instructions? Ethan, can't you stop telling everyone how to behave and how to act for one second? Can't you just let everyone be who they need to be?'

The red carpet is wrapping up and the awards are about to start. The crowd of sparkling dresses and tuxedos moves toward the auditorium.

'Next week you'll be back in your yurt and you can be whoever you need to be.' At this point I'm almost shouting at him.

'Ethan!' he shouts before immediately regaining his composure. 'Don't you get it? The person who needs to learn to be who they need to be isn't me, or all your viewers or anyone else. It's you!' he says. He takes one last look at me and then heads to the auditorium.

Chimes ring in the lobby and an announcer explains that we need to be in our seats for the scheduled broadcast. It's final call. The last place I want to be is in that auditorium, but I follow the other last-minute arrivals into the cavernous space and quickly find my seat next to Beau. He doesn't say a word. I'm about to ask him what he means by saying I'm the person who needs to learn how to be myself but before I can even search for the courage to ask him the music swells and the audience applauds. Massive cameras face the stage and portable versions with operators in formal attire run up and down the aisle.

The announcer begins. 'Everyone please welcome your host for tonight's award, the always hysterical and never forgettable, Delilah Kaufman.' I had forgotten she would be opening the show. I shrink in my seat hoping she won't be doing her usual roast of the audience.

I smile and applaud like everyone else in the room. I can almost feel the heat of Beau's body next to mine. My elbow grazes against him and he moves his away. I don't even have to see his face to know how disappointed he is in me. I look down and see his hand on his knee. What would happen if I just moved my hand toward his? I do it to see if he returns any signal that this might be all right. A camera person swoops down the aisle and points the lens at us. I let my hand touch his. The camera tilts to get a shot of what they think is a tender moment, but I guess it's all pretend.

What have I done? I've spent the last few years focusing on making sure everything looks right for the camera and now there's one inches from me and all I want to do is push it away. I don't want to polish surfaces anymore. The camera moves to the next shot and as soon as it's gone Beau moves his hand away, too.

Delilah is on stage doing her thing. She has the audience laughing loudly and I open my mouth and pretend to be joining in but no sound comes out. She makes her way through the audience picking on various celebrities.

I'm barely present mentally until she says: 'And we have Chase Myles with us tonight from the hit *Myles of Style.*' I'm at attention. The camera person runs back down the aisle to focus on us. I smile. It's fake. I've done it before but this time I struggle to keep the corners of my mouth up.

'I hear you're getting married. Congratulations!' I freeze. The audience applauds but I can't move. 'I have always supported gay marriage. I see no reason why gay people shouldn't be as miserable as straight people.'

The audience laughs and I can feel Beau next to me playing his part but I can't do it. I can't keep up the charade. The show cuts to a commercial. The entire auditorium shifts. I turn to Beau and say, 'I'm sorry. I have to go.' I don't look at him. I don't give him a chance to respond. I can't stay in the auditorium a second longer. The pressure is too much. I rush down the aisle and past one of the people hired for the night to fill any empty seats so the auditorium always looks full. The world I have been living in is nothing but seat fillers and stand-ins.

I exit the auditorium and start walking through the lobby. I'm so close to being out of there when I run into Keegan.

'Hey Ethan. Where's Chase? I want to make sure I connect with him off camera tonight.'

'I'm sure you do,' I say. I thought that maybe they didn't hook up on Fire Island but here's Keegan thirsty for more. Beau thinks he's all truth and integrity but when it comes to Saturday night in The Meat Rack he can't help himself.

'Did he tell you how we ran into each other after I saw you last weekend?'

'No, Keegan. Luckily he kept the lurid details to himself.'

'Lurid?' Keegan asks. 'There was nothing lurid about it. He could tell I was anxious and we sat on the dock and he showed me how to calm my breathing. He recommended some meditation teachers in Brooklyn that I looked up and they really helped. I couldn't tell him all this on camera. I told you he helped me when I saw you that morning. Starting to meditate really has been magic. I just wanted him to know too,' Keegan says and then heads into the auditorium.

Why did I assume they hooked up? Was I thinking about what his brother would do in that situation? Or maybe I just believed what I wanted instead of dealing with the feelings I was having for Beau. I feel my entire body deflating like someone has pulled the plug on one of those inflatable tube people outside a used car lot.

I think the night can't get any worse until I see Jeremiah headed right toward me. *People come and go so quickly around here.* I consider running away but I'm not sure where I

would go. The last place I can go is back into the auditorium.

'Hey there, Ethan,' Jeremiah says, and we air kiss.

'I really have to go,' I say.

'Shouldn't you be heading in the other direction? The
commercial break is almost over.'

'Ahh,' I mutter. I don't know how to answer him.

'I want to congratulate you,' he says.

'For what?' I ask.

'Maria Luisa told me you'll be the new VP of diversity
programming.' My mind is barely present. The fact is he's
announcing my triumph in a game I've worked so hard
to win and it barely has an impact on me. All I can think
about is Beau and how I didn't trust him and what he said
to me about how I need to learn to just be myself.

'I'm sorry,' I say, although I know that's the wrong
response. It's all I can think of to say.

'For what?' Jeremiah laughs but there is hurt behind his
cackle. 'The best *man* won. That must make you happy.'
He says the word 'man' with a vexed emphasis that makes
me uncomfortable.

'What's that supposed to mean?' I ask. I'm too
distracted to play our usual cat and mouse.

'Maria Luisa has been a great ally but when it comes to
the upper echelon of our network we both know there's
no way they're going to pick the producer of a group of
drag queens over you and your picture-perfect host. Let's
not kid ourselves,' he says. He isn't angry or bitter or even
sad. His tone is dry and matter-of-fact. It's not the first
time he's seen things go down this way. 'You hitched your
wagon to the right star. Congratulations,' Jeremiah says
and walks away. Before he's gone, he turns back and says,
'You deserve it.'

I feel hollow inside. I've waited for this moment for so long. Not just the promotion but winning, getting what I want. It's here now and I don't feel any of the things I thought I would feel. I thought if I did what I was told and followed all the rules I was given I'd get to where I needed to be. But I don't want to be here at all.

Soft chimes play, indicating the awards are about to resume. I can hear the muffled roar of fans cheering late arrivals. I think of them taking the same path we just finished. They get out of their cars and follow the red carpet like it's the yellow brick road, but maybe it's time to stop following?

I see a sign for the exit and I walk toward it. I need to get out of here. I can't be in the lobby of Radio City one second longer. I need to breathe. I escape through the side door that empties on to a dark side street where I inhale the night air. It takes me a second to get my bearings, but I don't stop walking. I hear the sound of the awards getting thinner in the distance. I wind through Rocke-feller Center and I'm suddenly in front of the *American Morning* studios.

The ground-floor studio is dark and the set pieces are covered but in my mind I can still see Beau trying to dance the Pride Pump and ending the segment on the floor wrapped in shiny ornaments. I remember the shudder I felt when I heard him say: 'You don't have to be perfect, you just have to be yourself.' At that moment I thought my body was reacting to the fact that he was blowing our cover but tonight, as I walk away from all the shimmering perfection of the awards show broadcast, I wonder if my reaction at *American Morning* that day was my body hearing something so true and authentic. Something that it needed to hear. I couldn't take it in then but it's beginning to penetrate now.

Dorothy didn't find her way home following the yellow brick road. It only led her to the Emerald City. She held the power the whole time. In her shoes. I look down at the glossy black patented leather loafers pinching my feet. Maybe I don't have to click them together three times; maybe all I need to do is be myself.

Chapter 36

I don't need to set an alarm to get up for Pride because I haven't slept at all. I've been working on a way to make everything right. My brain is on overdrive trying to find the right words for everything. But to seal the deal I also need to make some travel reservations. The first is easy as cake, or maybe gateau; the other is a much more bitter pill to swallow but it's been a long time in coming and needs to be done. I arrive at the apartment to pick up Beau so we can drive down to the viewing stand at Madison Square Park where his duties as Grand Marshal will officially begin before we start the live stream. Tina is meeting us at the location with our remote crew.

The car pulls in front of the building and Beau isn't there. I don't want to go up to the apartment – it's too painful. I ask the doorperson on duty to ring him. I hope he's okay. It's very unlike Beau to keep anyone waiting like this. After about ten minutes I ask them to ring again. They do and I wait again. I'm about to go up to see if he's okay when Beau comes out of the elevator and we get in the car. He's wearing the exact outfit we picked out for him with large sunglasses he must have found in the apartment. He's carrying the Beefy Boy envelope with the speech.

The car heads downtown and I find the courage to speak. 'Beau, I understand you're upset with me and you have every right to be.'

He nods but doesn't say anything. He's freshly shaved and the purple streak in his hair seems a bit more faded than it did yesterday. Looking at him stirs almost nothing inside me, which makes me wonder if any of it was real anyway.

'Beau, I know you have the Beefy Boy speech.' He nods again. No words. Fine. I don't deserve anything more after everything I've done. He keeps his sunglasses on so I can't even see his eyes.

'Don't read that speech,' I say, and I hand him a mauve envelope with the *Myles of Style* logo on it. 'You can throw out the other speech. Read this at the ceremony. It explains everything.'

He takes the envelope and puts it in his jacket pocket. I remain silent. I hope once he reads the words the ice between us will melt.

We step out of the car and the spirit of Pride embraces me, making me smile from ear to ear despite the daunting events about to unfold for me personally. I've been coming to the parade since I came out, but today I'm struck by the variety of different styles around. No two people seem to be expressing themselves in the same way and the range and diversity make me feel like I can finally be a part of everything on my own terms. Floats are making their way down Fifth Avenue and I can hear disco and house music from competing loudspeakers. The parade begins further uptown but it doesn't officially start until the ribbon-cutting ceremony when the first groups march past the viewing platform before ending just past the famous Stonewall Inn. The mood is always a party and today I want to be part of it, not just producing it for someone else. But I have to, for lack of a better word, straighten some things out before I can move on.

I meet Tina and the crew working on today's parade and we go over some of the logistics. We make sure the feed from the remote cameras to the giant screen is working so that everyone can see what's happening up on stage and get a better look at the details of the parade. We also have a hookup to the speakers surrounding the blocks near the reviewing stand. Beau is even more quiet than usual but I assume he's a combination of nervous and mad. I don't push it. I let him be quiet though the separation is killing me. A production assistant takes Beau up to the podium and I take Tina aside.

'Tina, I want to thank you for everything you've done this month. You've been incredible,' I say. 'I want you to know that you have two tickets to Paris and a room at a hotel on the Seine within walking distance of that patisserie you love. I've arranged everything. You just have to pick the dates.'

'Wow. Ethan, thank you. I can't believe it. I don't know what to say.' She deserves it. 'I appreciate this so much,' she says, and since chances are I won't be an employee of the network very soon and strictly obeying physical contact protocols, I hug her tightly and she hugs me back.

The sound of a marching band playing a brassy version of 'Born This Way' approaches. The organizers tell us it's time to begin the opening ceremony and our cameras roll. Beau is on stage with some local politicians and the mayor gives a very dull speech about how important the parade is. He then asks the man he thinks is Chase to say a few words before cutting the ribbon and starting the parade. I can feel small muscles up and down my body twitching as I wait for everything I set in motion to unfold.

I'm not worried I'll be fired when Beau reads my speech. I know I will be. I'm more worried that what I've written won't be enough to make Beau understand how important he is to me and how much he has helped me understand who I am and, more importantly, who I need to be.

'Without further ado,' the mayor says. 'I am pleased to have the star of *Myles of Style*, Chase Myles, say a few words before cutting our ribbon.'

The cheering crowd has doubled in size since we arrived. It feels like every queer person within a hundred-mile radius is part of this celebration. Beau stands on the podium in front of the microphone. He's become very good at pretending to be Chase. From where I'm standing it looks like this guy is eating up the applause. He can't get enough of it and waits until every last hand has clapped. I'm surprised. Beau has never shown a desire for that kind of attention since I met him. He reaches into his pocket and he takes out the envelope with the speech.

'Hello,' he says, his voice a bit higher than usual. 'Hello, ladies and gentlemen.' What's he doing? I hear a few grumbles in the crowd. *Ladies and gentlemen?* I'm sure I didn't write that down. I would never start a speech with those categories. Not at Pride. He must be incredibly nervous, but when I look up at the podium he doesn't seem nervous. His usual open smile is a bit more of a grin and he still hasn't taken off his sunglasses. He's enjoying being the center of attention way too much in this moment. He taps the microphone and feedback squelches through the enormous speakers and rattles the crowd. 'My bad,' he says and looks down at the envelope and takes out the paper.

'I'm so honored to be representing Beefy Boy,' he starts. That's the old speech. No, no. He keeps going and I wave my hands frantically. He sees me. I know he sees me but instead of acknowledging me and doing the right speech he keeps going. I start jumping up and down and waving my arms over my head. What is he doing? I look closely at the image on the giant screen above the stage and notice the color of the envelope isn't mauve at all.

'Beefy Boy has done so much for our community,' he says and the crowd groans. As they should. This is not the speech I wrote. This is not right on so many levels. I look more closely at Beau on the big screen. The bangs are too long and faded. His tan is too real. I pull out my phone and open up SecretSlam and see that MagicAss is… forty feet away.

'That's not Beau,' I say.

Tina turns to me and whispers loudly. 'No, it's not. It's Chase.'

'No, I mean it *is* Chase. I mean. It's not our Chase. It's Chase-Chase. It's not the good Chase. It's bad Chase.' I sound like I have lost my mind and I think maybe I have.

'Stop! Stop!' I yell as loud as I can. I run through the crowd and weave between the members of the marching band, dodging trumpets and sousaphones. I almost knock over a flautist but I don't care. I have got to get to that stage. I run up to the steps of the podium flashing my security badge as I go and I stand next to Beau – I mean Chase. This one is definitely Chase.

'What are you doing?' Chase asks, covering the microphone. I grab it away from him.

'Everyone, I'm sorry but this isn't Chase Myles. This man is an imposter.'

Even with the parade loudly approaching you can hear anyone within earshot gasp in unison. No one has any idea what is going on.

Chase laughs and grabs the mic back. 'Of course I'm Chase Myles. Everyone can see that. Do you want me to take out my driver's license? I'm Chase Myles, I tell you. I'm Chase Myles. Me.' He's on the verge of a tantrum. A babble rises from the crowd. The audience is confused and some are even scared. I don't blame them. The mayor is quickly escorted from the stage with the other dignitaries who must assume I'm a crazed gay activist and, in this moment, I am.

'Ethan, sit down. You're making a fool of yourself,' Chase says.

'What the hell are you doing here?' I ask, my hand over the microphone this time.

'I'm supposed to be here. My brother is not. I'm not the idiot you think I am. I put two and two together and you know what I got? Two. You're trying to make two of me. I came home last night and sent him on his way.' Chase and Beau together. I can't imagine how that went down. Poor Beau. I feel awful that I created this disaster for him.

'You're supposed to be in Babu Dobby as you call it.' He doesn't say anything but his eyes dart to the ground. 'You got kicked out. I knew it.'

'So what? I didn't know they had all those rules about nudity. I mean, it's a desert. It's hot!' I should have known that Chase couldn't hack it in a country with strict rules about indecency. His very being is indecent. I'm sure whatever movie mogul he may have lured got tired of his obnoxious outbursts. With nowhere else to turn he came back to his old life here.

He takes my hands off the microphone. 'Sorry, everyone,' he says, and I push him out of the way and grab the microphone off the stand and start walking around the stage.

'Folks. I'm sorry to do this during such an important event.' I swallow hard. I suddenly realize I'm speaking to a crowd of thousands, something I have spent much of my life avoiding. I look up and catch a glimpse of the magnificent spire on the Chrysler Building blocks away. Then I remember being up there with Beau and how he taught me to slow my breathing. I do that and try to gain my composure. I walk across the stage to Chase and grab the envelope I gave him out of his pocket. He tries to stop me, but my determination is too great and I grab it.

'That is not Chase,' I yell, pointing at Chase. I'm so loud most of the crowd can hear me without a microphone.

'What are you talking about? Of course I'm Chase.' Chase smiles and takes off his sunglasses. I move away from him and back to the podium.

'What I mean is that there is no such thing as Chase.' I speak into the microphone so the entire parade can hear me. 'He's no more real than The Boogie Man or The Tooth Fairy. He's something that has been designed and created.'

I rip open the envelope of the new speech I prepared last night. I'm able to read enough of it to keep going. 'Our show started off trying to lift you up, to make you feel empowered, but somewhere along the way we started doing the opposite. We displayed impossible ideals of beauty, showed you endless exercise routines to change your body and the perfect way to do everything. We let our sponsors dictate our content.'

The crowd is confused. It's like they thought they were going to the ballet but the circus pulled up. I see people literally scratching their heads. I want to run from the stage, but I remember what Beau said and keep focused on my breathing.

'It wasn't until recently that I realized nothing has to be perfect. Nothing has to look fabulous if it feels wrong. As queer people we grow up being told how we should behave and now we're on TV and in movies and we're told how we should be gay, how we should be queer. We have to stop allowing that. We have to start celebrating all the talents and gifts we already have. So Beefy Boy can take their dry, crusty sandwiches and shove them up their ass!'

I grab the scissors from the podium, cut the ribbon and shout, 'Let the parade begin!' At that the crowd erupts in cheers that seem to spread throughout the city.

But then I hear it.

A car horn goes beep. Beep. Beeep-beep-beep. I recognize the notes from the refrain of Sister Sledge's anthem. The Giblets had the horn tune replaced with 'We Are Family' years ago. I look out over the crowd and see the convertible down the block.

I jump off the podium and run past a float of go-go boys from Hell's Kitchen, a line of motorcycles from Dykes on Bikes and multiple contingents of various social service organizations. I feel the energy of the marchers pushing me toward where I need to be. I keep running. I'm out of breath when I reach the hot pink and aqua vintage Ford Fairlane Sunliner convertible with three drag queens, my best friend, her wife and child, their little black dog Otto, and the man who has made me realize what it means to have pride – Beau.

'Ethan!' they all scream together. I love every single person in that car but the one voice that rises above everyone else's is Beau's. He gets out and runs toward me. My stomach flutters as soon as I look into his face. He's Beau. It's not how he looks; it's how it makes me feel that lets me know I'm certain. I run to him. I have no idea what he's feeling right now but I know I need to be honest and let him know exactly how I feel about him. I put my lips on his hoping he's able to sense everything I'm feeling. He immediately kisses me back. His tongue searches for mine and I try to convey my regret over my actions and my appreciation for his entire being.

'I'm sorry,' I say. 'I'm sorry for everything. For thinking you would be with Keegan, for telling you to be with Keegan, for not listening to you, for not seeing everything that was right in front of me. I'm sorry for not kicking Beefy Boy out as soon as I heard what they wanted. I'm sorry for everything except one thing, and that's driving up and finding you and bringing you down here.'

I put my arms around him and kiss him. I can feel him smiling under my lips and then his mouth opens, inviting me in. I can feel his forgiveness and also his kindness, warmth and gentleness.

'You do realize this is Beau and not Chase,' he says as our lips part for a moment.

'Oh, yes,' I say.

'When he came back last night I...' Beau starts.

'I'm sorry you had to deal with him...'

'Actually, we wound up talking for most of the night. I told him how mad I've been at him and he told me how angry he's been with me. It was a hard conversation, but it was a good start. Thanks to you. He told me he was going to tell you the truth but, what can I say? Chase is still Chase.'

As long as Beau is still Beau it doesn't matter. 'I'm so glad you two were able to talk at least.'

'Me too. And I'm glad I was able to hear your speech. They broadcast it up and down the parade route.'

'I meant every word of it. Somewhere along the way I got lost. Thank you for reminding me who I am.'

He puts his hand behind my neck and gently pulls me in for another kiss, and for a few seconds the floats, the marching bands, the crowd all disappear and it's just me and Beau in the middle of Fifth Avenue with his lips on mine.

I'm about to get lost in his kiss when I'm suddenly aware of a chant growing louder and louder but I can't make out what they're saying. I keep my lips on his, but my eyes flutter open. Behind him on the giant screen I think I see Chase. But it isn't Chase. It's Beau. And me. We are locked in an embrace, our happy, smiling, gigantic faces towering over the crowd. I look around and notice Tina has the remote crew filming us. She's happy crying and the crowd is still chanting something incomprehensible. I look into Beau's eyes for a moment before pressing our lips together again and kissing him tenderly.

Now the crowd erupts in unison and the message is clear. 'Love is love! Love is love!' Anyone within the five boroughs can hear it clearly. 'Love is love!' It doesn't feel like a gimmick or a slogan or a platitude. I feel the power of the words all the way from my toes to my lips and I know Beau feels the same way as he kisses me even more deeply. I could spend the entire parade here but then my nose picks up an acrid smell coming from behind us. I hear the notes of 'We Are Family' again and turn to see small puffs of dark black smoke coming from under the hood of the convertible.

Clams, Amnesia and Joan are in the car dressed in their finest gowns. Clams is leaning on the horn as it blares. 'Can the two of you kiss and make up later? You have three gorgeous drag queens and an adorable queer family waiting to join the parade.' Otto adds a bark.

I look over at the overheating car and see everyone smiling but then I notice someone I wasn't sure I'd see here. Ever. I guess she accepted the car service I sent. My cousin Sheila is wearing a simple beige suit and holding the world's tiniest Pride flag between her fingers. She acknowledges me with a small smile. It's a start. It's a day of new beginnings.

Uncle Clams waves me over and I bend down to hear him. 'Ethan, I have no idea how you got her here but whatever you said worked.'

'It was easier than I thought,' I whisper. 'I just reminded her who you really are and what family means.'

Uncle Clams kisses me on the cheek and wipes a tear without smudging his makeup. Then he throws his hands in the air. 'Ethan, can you fix this heap of junk? We're stuck.'

Clams pops the hood and I look at the engine, trying to remember the basics from my high school automotive class. I run to the trunk where I know there are some tools and start testing some connections, maneuvering through the grease and dirt of the engine. It takes a minute but then I ask Clams, 'See if it starts now?' He turns the key and the motor starts without any smoke. We're in business.

Beau opens the door for me and gives me the sweetest, most tender kiss that has ever been given in the middle of

Fifth Avenue. I jump into the driver's seat where I should have been since the parade started.

I'm about to pull out when Beau starts looking around the car. 'Wait,' he says. 'Let me find something to wipe off your face. You're covered in grease.'

I put the car in gear and say, 'Nah, what's wrong with a little mess now and then? You don't have to be perfect. You just have to be yourself.' Beau reaches over and kisses my grease-covered cheek. I kiss him back and we join the parade.

Epilogue

You're invited!

Please join us for the grand reopening of The Starlight Inn on Fire Island.

Our recently refreshed rooms feature contemporary mid-century inspired decor and sustainable Belgian linen spa towels. The private decks overlooking the bay are the ideal location for yoga, meditation or just turning off.

The reimagined menu at our cafe offers seasonal organic specialties in a casual and welcoming atmosphere. We've partnered with Rainbow Roots Farm to provide ethically sourced local produce. Equality tastes better.

Help us toast the summer season at a special outdoor screening of The Wizard of Oz. We hope as the sun sets and Dorothy makes her way down the yellow brick road, you'll realize there's no place like home and that home is wherever you feel loved and welcome.

We hope you'll always feel at home with us.
Sincerely,
Ethan Wells, hotelier
Beau Myles, chef

A letter from Philip

Dear Reader:

When I was a kid growing up in the suburbs I'd stand on my bed and stick my nose out the window. My mother would ask, 'What are you doing?' I'd tell her, 'I'm trying to smell New York City.' All my life I wanted to live in The Big Apple. At the time I didn't know why but I had a feeling I'd find my people there. And I after I graduated from college, I made the East Village my home and then the Upper East Side, where much of this book takes place. New York was glamorous, gritty and erratic but I felt safe there because I could be myself. I felt like I belonged.

I often write about characters who are searching for a place where they feel at home, where they feel safe. I like to think I write chick-lit featuring gay male protagonists, something I call *kiki-fiction*. A *kiki* is a slang term that has come to mean a gathering of close friends in the queer community. I'm interested in stories about how love helps us find ourselves. I think people in marginalized groups, and all people, struggle to love themselves. I know I did. I still do. I think finding love is often about experiencing a deep connection with someone that helps you love and accept yourself for who you are.

In *The Problem with Perfect* Beau talks about wanting to feel the 'tug at the end of the line' as a chef. He wants to know that outside the kitchen there is a person enjoying the meal he created. Everyone wants to feel seen and heard. I think that's part of being human and that connection is the reason I write.

I'm looking to make a connection with you.

It means so much for me to know that my writing has had an impact on you in some way. Please consider sharing your thoughts by writing a review on your favorite website, posting about the story to your socials or simply carrying the book around on public transport in a way that invites inquiry.

I'd also love to hear from you directly. I answer every message I see. Please find me at any of these digital waypoints.

https://www.instagram.com/philipwilliamstover/
https://www.facebook.com/philipwilliamstover/
https://www.philipwilliamstover.com/
email: philipwilliamstover@gmail.com

I hope wherever you are today you feel safe, you feel seen and you feel like you belong. You are perfect just as you are.

Philip William Stover
New York City
January 2023